Roped ... **d**
tightly ... **e**
gasped ... **or**
and outrage, her fingers snarling
in desperation around the
harness.

But to no avail. He plucked her up with ease,
lifting her so high that her feet were far above
the ground. Under the sheer force of the
movement her grip loosened on the harness,
her fingers flailing in the air as he slammed
her against his solid frame to carry her away.

The jolting impact of the man's body against
her own sent shock waves coursing through
her. Her face was on a level with his, his chest
was hard up against her soft breasts, her hips
were bouncing intimately against his muscle-
bound thighs. A wild, hectic colour flooded
her pale skin; she wanted to die in shame.
Never, *never* had she been so close to a man!

Meriel Fuller lives in a quiet corner of rural Devon with her husband and two children. Her early career was in advertising, with a bit of creative writing on the side. Now, with a family to look after, writing has become her passion... A keen interest in literature, the arts and history, particularly the early medieval period, makes writing historical novels a pleasure.

Books by Meriel Fuller

Mills & Boon Historical Romance

Conquest Bride
The Damsel's Defiance
The Warrior's Princess Bride
Captured by the Warrior
Her Battle-Scarred Knight
The Knight's Fugitive Lady
Innocent's Champion
Commanded by the French Duke

Visit the Author Profile page at millsandboon.co.uk.

COMMANDED BY
THE FRENCH DUKE

Meriel Fuller

Published in Great Britain 2016
by Mills & Boon, an imprint of HarperCollins*Publishers*
1 London Bridge Street, London, SE1 9GF

© 2016 Meriel Fuller

ISBN: 978-0-263-91711-6

COMMANDED BY
THE FRENCH DUKE

Chapter One

Wiltshire, England—October 1265

'Thank you, Ralph, for coming today.' Alinor of Claverstock turned to the burly lad sitting beside her on the cart seat, a trace of relief in her voice. Despite the faint rays of a weak October sun, she shivered in the chilly morning air, her green eyes vivid, shining, as she threw him a grateful smile.

'Any excuse to break from ploughing in the stubble, mistress,' Ralph replied with a quick grin, flicking the reins expertly down the bristled backs of the oxen as they began to slow. His skin was ruddy, sunburnt from his constant work outside. 'Market day in Knighton is certainly a better option.'

'I probably could have managed on my own.' Alinor fixed her eyes on the rutted track ahead before it disappeared around the curve of the next hill, willing the oxen to move slightly faster than their current snail's pace. Leaning back against the wooden seat, she adjusted her slight frame to the incline of the cart as it lumbered to the valley bottom. 'I feel guilty for taking you away from your other duties; there's so much to do at the Priory at this time of year.'

Ralph twisted around, his muscled shoulder jogging into the towering pile of grain sacks behind them. 'I would have liked to have seen you try and shift this lot, mistress. Besides, it's not right, a lady of your—'

'We've been through this, Ralph.' Alinor cut off his speech abruptly. 'The nuns need my help and I'm happy to give it.' She flicked the uneven hem of her practical gown down over her boots, stained dark from the heavy morning dew. Through her silk hose, which she had forgotten to change in her haste to reach the Priory that morning, the coarse wool dress scratched uncomfortably at her legs. Around her waist, at the point where the knotted girdle pulled in the baggy garment, her skin itched. She glanced up at the sky where the sun was attempting to push through a rolling bank of pale-grey cloud. When the light broke through, the rays were hot, illuminating the mists that rose from the dew-soaked fields, polishing the grass to silver.

'Well, it's very good of you, my lady.' The cart

lurched over a large dried-up rut in the track, a sudden, jolting movement, and Ralph frowned as one of the cart's wheels began to squeak ominously. 'I knew I should have put some extra grease on that wheel before we left,' he muttered.

'Will it slow us up at all?' Alinor asked quickly, then bit down on her bottom lip, hoping Ralph hadn't noticed the urgency in her tone. Behave normally, she told herself. No one must suspect anything. Usually, she would take the whole day to attend the market in Knighton, selling the grain before buying any goods that the nuns might need. But today? Today she wanted to return to the Priory as soon as possible. Ralph had no idea what she had done and neither did the nuns. But if no one knew of the girl's existence, she would be safer. Only Alinor knew where she was hidden. Clasping her knees tightly, she willed her heart to stop racing. The sooner she could help the poor maid leave the country, the better.

'I'm sure we will reach the market,' Ralph reassured her, 'and I'll fix it while I'm there.' As they squeaked past a solitary hawthorn, branches thick with red berries, three magpies rose, squawking indignantly, blue-black feathers glossy in the sun, white flashes on dark tails.

Running a finger around the tight curve of her wimple, Alinor tried to loosen the restrictive cloth around her neck and temples. The thick white

linen wound about her throat, rising around her
face to cover every strand of hair, over which she
wore a piece of fawn-coloured linen which served
as a veil. Even now, her stepmother's mocking tone echoed in her skull; Wilhelma simply
couldn't understand why her stepdaughter would
choose to wear such sober garments: a plain, un-
dyed linen gown with a mud-coloured veil. But
then, Wilhelma failed to even comprehend why
she would help the nuns in the first place. Her
stepmother would never think of helping anyone,
apart from her wonderful son, Eustace. An invol-
untary shudder crawled down Alinor's spine; no,
she would not think of her stepmother now, of
what that woman had wanted to do. Elements of
that terrifying night at Claverstock shot through
her brain: desperate, splintered images that sent
ripples of anxiety through her slight frame. She
smoothed out the fabric of her gown across her
knees, plucking at a stray thread. Dragging her
thoughts to the present, she forced her brain to
focus on her task today. The market. Selling the
nuns' grain at a profit. The sisters would need the
money to get them through the coming winter;
she needed to concentrate on that.

As the sun rose, the air became unseasonably
muggy, oppressive. Clouds of midges rose up,
dancing above dank wet spots beside the track.
Parched leaves, edges curled up and blackened,

drifted down from the few trees dotted here and there in the sloping fields that ran down to the path, catching under the cart wheels with a dry rustle. The scant, shifting breeze carried a sharpness, a forerunner of winter.

'It's not far now, mistress,' Ralph said, across the incessant noise of the squeaking wheel. 'The bridge is around this next bend.'

And then the river was before them, startling, glinting silver. Water rushed, cackling throatily across the stones at the shallow, stone-strewn edges. In the middle, the river was deep and fast-flowing, the surge of current too dangerous for a horse or person to cross safely. A narrow pack-horse bridge spanned the gurgling flow with four stone arches, rising steeply at the centre to counter any problems with flooding in winter.

Clusters of brown-winged seeds bunched beneath the yellowing leaves of the sycamores by the river's edge; a few spun down, circling crazily around her, landing on her shoulders, her lap. 'Quick, let's cross it before someone comes the other way!' Alinor grasped at Ralph's arm. 'I want to get to the market before noon.'

'There's no one around, mistress,' Ralph said, pushing back his chestnut hair, the smooth strands flopping across his brow. 'It's too early for most folks.' Pulling on the reins, he guided the oxen towards the flared stone entrance of the bridge, their hooves slipping on the steep ascent of greasy cobbles. He drove the animals along carefully, their heads nodding in unison as he steered them between the stone parapets. As they passed the middle of the bridge, an ominous crack sounded from the squeaking wheel, followed by a sickening sound of crunching wood. The cart tipped violently, the right side dropping down with a significant jolt.

'Oh!' Alinor's arms flailed outwards, instinctively seeking to steady herself as she was thrown to one side. For one horrible moment she thought she would lose her balance and tip straight into the whirling river below, but Ralph grabbed her arm, hauling her back.

'Damn it!' he cursed in annoyance, pushing distracted fingers through his hair. 'Wait here, my lady, and hold the animals while I see what's happened.' Squeezing his brawny frame between the stone parapet and the cart, he ducked beneath.

She heard a muffled groan. 'The axle's broken,' Ralph shouted up to her, coming back. 'I'll have to fetch some help before we can shift this thing.'

'Then I'll come with you,' Alinor said, shuffling to the edge of the seat.

Ralph held up a hand to forestall her. 'Probably best if you stay here, my lady.' He glanced at the voluminous fabric that spilled out from her girdle and draped over the seat, material that would hamper her stride. 'With the greatest respect, I can move more quickly on my own. Besides, someone needs to stay with the cart; those sacks of grain are worth a lot of money.'

'A whole winter's worth,' Alinor agreed. Ralph's words made sense.

'Will you be all right on your own, my lady? I'll not be gone long. I seem to remember passing a farmstead a couple of fields back.'

'Of course,' she replied confidently. 'I have my dagger—' she touched the leather scabbard hanging from her plaited waist belt '—and no one would ever dream of attacking a lay sister, or at least someone dressed as one!'

Ralph laughed. 'Not unless they wanted to risk eternal hell and damnation!' He waved casually and loped off along the way they had come.

Alinor sighed. Wriggling her spine against the cart seat, she allowed the reins to drop beside her. Out of habit, she kneaded her left forearm, trying to alleviate the slight, constant ache that had plagued her since her accident, a small frown crinkling the skin between her finely etched brows. The oxen stood patiently, ears flicking idly at the flies massing above their heads. There were more trees now, along the river: sturdy beech, willow, stubby hawthorn dotted the flat, wide valley. The earlier cloud had dispersed and now the rising sun filtered through the shifting leaf canopy, casting a dappled glow.

A warmth suffused her body. Closing her eyes, she lifted her chin, drinking in the balmy heat across her skin. If only she could forget, for a moment, what had nearly happened. The breathless rush as she had helped the girl into her clothes; the headlong sprint across the moon-soaked land, huddled together in hooded cloaks, hiding behind trees, stealing along ditches like thieves. A long, juddering breath caught in her chest at her own daring, the subterfuge. There was no knowing what her stepmother would do if she discovered the truth of what Alinor had done.

'Make way, in the name of Prince Edward!' A harsh, guttural voice barged into her senses. Alinor's eyes popped open in horror; she jumped to her feet, panic slicing her innards. A group of horsemen were gathered on the other side of the bridge; nay, not horsemen, knights, for they wore helmets and chainmail, their red surcoats emblazoned with three gold lions. The mark of the King, and his son, Prince Edward!

Her chest hollowed out in fear, a debilitating weakness hammering through her knees; she wondered if she would fall. God in Heaven, where had they sprung from? They had approached so quietly, it was as if they had materialised from the very trees, like ghosts, ghastly apparitions!

'We need to cross this bridge,' one of the soldiers shouted up at her, hoarse tones emanating from a shiny metal helmet. 'Move the cart now, Sister!'

Sister. Of course, from her garments they believed her to be a nun. Alinor stared at them, terrified, trying to find the words, the courage to address this formidable group. A dozen men or so, chainmail hauberks glinting and winking in the sunlight, lower legs encased in riveted plate armour. They were armed: swords, pikes, maces and shields; the lead knight carried the King's red banner on a pennant. Her mouth was parched, fear cleaving her tongue to the roof of her mouth. What would they do to her, these soldiers of the King? 'I... I cannot,' she managed to say, but her voice emerged as a pathetic whimper and they failed to hear.

'Speak up, woman,' the lead soldier bawled at her, leaning forward in his saddle as if to hear her more clearly. 'What ails you? Why do you not move?' He threw a comment back to his companions; they laughed in response.

Alinor flushed; no doubt the soldier's words had been derogatory. She cleared her throat, summoning up the power in her lungs, the nerve to speak more loudly. What was the matter with her? It was not like her to be intimidated by knights; she came from a high-ranking family who had entertained the King and Queen and their entourage on several occasions. She had a perfect right to be here, on this bridge, as much as the next man, and anyone could have an accident, couldn't they?

'The axle is broken on the cart,' she shouted out in loud, clear tones, tilting up her nose in the hope of projecting an air of superiority. 'The servant has gone to fetch help; he should be back very soon.' Beneath the folds of her gown, she crossed her fingers.

'Then it seems we have a problem,' the soldier replied, throwing his thick-set body down from his horse and moving towards the bridge. 'Prince Edward rides not far behind me and expects us, as his outriders, to clear the way for him. He's in a hurry, Sister, and does not like to be held up.'

Standing on the cart, Alinor shrugged her shoulders, her arms spread wide, palms upturned. 'What can I do?' she replied. 'I cannot move the cart by myself…'

'Then we'll have to help you.' The soldier strutted boldly towards her. 'First, we need to lighten the load.'

'The sacks are quite heavy to carry,' Alinor explained, 'but two of you would manage…' Her mind tacked back to earlier in the day, her breath fanning out like a veil in the pre-dawn air, when Ralph and his younger brothers had loaded the cart. It had taken two of them to lift each sack…

'I have no intention of carrying your measly sacks anywhere,' the soldier replied, his voice muffled by the helmet as he squeezed past the oxen to the back of the cart. Drawing his short sword, he slashed violently at the first sack, cutting the coarse hessian from top to bottom. Grain poured out, spilling over the side of the bridge, down, down into the rushing water. A whole field's worth of harvest.

'What are you doing?' Alinor squawked at him in disbelief. Anger rose in her gullet, mirroring her fear. Panic rattled through her veins, but she had to overcome it, to fight it, for how could she let this thug, this ruffian, behave in such a way? How could she allow the nuns' hard work to disappear beneath a river's churning current? 'How dare you!' As the sack emptied, the soldier tossed the flapping remnants of the sack over the stone parapet and moved on to the next sack. At this rate, the nuns would lose everything!

'Come on, men!' The soldier ignored her furious words, curving one heavy arm upwards to summon his companions, as he moved along methodically. 'Come and help me!'

'No! No! Stop! You cannot do this! You have no right!' Alinor yelled at the soldier, jumping down from the cart. Grabbing at the soldier's arm, she pulled down hard, preventing him from slashing into the next sack. Pausing, he twisted around, holding the flashing blade up to her face, foetid breath wafting over her from the crossed slit in his helmet.

'Take care, Sister,' he warned. 'I'm not in the habit of killing innocent nuns, but I'm sure I can make an exception on this occasion if you continue to goad me.'

The knife-point quivered beneath her nose. Silver in the sunlight, glinting, dangerous. How easy it would be to run away now, to acknowledge the fear that dragged at her belly, the fear that sapped the ligaments in her knees. She could simply turn tail now and hear the soldiers' taunting laughter pursue her as she stumbled away. But it wasn't in her nature to give up, to give in to people like this. They were bullies, pure and simple, and she wasn't about to let them get away with this.

'You don't scare me,' Alinor scoffed back at him. 'I'm sure your Prince would have something to say if he knew what you're doing!' Her fingers scrabbled for her scabbard, fumbling for her dagger within the leather holder.

Within the shadowed confines of his helmet, the man scowled. 'The only thing the Prince is thinking about is beating the rebel Simon de Montfort and he doesn't care how he goes about it,' the soldier hissed. 'He wouldn't give a fig for the likes of you. So step back, Sister, and let me do my work.'

He turned away again, about to cut into the next sack.

Rage boiled through Alinor's veins, hot, surging; drawing her knife, she slashed down on to the soldier's bare hand, cutting into his palm. He cried out in pain, blood spurting from his callused flesh; her attack was so unexpected that he dropped his short sword in surprise, blade clattering to the stone cobbles below. In a trice, she had kicked it away, sending the weapon spinning into the gloom beneath the cart. In the same moment, she saw her opportunity: the jewelled helm of the soldier's long sword gleaming out from his scabbard. Her nerves jittered —was she really about to do this? There was no time to think about it. With both hands on the sword helm, she wrenched upwards, withdrawing the shining metal blade easily, and stepped back so the tip waggled dangerously towards his throat. She had helped her father on with his chainmail enough times to know where the weak spots were, where a blade could pierce the skin.

'Step away from the cart!' Alinor fought to contain the wobble in her voice. Fear washed her mind blank. How was this going to go? She had stopped him from ruining the sacks, but now what? Glancing behind quickly, she checked that no other soldier was creeping up behind her. But the rest of the group remained gathered beyond the bridge, pointing and laughing at their unfortunate comrade. They obviously didn't think he needed any help, fully believing he would best her in the end; it was purely a matter of time. Come on, Alinor, think, she told herself firmly. Use your wits! Her slim fingers wound around the cross that hung across her bosom.

Cradling his bleeding hand, the soldier's eyes blazed with annoyance through the slit in his helmet. 'Give up now, Sister, and give me my sword back; there's another dozen soldiers back there for you to fight before this is over. Your prayers are meaningless—your God cannot help you now.'

And there she had it: the dart of an idea. Let them think that she called on darker beings to help her now. Her pearl-studded cross hung down on a rope of thin wooden beads; she held it out and aloft, narrowing her eyes in what she hoped was a suitably threatening expression. 'I agree...' she lowered her voice to a sibilant hiss '...but I summon the Devil to help me now.' She began to murmur in Latin, first softly, then louder and louder; unless he was a proficient Latin scholar, the soldier would have no idea that her words were complete nonsense. It was fortunate for her that at the same moment, a large black cloud moved slowly across the sun, dimming the landscape, sending a dusty gust of wind to scurry crisp leaves along the river bank, bouncing wildly. The soldiers fell silent; they watched Alinor, open-mouthed, faces greying as they realised what she was doing. As she spoke, she jabbed the sword in the man's direction and slowly, slowly he backed away, around the other side of the cart, before staggering back to the other soldiers.

'She's put a curse on me!' Alinor heard the soldier shout, pointing back to her. Her wrists ached from holding up the heavy sword, but she refused to let it drop. A curious bubble of laughter, or was it hysteria, welled up within her; she clamped down on it, hard. These men couldn't see her laugh. Let them continue to think I'm giving them the evil eye, she thought. I'm safe here on this bridge as long as they believe that and so is the grain. But she lifted her eyes briefly skywards and prayed for Ralph's swift return.

Suddenly, she felt very, very alone.

'Where in the Devil's name are we?' Edward, son of Henry III of England, thrashed petulantly at the arching brambles with his sword, eventually pushing his horse into a small, shadowed clearing in the beech forest. He pulled his helmet off with an angry movement; sparse strands of pale blond poked out from around the edges of his chainmail hood. 'And where are my outriders? I thought they were scarcely half a mile ahead? They're supposed to come back and lead us through!' He scowled, thin mouth rolling down at the corners like a spoiled three-year-old.

Guilhem, Duc d'Attalens, shrugged his massive shoulders as he reined in his glossy destrier to stop beside Edward's horse. The three golden lions embroidered across his surcoat gleamed in the sunlight as he drew off his leather gloves and tucked them beneath his saddle front, lifting off his own helmet and pushing back his chainmail hood to reveal a shock of vigorous dark-blond hair. He shook his head roughly, relishing the kiss of balmy air against his hot scalp.

'Well?' Edward regarded him irritably, swatting at a fly buzzing lazily around his face.

'Your guess is as good as mine,' Guilhem replied, rolling his shoulder forward, trying to relieve the itch beneath his chainmail. 'Although as we've been riding half the night, I suspect they might have taken the opportunity to grab a short rest.'

'We haven't got time for a rest!' Edward spluttered, yanking on the reins as his horse skittered nervously beneath him. 'There are rumours that de Montfort might have crossed the River Severn; if that is the case, then they'll be heading east as we speak!'

'I know. But they are only rumours, Edward. If the men are tired, they'll be in no position to fight and we'll lose anyway.' Guilhem's blue eyes regarded Edward calmly. He was used to his friend's moods, the excitable energy that few men could match, the intense, determined stamina on the battlefield.

'I could fight now,' Edward muttered sulkily, 'and so could you.'

Yes, he could fight, Guilhem thought. But then he could always fight, night or day. He never seemed to feel the cold, or to experience hunger or fatigue. Fighting suited him, suited his personality—to be in the fray, driving onwards relentlessly, to have no time to think or feel. It was better that way.

'We both could, Edward, but I suspect we're in the minority. The soldiers need to rest.' He flicked his head around to watch the remainder of the men gather behind them at the edge of the clearing; knights on horseback stretched back in single file into the shadows of the forest, Edward's royalist army. Exhaustion etched their faces. 'I suggest you take the men to your mother's palace at Knighton and beg some board and lodging. The rebels can wait.' He tilted his head on one side. 'What do you say?'

'You suggest I take the men? Why, what are you going to do?'

Guilhem sighed. 'I promised my mother I would visit my sister. She has travelled over to be married to an English noble and I believe his castle is not far from here.' He grinned as Edward's mouth turned down sulkily. 'It'll only be one night and then I'll join you at Knighton.'

"You need to rest as well. Why not come with us now and see your sister on the morrow?"

"Alright." Guilhem nodded, then tilted his head, listening intently. 'Someone's coming,' he said softly, drawing out his long sword from the scabbard. The steel blade rasped along the leather, a sibilant hiss. His eyes searched the area swiftly, body poised, tense and alert in the saddle. The sound of twigs breaking, of horse's hooves thumping heavily, came from the other side of the clearing. One of Edward's outriders came flying towards them, his helmet gone, face red and excited. He pulled so violently on the reins that his horse skidded to a stop, the whites of its eyes rolling back wildly. 'There's a problem!' he managed to gasp out.

Chapter Two

The only problem, as far as Guilhem could gather, seemed to be a diminutive nun dressed in what looked like a grey baggy sack and holding a large sword which he suspected did not belong to her. The substantial blade dwarfed her neat frame, semi-precious stones winking dully at the leather-bound helm. The maid stood at the apex of a packhorse bridge, legs planted wide, a laden ox-cart tilting precariously behind her; at intervals she would swish the sword from left to right in a vaguely threatening manner. From what he could work out, not one soldier had made any attempt to overthrow her; instead, they stood in a miserable group on the river bank, helmets off, horses plucking in desultory manner at the spindly grass. Why were they holding back? Surely it was a simple matter to take her down?

'What is going on here?' Edward said, dismounting swiftly, reddish-blond brows held together in a deep frown.

'Er…well, this…this lay sister…' one of the soldiers began to explain, clutching at his hand. The other men collected around him, shuffling their feet, nodding encouragement to their companion.

'Are you bleeding?' Edward demanded roughly, snatching at the man's hand and opening the stubby fingers. Blood trickled slowly from a deep cut across the soldier's palm.

The soldier flushed to the roots of his hair. 'She did it.' He nodded in the direction of the bridge.

Edward glared at him, pale blue eyes narrowing to slits. 'She did it? Are you trying to tell me that a nun attacked you? God in Heaven, call yourself knights?'

'Look at her, sire. She's giving us the evil eye, muttering godforsaken words at us. Words of the Devil. We tried to make her move the cart, but she slashed at my hand and took my sword! Then she raised her cross and…and put a curse on us! I swear, it's the truth, sire. We daren't touch her.'

'What utter nonsense,' Edward shot back. 'Let me deal with this.'

'Allow me,' Guilhem said, stalling Edward's forward step with a burly arm across his friend's chest. Shoving his helmet towards a soldier, he pushed back his chainmail hood so it settled in loose folds across his shoulders. 'It wouldn't do to have the King's son cut down by a woman.'

'As if!' Edward snorted. But he stopped, sweeping his arm out with mock courtesy. 'However, I have no wish to be cursed, either. Be my guest.'

The knight who walked towards her was tall, a red woollen surcoat covering his muscled torso and broad shoulders. Despite his height, he carried his body with graceful athleticism, like an animal: powerful, self-assured. Beneath his surcoat, glittering chainmail covered his massive arms, but, in contrast to the other soldiers, he wore no plate armour on his shins. Instead, calf-length leather boots and woollen trousers covered his long legs. His head was bare, chainmail hood pushed back to reveal a thatch of burnished hair, more dark blond than brown, strands thick and wayward, framing a lean, tanned face, prominent cheekbones dusted with sunburn.

Alinor licked her lips rapidly, desperate for a drink of water, for something to calm her, to quell the rising tide of fear that filled her chest, that channelled her breathing into short, quick gasps. Her wrists were weak, fatigued from holding up the cumbersome sword. Her left arm ached, the scar pinching painfully. Where had *he* come from? Suddenly the short, rotund soldier who had first accosted her seemed infinitely preferable to this approaching barbarian! Everything about him frightened her: those fierce, glinting eyes of midnight blue; his stern mouth set in a grim, intimidating line and that imposing height—all made her innards quail, leap with terrified anticipation. Her heart fluttered incoherently. Have courage, she told herself. You've managed to hold them off so far, you can do it again. This is not your grain in the cart and the nuns need the income from it in order to survive. If you let it go now, they will have nothing.

The knight had reached the head of the oxen.

Blood thrummed in her ears. 'Go away!' she stuttered out, waving the sword threateningly in the direction of his chest. The heavily embroidered gold lions danced before her eyes. *'Olim erat urbs magna, nomine altum est!'* The Latin speech poured out of her, nonsensical.

To her utter surprise, the knight laughed, his wide mouth breaking into a smile. Small lines crinkled at the side of his eyes. 'Your curses don't scare me, Sister. I don't believe in God, or the Devil either. We have no intention of hurting you; we merely want to cross the bridge, but you seem to be blocking it.'

'The wheel is broken,' Alinor explained. Her voice juddered out, high-pitched. 'Your men know that already! And that one over there...' she jabbed the sword point in the direction of the first soldier who had come across to her '...started cutting at the sacks, spilling the grain, pouring it into the river!'

Guilhem stuck his thumbs into his sword belt. The supple leather around his slim hips emphasised the bunched muscle in his thighs. He frowned, blue eyes sweeping across the damaged sacks behind her. A lock of burnished hair fell across his brow, blond tips grazing his tanned forehead. 'And for that I can only apologise,' he replied. 'The man overstepped the mark, but I think he has paid the price; you've cut him quite badly.'

'He deserved it!' A vivid colour flushed Alinor's cheeks. 'I thought he was going to help me and then...to waste the grain like that!'

Her eyes were truly the most astonishing colour, Guilhem thought. The wimple wrapped around the perfect oval of her face seemed only to enhance the clear, brilliant green of the irises, glowing like huge emeralds, translucent glass. His heart lurched suddenly, unexpectedly.

'Just give me the sword, Sister,' he demanded gruffly, annoyed at the unwelcome nudge in his groin. A nun, for God's sake! What had got into him? She was nothing to look at: short, no doubt with a vast mountain of flesh beneath that unbecoming gown and a shaved head under that headcovering. A bride of Christ, married to Our Lord. Untouchable. He should know better.

'Never!' Alinor hissed out. 'Why should I trust you...or them—' she nodded mockingly over at

Edward's men '—to do the right thing? Your reputation, or should I say, your notoriety, precedes
you! Everyone knows what Prince Edward is like!
He's a devil and a rogue, and that goes for all who
serve him, as well! I'm staying here and I'm not
moving until my friend comes back with help to
mend the wheel.'

Irritation burned through him at her rudeness.
'Be careful, maid.' His voice lowered in warning.
'Your accusations are treacherous and based on
ignorance; you would do well to remember who
you're dealing with, lay sister or not. Edward does
not take kindly to those who defy him...' his sparkling eyes roamed over her '...and neither do I.'

Alinor reeled back in fright as he lunged forward, wrenching the sword helm easily from her
and lobbing it back along the bridge with a clatter. The blade spun away, sliding across the flat
cobbles. 'No...o...o!' she protested weakly, senses
spinning; for one sickening moment, she thought
she might faint. Quickly, she wound her fingers
into the oxen's leather harness, thinking to stay
close to the cart that way.

'Forgive me, Sister,' the knight said, but there
was no forgiveness in his tone. 'But if you refuse
to move, then I will have to move you.'

Roped, muscular arms looped tightly around
her waist; she gasped out, a mixture of terror and
outrage, fingers snarling in desperation around

the harness. But to no avail. He plucked her up
with ease, lifting her so high that her feet flailed
above the ground. Under the sheer force of the
movement, her grip loosened on the harness, fingers flailing in the air as he slammed her against
his solid frame to carry her away.

The jolting impact of the man's body against
her own sent shock waves coursing through her;
her face was on a level with his, his chest hard up
against her soft breasts, her hips bouncing intimately against his muscle-bound thighs. A wild,
hectic colour flooded her pale skin; she wanted to
die in shame. Never, never, had she been so close
to a man before!

'You let me go! This instant!' she demanded,
fury and humiliation shunting aside her fear. Bat-
tering small fists down on the top of his shoulders, she wriggled violently in his fearsome grip,
wanting him to drop her, kicking at his shins and
stubbing her toes against the inflexible muscle.
'Put me down! I'll make you pay for this!' Beneath his tunic, the tiny links that made up his
mail coat poked into her raging fists.

He chuckled, a throaty sound rippling upwards from his chest. 'You make a lot of threats
for someone supposedly from the house of God.
And for a woman.'

Bashing furiously at his shoulders, Alinor failed
to hear him. 'Let me go,' she shrieked again, 'let

me go!' Sanity fled, as if snapped away in a sharp breeze. She would do anything to extricate herself from his punishing grip. Instinct drove her, the instinct to survive. Leaning forward, she sunk her teeth into the soft, downy lobe of his ear, senses poised for the smallest release of his arms so she could wriggle away.

It didn't come.

'Why, you little....!' Guilhem roared at her, outraged, his brawny arms still clamped around her, muscles like iron rivets against the small of her back. 'You bit me!' His eyes flared across her white, fearful face.

Her confidence shrivelled; convinced he would release her after she had bit him, she had given no thought to the consequences. Why had she not been meek and mild, subservient? How foolish she had been! What would they do to her, a single maid in a group of royalist soldiers? My God, it didn't bear thinking about! A shriek rose up on an engulfing tide of fear, a high-pitched screeching welling in her chest, bursting out from her mouth in incoherent splutters, gathering strength; her mind blanked completely, washed through, crumpling into a vast wasteland of utter terror.

Her screams, shrill and anguished, made his ears hurt. Wincing, Guilhem reached the riverbank with the struggling bundle in his arms. He wanted to assure the maid that everything would be fine, that they had no intention of hurting her, and that all they wanted to do was be on their way, but he knew his words would make no impression. Given the noise the nun was making, she simply wouldn't hear him.

'Sweet Jesu! Will you stop that caterwauling?' Edward said as he strode towards the pair of them. 'I've had enough of this!'

The blow came out of nowhere, a large fist slamming into the side of Alinor's cheek.

The maid's body reeled sideways at the violent impact, limp in Guilhem's arms, unconscious. Her head lolled forward on to his shoulder, linen veil fanning out across his surcoat. He didn't even have time to step back, to pull her away from Edward's damaging swing, the full force of his blow. 'I'm sorry,' Edward said, staring with dismay at the senseless maid in Guilhem's arms, 'but that infernal screeching was crawling under my skin; it made me mad.'

'Really?' Guilhem replied, his tone constrained, dry. He adjusted his arms so that the girl's body was more evenly balanced against him. God, when would Edward learn to control his temper? He swung her legs up towards his chest, so that she lay secure against him, her weight light, surprisingly delicate. Her voluminous gown concealed a trim figure, a slender indent of waist. The curve of her hip nudged against his forearm.

'It was completely unnecessary. To hit a woman, Edward, and not only a woman, a lay sister!'

'I know, I know,' Edward said, pale eyes immediately contrite. 'I wasn't thinking.'

Guilhem's eyes lowered, scowling at the mass of purple bruising on the woman's cheekbone. Blood trickled down towards her wimple, staining the white cloth, blooming steadily across the fabric like a blossoming flower. Her eyes were closed, long velvet lashes fanning her cheeks. But her breath puffed against his jawline, warm and regular. Thank God. Ignoring Edward, he carried her over into the shade of a beech tree and laid her down, carefully, on the ground.

He walked over to help the other soldiers unload the grain sacks, stacking them neatly at the side of the bridge. Unhitching the oxen, they led the animals over to the trees, securing their reins to the lower branches. Watched by Edward, grim and unsmiling on his horse, they managed to half-drag, half-carry the ailing cart from the bridge, depositing it safely on the river bank.

'What I can't understand is, what was the stupid chit doing on her own?' Edward said suddenly, exasperated, trying to mitigate his guilt, as if he were less likely to hit a woman if she had a man with her. 'I mean, what woman travels alone, these days? It's unheard of. Foolish. Stupid.'

'I couldn't agree more,' Guilhem said. 'But apparently she told the soldiers she had sent her man to fetch help with the broken axle.' He flicked his gaze over to the spreading beech tree, at the prone, motionless figure, the stark white face.

'My mother would tear a strip off me if she found out that I'd hit a woman,' Edward said, his narrow mouth turning down ruefully.

'I doubt it,' Guilhem replied. 'The Queen adores you and well you know it. She would blame the girl for bringing it upon herself.'

Edward threw him a curious lopsided smile. 'Well, her behaviour was completely out of order...'

'It was certainly...unusual,' Guilhem replied. Most women would have run away at the first sight of the soldiers, rather than guarding the cart with its mediocre haul of grain. She had been horribly frightened, but had held her ground, hitting out like a cornered animal. Admiration threaded through him, a grudging praise; although she had been foolish, it had taken a great deal of courage to do what she had done.

'Anyway...' Edward adjusted his leather gauntlets around his wrists '...let's move; we've wasted enough time in this godforsaken place. Let's rideto Knighton. To the palace.' He looked around the clearing, satisfied that the other soldiers were mounting up. 'Where's your horse?'

'I'll catch you up,' Guilhem said bluntly.

'Wh-what? Please don't tell me you intend to

shilly-shally around a common nun? Her manservant will be back in a moment!'

Guilhem patted the neck of Edward's horse, rubbing his calloused thumb against the soft pelt. 'I want to make sure she's all right.'

'An attack of conscience, Guilhem? What's the matter, feeling guilty on my behalf?'

Guilhem shrugged his shoulders. 'No, merely concerned.' The feeling of guilt was nothing new to him, hanging constantly from his shoulders like a grey shroud. 'She's vulnerable lying there like that, unconscious; any woman would be.'

'Oh, for God's sake, leave her! Get on your horse and come with me'

'I'll follow on.'

Edward's mouth drooped with disappointment. 'You've gone soft, Guilhem,' he said bitterly. 'Ever since that day at Fremont—'

Guilhem shook his head, a swift, decisive moment, stopping Edward's speech. He had no wish to be reminded of that awful day. Remorse lurched through his heart. The burning castle. That child...

Edward eyed his friend's stony expression. 'Don't let it affect you so, Guilhem. You paid the price.'

'I set the fire that killed him,' Guilhem replied tonelessly. A child's life lost through his thoughtless actions. 'I'll follow on.'

Edward slumped in the saddle. Hazy shadows cast by the beech trees dappled his skin, sunburnt and freckled. Guilhem was indispensable, his best commander. But he had no authority over him: Guilhem was not a knight in Edward's pay, he was a rich man in his own right, a man who chose to ride by the Prince's side from a sense of loyalty, of friendship. Because Edward had helped him. Saved him.

'Oh, if you insist,' Edward said finally, resigned. Raising his arm, he gave the order for his soldiers to mount up and follow him. Kicking his heels into the destrier's flanks, he rode away, clattering across the flat square stones of the bridge, horse's tail swishing in his wake.

The sun had moved behind the clouds again. Beneath the tree the light was dim, streaked in shadow. Ducking his head beneath the low swaying branches, Guilhem crouched beside the girl's prone figure, pillowed in a mass of spent beech leaves, her gown billowing out from a girdled waist, the cloth sinking down around her limbs to display the rounded curve of her hips, slender thighs. Leather boots poked out from a rickety hemline. And hanging from her belt, a dagger, carried in a leather scabbard! Surprising, for a lay sister to carry a blade; he thought they believed that prayers and the Cross would protect them in all circumstances. Obviously, this one had other ideas.

He knelt in down in the spongy ground, shins sinking into the mess of decaying coppery vegetation. A single leaf, burnt orange, fluttered down from above, landing on the coarse cloth covering her midriff, the concave hollow of her stomach. His nails dug into his palms, resisting the urge to brush it away.

'Come on,' he said brusquely, stroking the side of her cheek. His breath hitched at the silky sensation spiralling upwards through his blood. Her skin was like goose down, delicate, milk-white, a single freckle above her top lip. His big body hulked over her fragile frame, awkward, graceless, like some giant about to devour its prey. Most of his life had been spent bawling at soldiers, training them to fight, to battle harder, faster, longer. He'd been fighting for so long, he couldn't remember the last time he'd spent in the company of a woman, had forgotten how to treat them. 'Come on!' he repeated, more loudly this time. Moving closer, his knees snaring her skirts, he seized her shoulders, shaking her gently. Her head rolled back against the leaves; she moaned softly.

Her eyes opened slowly.

At first, Alinor's vision was hazy, clouded; above her head, a trembling latticework of leaves, yellow, brindled, scuffing gently in the breeze. Where was she? Why was she lying here? Damp seeped upwards from the ground, soaking through the thin fabric of her gown. She wriggled her shoulders, trying to reduce the uncomfortable feeling. Her cheek ached incessantly; she examined the smarting skin with tentative fingers.

'No,' a gruff voice said, 'leave it.' Firm, decisive fingers pushed away her hand.

Alinor's stomach lurched in recognition. Oh, God, not him again! The man knelt above her, face tough and brutal, slanted grooves carving down from his cheeks to the square angularity of his jaw. Fear whispered through her veins. She pushed her hands down into the ground, trying to push back from him. 'You, go away!' she stuttered out. His knees pinned her skirts; she was trapped. 'Get away from me, you...you barbarian!'

To her surprise, he laughed. 'I'm not going to hurt you.' His voice was low, melodious, curling through her veins like velvet smoke.

'You hit me!' she spat out weakly, eyes flaring with accusation.

'Not me,' he replied calmly. 'The Prince. You wouldn't stop screaming.'

'And that makes it all right, does it?' she flung at him, her tone brittle. 'To hit a woman because she's making too much noise?' Anxiety knotted her heart; she wished she had the strength to leap up, to push the man away.

'I don't agree with what he did...' the man hulked over her like a huge bear, shining chainmail wrinkling across his shoulders '...but you must admit, your behaviour was extreme, and discourteous. It's customary to defer to royalty, to show respect, but you, you showed anything but!' His eyes pierced her, twilight blue, intense and predatory.

'I had to protect the grain,' she mumbled. The rounded bulk of his knees brushed against her midriff, hot through the thin stuff of her dress. Too close! What was she thinking of, lying sprawled out beneath him, like some wanton? Vulnerability surged through her, her pulse fluttering insanely. 'I need to sit up,' she muttered. 'And you're on my skirts!'

He looked down to the point where his knees trapped the fabric of her gown, mouth twitching with humour at the nun's temerity, her constant spurning of any help from him. Surely she should be pleased that he had stayed? Ignoring her, he clamped strong fingers around her elbow.

'I can do it myself!' she hissed at him, jerking irritably at his hold. But to no avail. He released her when she was sitting upright. Her vision wobbled dangerously, but she compelled herself to concentrate on the details in front of her: his horse, the bridge, the oxen waiting patiently.

'What have you done with my grain?' Raising her knees, she planted her boots flat on to the ground, scrabbling to stand, fighting the bubbling sickness in her stomach. 'If you've done anything, you'll...oh!' Collapsing back, she clutched at her mouth. 'I don't...'

'Take it easy,' Guilhem said, pressing down on her shoulder. 'Your grain is safe, stacked by the side of the bridge.' In contrast to the maid's hostile behaviour, her collarbone was fragile, bird-like against his palm. He had a sudden urge to unwind the cumbersome fabric of her veil, her wimple, and trace the line of bone into the dip of her throat. He frowned, rising swiftly and strode over to his horse, extracting a leather water bottle from the saddlebags.

'Here.' Pulling the cork stopper as he walked back, he held the bottle out to Alinor.

Reaching upwards, she was shocked to see that her hand was shaking. Inadvertently, her finger-tips jogged against his wrist, muscled and sinewy, and she snatched her hand away, horrified at the flare of sensation arcing straight to the pit of her belly. Hell's teeth, the Prince must have really punched her hard to make feel so strange!

'Take it!' he insisted, gruffly. 'Stop acting as if I'm about to poison you!'

She glared at the firm, tanned fingers holding the bottle out to her, then reached up to grab the flagon quickly, to avoid all touch. He raised his eyebrows at her desperate movement, but said nothing. She took a sip, relishing the cool water slipping down her throat, quelling the unstable feeling of nausea in her belly.

'Thank you,' she said, giving the bottle back. Tilting her head on one side, the fawn linen of her veil draping across one shoulder, she swept the empty clearing with a wide-eyed, luminous glance. 'Where have all the soldiers gone?' And him, she wanted to add. Prince Edward, the thug who had punched her.

'They carried on.' The knight stood over her, his expression stern, implacable, long legs planted wide, arms crossed over his chest. His calf-leather boots were scuffed, well worn. The woollen trousers that clung to his knees and the lower half of his thighs emphasised the bulky, contoured muscle of his legs. Pinioned beneath his blue gaze, Alinor drew a deep shuddery breath. She hated the way his sheer size made her feel self-conscious, her outer layers peeled away: a quaking shadow of her former self.

'Then why didn't you go with them?' She switched her eyes away from him abruptly, a flag of colour staining her cheeks, annoyed at her reaction. Having lived with the unwanted advances of her stepbrother in the last few years, not to mention the harsh callousness of her father for all of her life, she prided herself on being able to ignore or dismiss most men. They were dispensable, as was this man. She frowned intently at a silver-backed beetle crawling slowly across the coppery leaves on the ground.

'You were unconscious. It wasn't right to leave you alone.'

The note of care in his voice startled her. 'Well, I'm fully conscious now,' Alinor replied with finality. She fiddled with the plaited strings of her girdle, her leather scabbard. 'So you can go.'

Laughter blossomed in Guilhem's chest. Her outright repulsion of him was so blunt, so churlish. 'I could,' he replied, infuriatingly, his eyes twinkling. The chit made him curious, keen to linger; she was feisty and obdurate, and not at all grateful for the fact that he had elected to stay and make sure she was safe.

'Go then!' she snapped as he continued to stand beside her. 'I'm fine, can't you see that? I'm sure your Prince Edward would have something to say about you wasting time over me.' Shuffling her legs impatiently, Alinor tried to ignore the chill creeping in from the wet leaves on the ground, through her skirts, her silk hose.

'He's already said it,' Guilhem replied. 'And he's your Prince as well. You would do well to show him a little more respect. He is in charge of the country now that his father King Henry has been taken prisoner.'

Alinor flinched, pursing her lips. Tipping up her neat, round chin, she flicked her eyes briefly across his lean, impassive face, regretting her runaway tongue. 'Well, he certainly didn't act like a Prince!' Defiantly, she probed the pulpy bruise on the side of her cheek as if to emphasise her point. Throwing her knees to one side, she clambered messily on to all fours, struggling to her feet, clamping her weak arm to her side. Her head swam, shifting unsteadily, iridescent points of light bobbing before her eyes. The knight seized her and, to her dismay, she clung to him, gripping tightly for support as she swayed, fighting for balance.

He pulled her towards him, manacling her wrists. His face loomed close to hers. 'And you, chit, do not act like a nun. So I would be careful if I were you.'

Her heart quailed beneath the questioning look in his eyes, the suspicion held in those glittering depths. Eyes like the sea. His eyelashes were black and long, almost touching his high cheekbones, silky threads splayed out across tanned skin. Yanking away, Alinor forced herself to breath evenly, making a great play of adjusting her linen veil around her shoulders.

A shout caused them both to look across to the bridge and she sagged with relief. Her scattered senses gathered, her mind clearing, focusing on the need to pull away from this man. There was Ralph, grinning, one arm raised in greeting as he plodded towards them carrying a piece of wood, and what looked like a hessian sack of tools. Thank God.

'That's him!' she almost shouted at the knight beside her. 'That's Ralph!' In her eagerness to reach the lad she charged past Guilhem, jogging her elbow into his forearm.

He watched her go, her step light and purposeful across the grass, flowing skirts dragging brindled leaves in her wake. He smiled softly; why, she had practically shoved him out of the way in her eagerness to reach the boy. A maid half his size, who barely reached his shoulder! She couldn't wait to be rid of him! He should have been annoyed, furious with her for her lack of courtesy and respect, and yet, he was not. Curiosity chipped the mantle of his soul, dug beneath the impenetrable crust that had lain numb, dormant for all these months. Mounting up, he steered his horse towards the bridge, and up over it, his horse's hooves clattering over the cobbles, glancing down briefly at the maid and the boy beside the broken cart. They didn't look up and he had the distinct impression that the little nun was studiously ignoring him. Something else was going on here; it was a pity he wouldn't be around to find out what it was. Kicking his heels into the destrier's flanks, he rode off without a backwards glance.

Chapter Three

Layers of mist veiled the huge, creamy moon: a harvest moon, full and orange, inching upwards above the horizon. Brilliant stars pinpricked the dimming sky. The chapel bell attached to Odstock Priory tolled slowly for the last service of the day, sweet, melancholy notes ringing out across the flat, undulating land, the occasional screech of an owl disrupting the regular chimes. Crosses swinging from their girdles, the nuns walked in single file, heads bowed, towards the chapel from the Priory; their fawn-coloured veils shone white in the moonlight.

Hidden in the shadows of the gatehouse, Alinor watched them, pale wraiths silent as ghosts, some hunched over with old age, others graceful with spines ramrod straight, gliding across the cobbled courtyard and into the light-filled chapel. At this hour, every windowsill, every niche in the stone walls held a flaming candle, shining on the pewter plate, the jewelled cross on the altar, on the nuns' faces bent in prayer. Alinor knotted her fingers across her stomach. As an honorary lay sister, she had the choice as to whether she would join them or not; tonight, she would not. As the last nun stepped over the chapel threshold and the great arched door closed against the night, Alinor darted out, skipping across to the main Priory: three double-height rectangular buildings constructed from limestone blocks, arranged around cloisters and an inner courtyard garden. Climbing the wooden steps, she pushed open the iron-riveted door which led directly on to the first-floor hall, open to the roof rafters.

Pausing, she tried to still her quickened breath, the sound from her lungs roaring in her ears. Her keen eye absorbed the sparse, familiar details: glossy elm floorboards, gilded by the light from a single candle burning on an oak coffer; a fire smoking fitfully in the wide, brick-lined fireplace. A long trestle table and benches dominated the hall; this was where the nuns ate and any guests that might join them. But now, the hall was completely empty. All was quiet.

Extracting two lumpy bags of gold coins from her satchel, Alinor dumped them on the carved-oak coffer beside the door, the money earned today from the sale of the nuns' wheat. After her unwanted encounter with the Prince and his soldiers this morning, the remainder of the day had passed in a blur; she could scarcely remember the noise and bustle of the market, the bartering, of which Ralph had done the most. She had stood by and watched, her body shocked and reeling, her mind constantly playing the moment when a pair of powerful hands had grabbed at her waist and thrown her up against a hard, unyielding torso. The image taunted her, dragged on her senses. She had been useless at the market, no help at all.

Seizing a rush torch from an iron bracket, Alinor held the blazing twigs aloft as she crossed the hall diagonally, moving through a narrow arch in the far corner, twisting down a spiral staircase. She entered the storeroom below, full of earthenware pots, casks, sacks of flour, wriggling carefully through the clumsy towers of hessian bags, the stacked barrels, to reach another door that squeaked on its hinges as she dragged it open. Holding the spitting, crackling light aloft, she descended the steep, rickety steps. None of the nuns came down here; the cellars were a labyrinth of hidden chambers and torturous passageways, formed from the vaulted foundations of the original, much smaller, Priory. Only the hefty barrels of mead which the sisters needed occasionally were situated in the first shallow-arched alcove, close by the bottom of the steps.

Alinor was going further, down into the basement. She knew her way around these cellars. As a frequent visitor to the Priory, the nuns had offered her space in the vaults to hang and store her herbs. Long stalks, tied with bristly twine, hung from iron hooks in the ceiling, crispy flower heads rasping at her veil, scattering seeds as she moved along the corridor, careful to keep the flickering, spitting torch away from the precious harvest above. The nuns' offer had been a godsend; after her stepmother had ordered a whole roomful of her herbs to be destroyed, claiming they were 'the work of the Devil', Alinor had been desperate to find another place to keep them. Any place away from her stepmother's prying eyes. The nuns, friends of her mother, and now her, had come to her rescue and she repaid them in kind, using her tinctures and ointments to heal them, as well as the many villagers who came to her for help.

'Bianca?' Alinor called out quietly, pausing in front of one of the wide shallow arches. 'It's me.' Her whisper echoed eerily around the limestone walls, stone the colour of pale honey. A cobweb tickled her cheek; she brushed it away. There was a rustle, the sound of breathing, and then a voice.

'Alinor?'

She peeked inside the chamber, thrusting the light inside. The girl, Bianca, sat huddled in a blanket on the flagstone floor, blinking rapidly

with the unexpected surge of light. The silver embroidery on the hemline of her gown winked and
glistened, the rich silk fabric rippling out around
her.

Thrusting the burning torch into an iron bracket
on the wall, Alinor knelt down beside the maid.
'I'm so sorry I left you alone for so long,' she said.
'I had to go to the market today, for the nuns…but
here, I brought you some food.' Delving into her
baggy leather satchel, she extracted the packages
she had bought, placing them on the uneven stone
floor. 'I hope it's enough.'

Bianca placed her hand on Alinor's shoulder.
The hanging pearls decorating the silver circlet on
her tawny hair bobbed with the slight movement.
'It's more than enough…you've…oh, what happened to your face?' Her blue eyes flared open in
horror at the mottled bruising on Alinor's cheek,
the dried blood. 'Did she work out what happened,
your stepmother? What you did?'

'No, no, I haven't seen her,' Alinor reassured
her.

'Then what happened to you?'

'It's nothing,' Alinor mumbled, drawing her
stiff linen veil forward, a self-conscious gesture,
embarrassed by the girl's concern. She had managed to rewrap her wimple on the way to the market, so the bloodstained cloth was hidden. But
nothing could conceal the damage on her cheek.

A pair of sparkling midnight eyes, a teasing smile, flashed across her vision and she bit down on her bottom lip, hard. Do not think of it, do not think of *him*, she ordered herself sternly.

'Looks like it was a bit more than nothing,' Bianca said, frowning critically at Alinor's face. 'You've risked your neck for me already; please don't take any more chances.' She shifted her position on the blanket, her blue-silk overdress sliding over her knees. Hundreds of tiny seed pearls had been stitched into the curved neckline, matching the intricacy of the maid's circlet and fine silk veil.

'It wasn't anything like that,' Alinor said, untying the packages with brisk efficiency. 'Ralph, you know, the lad from the village who went with me, and I, well, we ran into a bit of trouble on the way to market.'

'Trouble?'

'We crossed paths with Prince Edward and his entourage. And our cart had broken, so they couldn't cross the bridge. Ralph went to fetch help and left me there.' Her breathing quickened and she shook her head. 'I was stupid, thinking I could brave it out against them. I should have run, hidden somewhere.'

'Why didn't you?' Bianca asked softly.

'I thought they would destroy all the grain, all the nuns' profits. But, thankfully, I held them off until the Prince arrived.' She closed her eyes briefly, remembering. The thick arms folded about her slim waist, thumbs splaying against her spine, pulling her close. The mail-coat links pressed through her clothes, digging into her soft flesh. The way his muscular legs bumped against her toes, flailing uselessly above the ground. Blue, blue eyes, sparking fire. A shivery breath gripped her lungs, surging, alive. 'And then one of the knights grabbed me and carried me off the bridge, out of the way.' She grimaced, balling her fists defiantly in her lap. 'I put up a good fight though. I bit him.' Her mouth tightened. 'I bit his ear.'

'Oh, Alinor!' Bianca said, clapping her hands to her mouth. 'So I suppose he walloped you for that?'

'No, it was the Prince. I just kept on screaming.' A delicate colour brushed her cheeks as she recalled her outrageous display. She shrugged her shoulders. 'What was I supposed to do? Go quietly?'

Bianca laughed, dipping her head. 'Alinor, I have only known you a short while, but something tells me you would never go quietly. What you have done for me…your bravery; I'm sure I wouldn't have the courage to do the same. You were lucky, though. The Prince has a fearsome reputation; he could have killed you.'

It's not him I'm worried about. She shifted un-

comfortably, fiddling with the strings on the packages. She couldn't seem to undo them, her hands
clumsy, muddled. 'Then thank God he didn't.'
Alinor smiled wanly, her fingers tangling in the
knotted strings. Sweet Jesu, the thought of that
man was affecting her even though he was nowhere near! What was the matter with her? She
wasn't ever likely to see him again.

'Here, let me do it,' Bianca offered. 'I'm starving and you're taking too long.' She opened up the
squares of muslin to reveal fresh rounds of bread,
lumps of crumbling cheese, an apple. 'Oh, you've
brought me a feast!' She bit into one of the bread
rolls. 'This bread tastes like Heaven! Thank you
Alinor, thank you for everything.'

Alinor smiled at her enthusiasm, the girl's good
humour despite her desperate situation. Bianca
had arrived at Alinor's home with an escort of
French knights, sent by Queen Eleanor, King Henry's wife, in order to marry Alinor's stepbrother
Eustace. A marriage arranged by the Queen, with
the Savoy family of Attalens in France, a marriage
that could not be unarranged. Her stepmother disapproved of the match, violently disapproved, but
how could she openly contest a queen's edict? She
wanted Eustace to marry Alinor, as Alinor was
the sole inheritor of her father's vast wealth, his
many castles and estates. On her father's death she
would be a wealthy woman in her own right. And

her stepmother would do anything for Eustace to have all that and, so it seemed, she would stop at nothing, nothing, to achieve that end.

'Have you been able to find anyone to take me to the coast yet?' Bianca widened her large blue eyes in question as she nibbled delicately at the cheese. 'It was a shame your stepmother sent my escort away so quickly, otherwise they could have taken me back. And my poor maidservant as well, having to travel back with them!'

'Wilhema wanted them all out of the way as quickly as possible. She didn't want them to find out what she was planning for you,' Alinor said. 'But don't worry, I have someone in mind to take you back to France, someone I can trust.' Ralph, she thought to herself, or someone in his family. They would help. 'Remember, you are supposed to be dead. Wilhelma truly believes that I did what she asked of me, that I poisoned you. If she, or one of her friends, should see you…'

'It won't happen; I can disguise myself.' Bianca turned her mouth down ruefully. 'I need to wear your lay sister's clothes and possibly cut my hair, darken down the colour?'

'Yes, all of those things. You cannot risk being recognised. But you must stay here for the moment; I promise, I won't take long to ask my friend to take you home.'

'I'm surprised you're not offering to do it

yourself,' Bianca teased. 'After all, you seem to demonstrate exceptional skill when it comes to dealing with potential attackers.'

Alinor laughed, touched her check self-consciously. 'Don't worry, he will be a proper escort.'

'Just make sure he's good looking,' Bianca said. 'That's all I ask.'

Such a request seemed so idiotic in the face of the huge risks both girls were taking that they both dissolved into laughter, heads bobbing together in the flickering half-light.

Hiking up her skirts, Alinor scrambled on to the stone window ledge, angled deep into the infirmary wall. Standing, she reached for the ornate iron latch on the leaded window, pushing the casement open. Fresh air flooded the chamber, cutting through the fuggy, foetid air. The nuns' hospital, a double-height building set apart from the Priory, held about twenty pallet beds, simply constructed and lifted a few inches from the flagstone floor by a block of wood at each end. Mattresses and pillowcases were stuffed with straw, which could easily be replaced; coarse linen sheets and a motley collection of woven blankets lay on top of each bed.

Only one of the beds was occupied at the moment. Sister Edith, one of the more elderly nuns, had come in a few days ago complaining of stomach pains, which had developed into vomiting and fever. Now she lay on her back in the bed, a motionless doll-like figure under a heap of blankets. She had stopped being sick, yet still she shivered, moaning occasionally. Alinor jumped down from the window ledge and moved over to her, dipping a flannel into a bowl of cool water beside the bed, and placing it gently across Edith's forehead. She was worried about her; so worried that she had stayed the night at the convent, lying restlessly in the pallet bed next to her, alert and wakeful to Edith's shallow breathing. She hadn't even had time to visit Bianca today. She would go this evening, when there would be more sisters around to tend to Edith.

'Any change?' Maeve, the Prioress of Odstock, swept into the infirmary, flanked by two young novices. A tall, imposing woman, Maeve had a reputation for being strict, but fair. Alinor held a great deal of respect for her; the Prioress had held her mother in her arms as she had finally succumbed to the fever that had gripped her for days, and would help Alinor whenever she could. And in return, Alinor helped the nuns with her healing skills, learned from an early age at her mother's knee; she even had her own bed at the Priory, which allowed her to come and go as she pleased.

Alinor tilted her head to one side. For a fleeting moment, she wondered what Maeve would say if she told her about the girl hidden in the cellars. But the Prioress was a stickler for rules; if she found out about the Queen's wish for Bianca to marry Eustace, she would probably send the poor girl straight back to Alinor's home and to her conniving stepmother. No, she couldn't risk that. Helping Bianca leave the country was something she would have to do on her own, hopefully with Ralph's help.

'Have you put any ointment on that bruise yet?' Maeve barked at her, her light-brown eyes swiftly assessing the patchy marks on Alinor's cheek. The sparseness of her eyelashes made her facial features more prominent: a large, beak-like nose, the white expanse of lined forehead, shaved eyebrows.

'Yes, yes, I have,' Alinor reassured her. She had dabbed her cheek with foul-smelling unguent that very morning, when she had woken in the pallet bed next to the ailing nun.

Maeve peered at her critically. 'It looks nasty. How did you say it happened again?'

'I was stupid, I knocked it on one of the outposts of the cart, yesterday.' She threw her a twisted smile. 'As usual, I wasn't looking where I was going.'

Maeve smiled. 'Oh, Alinor, as clumsy as your mother was.' She clasped her bony fingers in front of her swinging cross. 'But also as good at selling. Your mother also knew how to drive a hard bargain. Thank you for all that coin; it will certainly keep us through the winter.'

And to think I nearly lost it all, thought Alinor. The risks I took. A hollowness suddenly emptied her stomach, the washcloth tightening between her fingers, drips running down on to the woollen blanket.

'You look pale, Alinor. Go and fetch yourself something to eat; there's food out in the refectory. I'll watch Edith for a while.' Maeve eased the washcloth from Alinor's fingers and settled herself on the three-legged stool next to Edith's bed.

'I need to pick one other plant which might help her,' Alinor said.

'Fine, but don't leave the Priory at the moment. There have been reports of fighting between the royalists and the rebels nearby. I wouldn't want you to become caught up in something like that.'

A surcoat of red and gold surged in her mind's eye; she dashed the vivid memory away. 'No, I won't go home today. I wanted to see how Edith fares.' And to make sure Bianca leaves safely, she thought. Besides, she had no wish to return home to face her stepmother. She was better off at the Priory.

During the morning, the cloud had thickened steadily; the day was sunless, overcast, with a fitful breeze. As Alinor walked through the arch in the ivy-clad wall to the vegetable gardens, leaves chased along the cobbled path before her, silver-backed, yellowing, as if tossed by an unseen hand. A gust of wind eddied around her skirts, blowing them sideways, but after being cooped in with Edith all morning, she relished the fresh air against her skin. From a line of billowing oaks to the north, a gaggle of black crows flew up, sharply, wings beating furiously against the powerful currents of air.

Eyes watering in the cool air, Alinor strode briskly, past the neat rows of root vegetables: the carrots, turnips and swedes ready to be lifted and stored for winter. Her herb plot lay to the rear of the gardens; here, she grew the flowers and plants that went to make up her tinctures and ointments. Leaning over, she plucked several leaves of fever-few, and some mint as well, for flavour, stuffing them in the linen pouch that hung from her girdle.

'Alinor! Alinor!' Her name, carried along on the brisk breeze. Someone was calling her! Turning abruptly, she glanced back at the Priory windows and then over to the infirmary. A drab white veil blew out from the window; one of the novices was waving at her, yelling her name. Oh, God, she thought, it must be Edith! Alinor sprinted back across the gardens, her slender legs carrying her through the inner courtyard of the Priory, past the cloisters and out through a small arched doorway on the southern side which would lead her back to the infirmary.

She stopped.

Her heart clenched, squeezed with fear.

Fingers searching wildly behind her, she scrabbled, clutched at the door, the doorframe, the surrounding stone arch; anything that would give her some support, some stability. No, no, no! It couldn't be! Her inner voice screamed denial even as her eyes told her what was true. Breath surged in her lungs; she sagged back against the cold stone. Before her, clustered in front of the infirmary was a group of about thirty knights, dusty, dirty, bloodied. Some sat on the ground, propped up by others, obviously wounded; others lay flat out on makeshift stretchers, faces drawn and white, eyes closed. Several soldiers held the large-muscled warhorses in a group, the animals obviously nervous, pawing the ground, enormous eyes rolling.

At the centre of the mêlée stood Prince Edward, head bent in conversation with the Prioress.

And him.

The broad-shouldered knight who had carried her kicking and screaming from the bridge, with his eyes of midnight blue, his shock of tawny hair. He was there.

Chapter Four

Fear spiked her veins; she rocked slightly, wondering if she could sink back into the shadows without anyone noticing her. But before she had the chance, Maeve turned her head, brown eyes homing in on the figure in the archway. Bony, arthritic fingers beckoned imperiously, signalling to Alinor. Straightening her spine, Alinor blundered out into the open, wobbling legs scarcely carrying her across the cropped wispy grass. These men wouldn't recognise her, surely; even now, the other sisters were coming out to help, streaming out from the cloisters, from the chapel, all dressed in exactly the same way as Alinor. She would blend in, hidden amongst the rest of the nuns.

Edging her way through the soldiers, she reached Maeve. Prince Edward was already moving amongst his men, shouting orders, commanding the more able knights to carry the injured soldiers into the infirmary. Of the other knight, there was no immediate sign; Alinor kept her eyes pinned to Maeve, unwilling to twist her head and find him right behind her. Her muscles hummed with the strain of keeping herself held tightly in, wanting to remain unnoticed, slipping through this crowd of soldiers like a ghost.

'Come, let us help these soldiers before they bleed to death on our doorstep,' Maeve ordered the nuns who clustered about her. Her keen gaze whipped about, directing the sisters to the men who needed the most help, making sure her commands were carried out. As Alinor moved to follow out Maeve's orders, her head lowered, the Prioress caught her arm. 'Alinor, wait, go into the infirmary and ask one of the novices to help you carry Sister Edith up to the bed on the second floor; I can't have her downstairs with all these men.'

Alinor nodded gratefully, almost running along the path towards the infirmary, desperate to be out of the immediate vicinity of the soldiers. She grasped at the sturdy handle of the infirmary door, about to push it open.

'Alinor? Is that your name?

She gripped the iron ring, knuckles frozen.

'Can I help at all?'

The male voice was low, well-modulated, *familiar*. Shock scurried through her. He must have overheard her name when Maeve talked to her.

She bristled at his use of it, the impertinence; her name sounded like treachery on his lips, a betrayal.

'Er...no, it's—it's quite all right,' she stuttered out, steadfastly facing the door, breath caught in her throat like a stone.

'You can turn around, you know,' the voice said. 'I know it's you.'

Sweat pricked her palm. A shudder rippled through her slender frame. 'I don't know what you're talking about,' she replied haughtily. 'Now, if you'll excuse me...'

He leaned over her. 'You're the screaming banshee from yesterday, aren't you?' he murmured.

The hot push of breath tickled her linen veil, her ear. So close. Excitement whipped through her veins, a wild heat suffusing her flesh, turning her limbs to pulp. She glowered at the wooden planks of the door, the yellow-green lichen spotting across the weathered oak, resenting the physical response of her body towards him. Defiance ripped through her; she flipped around to face him, to the beautiful savagery of his face. 'So what if I am? What are you going to do about it?' Blood thrummed in her ears. She was frightened of him. That was it. Frightened of the trouble these men could cause.

Blue eyes sparkled over her, a generous grin lighting up his sculptured features. His bottom lip held a wide curve, a surprising softness in the hard angle of his jaw. 'Nothing, as long as you don't start screaming again. Or steal my sword.' His eyes drifted over the mark on her cheek. 'Still hurting?'

'What do you think?' she asked truculently, crossing her arms across her chest.

'You're remarkably badly behaved for a woman who has taken her vows.' He ran one thumb along the underside of his sword belt, assessing her slowly. 'And aggressive.' He touched his ear, the one she had bitten, and she flushed, noticing the bluish bruise on his earlobe.

'Then you'd better keep away from me,' she warned, trying to inject an element of fierceness into her tone. 'There's no telling what I might do next.' Turning smartly away from him, she pushed into the infirmary, the door thumping behind her. She paused in the gloom, senses skittered, her breath easing out slowly by degrees. She needed to calm herself. How dare he creep up behind her like that? His blatant masculinity, so close, had pushed her mind from her task. If she didn't pay heed, the soldiers would be in here before she had managed to move Edith.

The infirmary was deserted. All the novices must have run out to help with the injured soldiers. Darting over to Edith's bed, she quickly evaluated the frail woman beneath the bedclothes.

The old nun had no spare flesh on her, just skin and bone, like a little bird. She would be able to carry her. 'Let's wrap you up, Edith,' Alinor said gently. Bundling the bedsheets and blanket around the nun's thin body, she eased her forearms beneath Edith's hips, the other around her shoulders. The old nun moaned softly, her skin stretched like translucent parchment across her jutting cheekbones.

'It's all right, Edith...' Alinor whispered. 'I'm going to move you upstairs.'

'Let me carry her.'

Twisting around, Alinor scowled, then straightened up, irritated that she hadn't heard the knight following her. She should have bolted the door! He stood beside her, his large frame spare and rugged, eyes shining like dark coals in the gloom. He smelled of woodsmoke, the tangy scent of horses. Her belly seemed to turn in on itself; a curious pang of longing dragged at the very core of her.

'I can do it!' she spat out, angry, intimidated. 'We can fend for ourselves here. Go out and help your men, and stop bothering me!' How jittery he made her feel! He prised away her customary self-confidence, this man whom she barely knew, throwing her off balance, burrowing beneath her practical level-headedness to make her nerves dance with an uncharacteristic anxiety.

Guilhem tilted his head on one side, his mouth

twitching up in a half-smile. Her behaviour was extreme, argumentative and stubborn. She reminded him of his sister: the same wayward truculence, the same self-reliance, wanting to do everything herself and fully believing that she could do so. The flash of defiance in that beautiful face, the hostile tilt of her pert little nose. He folded his arms slowly across his chest. 'Go on then.' Challenge sparkled in his eyes.

Ignoring him, she bent over Edith again, attempting to hoist the frail body from the bed, praying that her weak arm wouldn't let her down now, not here, not in front of this man. The ligaments in her spine gripped and stretched; her stomach clenched tightly. Sweat prickled on her brow, but Edith didn't budge.

'Out of my way.' The big man moved in beside her impatiently, shoving at her with a swift nudge of his hip, his expression grim. Alinor tottered backwards, knocking into a stool, scowling furiously as he lifted Edith carefully from the bed, wrapped tightly in a heap of linens and blankets. Only the nun's poor, bald head peeked out from the top of the blanket.

'Where do I take her?'

'I would have done it!' she protested limply. 'You didn't give me enough time!'

Guilhem glanced at the main door, his mouth fixing into a firm, impenetrable line. 'The other soldiers are being carried in now, so I suggest you lead me in the right direction or this old lady is going to have more of a shock than she deserves.'

He made her sound like a spoiled brat, thinking only of herself! 'This way,' Alinor bit out, fuming, swishing her skirts around with a brisk movement. She led him to a curving alcove set in the infirmary wall, indicating the uneven stone steps winding upwards from a central pillar. Daylight flooded down from a narrow, arched window set halfway up the stairwell.

'It leads up to the second floor; there's a small bedchamber up there.'

He ducked his head beneath the low lintel, powerful legs ascending the stairs easily, Edith's head lolling against his thick upper arm, white skin pallid against silvery chainmail. Alinor's breath caught in her throat; is this how he had carried her, after the Prince had hit her, senseless, unknowing, his hands clasped intimately about her body? Briefly, she closed her eyes in shame.

Kneeling on the bare floorboards, the knight laid Edith down on the pallet bed, adjusting the bedclothes so that they covered her bare feet. As he rose, his hair almost touched the serried rafters of the ceiling. Alinor hovered in the entrance to the stairwell, lips set in a mutinous line, rebellion coursing through her body. What was it about this man that made her behave so badly?

She jerked out of the way as he approached the stairs, whisking her skirts away dramatically to avoid all contact with him. 'I suppose I should say thank you,' Alinor bit out, grudgingly. 'But I could have carried her.'

'My God, you never give up, do you?' he said, the toe of his boot knocking against her slipper by mistake. 'It's fortunate that you decided to give yourself to Christ, because I can't imagine any man being able to deal with you. Your father must have blessed the day he sent you to the nunnery!'

Sadness whipped through her, sudden, violent. Her eyelashes dipped fractionally. 'My father cursed the day I was born,' she blurted out suddenly, her voice bitter. 'Not that it's any of your business.'

Guilhem thrust one hand through his tousled hair, the colour of rain-soaked wheat. 'And for that I am sorry,' he said, watching the raft of sorrow track across her pearly skin. He cupped her chin with one big hand, wanting to smooth the sadness away. His thumb swept across her cheek and, for a fraction of a moment, she stood there, savouring the sweet caress. The temptation to turn her head, to press her lips into the warm skin of his hand shot through her; her lashes fluttered downwards, momentarily. Her flesh hummed, treacherous.

What was she doing? Had she truly taken leave of her senses?

'No,' Alinor stuttered out. 'I must go!'

She whipped away from him then, plunging down into the darkness of the stairwell, hand pressed tight to the spot where he had touched her, tears stinging her eyes.

The day slipped quietly into evening. Outside the tall infirmary windows, the sun sank, descending into a riot of luminous pinks and golds that streaked the darkening sky. Inside, the infirmary blazed with light: candles flickered and jumped in stone niches, rush torches had been slung into every iron bracket around the walls, revealing every lump and crack in the uneven plaster. A huge fire burned at one end of the chamber. Badly wounded soldiers filled the beds, heaped under linens and coarse woollen blankets, some shivering, some unconscious. Others rested on piles of straw near the fire, conversing in muted tones, or simply staring into space, eyes blank.

'We were fortunate to find this place.' Edward sighed, stretching his legs out towards the hearth, crossing his leather boots at the ankles. He brushed at a scuff of earth across his fawn-coloured legging. On a stone mantel, above the hearth, a gold cross glittered, set with pearls.

Sprawled in the oak chair, Guilhem flexed his fingers around the scrolled end of the armrest, the intricate wood carving knobbly beneath his thumb as he surveyed the nuns bustling around the men, amazed at the stoicism, the practised efficiency with which they worked. The sisters moved about gracefully, never hurrying, stiff linen veils like angel wings as they bandaged up bloody limbs and stitched up wounds with fine needles and sheep's-gut thread. They never baulked at the enormity of the task; none of them had fainted, or turned squeamishly away at the sight of an ugly wound. As his eyes drifted across the space, he knew who he was searching for. The little nun with emerald eyes like limpid pools, whose tough and hostile manner intrigued him. He had seen the dip of her eyelashes as he had cupped her face, the slight parting of her lips, the faintest release of her breath at his brief touch. And yet here she was, trapped behind the veil, never to know of a man's desire. His loins gripped.

'Yes, we were lucky,' he agreed finally, turning his attention back to Edward. What a senseless waste the day had been. They had met some of Simon de Montfort's rebels on their way to Knighton. Forced to fight, there had been no winners, no losers; after that first terrifying skirmish, each side had slunk away to nurse their wounds, to recover. He accepted that Edward wanted to extract his father, the King, from the rebels, but at what cost? How many more men would they have to lose before they achieved such an aim?

'You should ask one of the sisters to look at your injury,' Edward said, his eyes swivelling to the rip in Guilhem's tunic.

'It's nothing, just a scratch,' he replied. 'I'll see to it myself.'

'Here, you, come over here!' Edward gestured towards a sister who carried a bowl of steaming water towards one of the beds. A sister with a large bruise on one cheek. The nun stopped and stared over at Edward with a haughty expression, clear, intelligent eyes mocking his command, the arrogant snapping of his fingers. 'Yes, you!' Edward demanded. 'Bring that bowl of water and come over here.'

Guilhem's breath quickened as she approached. Alinor. 'God, Edward, will you leave it? That one would rather kill me, than cure me. It's her, the nun from the bridge yesterday. Don't you recognise her?'

Edward narrowed his eyes. 'So it is. The squalling termagant. I'm sure she'll do as she's told after what happened.'

'Don't count on it,' Guilhem said. But his heart stirred in anticipation of her approach.

Alinor stopped by the chairs, setting the bowl of water down on an elm side table with deliberate slowness. Straightening, she bowed her head in deference to the Prince. 'How may I help you, my lord?'

'Guilhem has a wound that needs looking at.' Edward tilted his head towards the man sitting next to him. 'You need to sort it out.' He yawned, turning away, uninterested.

Guilhem. So that was his name. Unusual, reminiscent of a calmness, a serenity, both qualities in which this knight seemed wholly lacking. Shadows carved out the hollows beneath his cheekbones, emphasising their prominence; blond stubble glinted on his chin, giving him a dangerous, devilish appearance. Breath shuddered in her throat, her belly plummeting. The skin on her face still smarted from his earlier touch. What was the matter with her? Men did not normally affect her like this: her father, her stepbrother, the various knights who visited her father's estates—they were all the same, weren't they? Either autocratic and boorish, or weak-willed and incompetent; sometimes all of those things. Her tongue wallowed like padded wool in her mouth, muffling words, stifling her speech. A wave of fluctuating uncertainty crashed over her; how did this man, this stranger, manage to burrow beneath her customary self-confidence and make her behave with such uncharacteristic vulnerability?

'I'll fetch one of the other nuns,' Alinor stuttered out, lamely. 'I need to finish stitching up the soldier over there.' She indicated the bed nearest the fire.

Edward's arm snaked out, seizing her wrist. 'I want you to do this. You will do it.' His voice was savage, his fingers grinding into the fine bones on her forearm. Releasing her, he slumped back into his seat, closing his eyes.

Guilhem caught her eye. 'Be very careful, maid,' he murmured. 'Others are not so lenient as I.'

Alinor scrubbed furiously at the red marks on her wrist, hating Edward, hating the man who sat before her. Uncouth barbarians, the whole lot of them! Used to fighting and killing their way to victory, uncaring who or what stood in their way. But knowing this fact, knowing what these men were, would not help her out of her current predicament. Aware that Guilhem studied her closely, she drew on every last drop of her courage, drawing her spine up into a rigid, inflexible line.

She forced herself to meet his eyes. 'Where is it?' she asked, managing to make her tone bossy and defiant.

Guilhem frowned, uncomprehending. 'I beg your pardon?'

'Where is the wound?' she hissed back at him, churlish.

In response, he sat forward abruptly, hauling his scarlet tunic over his head, followed by the heavy chainmail hauberk, and threw them into a glittering jumble on to the floor. Beneath his chainmail he wore a white linen shirt, slashed open at the neck, the ties loose, undone.

'Here,' he said, pointing to a bloody stain on the white cloth. His tousled hair glimmered in the firelight, tawny, golden. A delicious scent lifted from his skin, like woodsmoke, musky and dark. Sensual.

'You need to take your shirt off,' Alinor barked at him, her voice strangely hoarse. 'I can't bandage it like that.'

He shrugged. 'As you wish.' Grasping the sagging hem, he dragged the shirt upwards, revealing his naked torso. In the firelight, his skin seemed polished, like molten gold. His upper body was lean, with no spare flesh, his neck corded and strong, rising up from the powerful jut of his collarbone. Panels of taut, honed muscle covered his chest, ridging his stomach across a narrow waist.

A savage, boiling heat shot through her, dancing with treacherous excitement. Immediately she ducked her head, hiding the flame of colour across her cheeks, muttering something about bandages. She scooted away across the flagstone floor, skirts slithering in her wake.

Edward rolled his head lazily along the chair-back, contemplating Alinor's bobbing flight. 'God, what is wrong with that chit? Why can't she perform a simple task? Did you see her face? It's as if she's never seen a naked man before!'

Guilhem observed him with a slow grin. 'She's a nun, Edward, do you think it's likely?'

Edward quirked one eyebrow upwards. 'No, but I thought these religious women were immune to men; sworn themselves away from earthly pleasures and all that sort of thing.' He rubbed his belly, suddenly bored with the subject. 'God, I'm hungry. Do you think these good sisters are going to offer us anything to eat?' Levering himself up from the chair, he turned to Guilhem. 'I'll leave you with her; don't take any nonsense. I'm off to find some food.'

Plunging trembling hands into the wicker basket full of rolled-up bandages, Alinor chewed fractiously at the inner lining of her cheek. Sort yourself out, she told herself sternly. He's a man, just a man, like your father and your stupid, mulish stepbrother. No different. Treat him exactly as you would treat Eustace and everything will be fine. Grabbing a pot of salve, balancing it unsteadily on top of the pile of bandages, she spun on her toes and marched back to the fire, plonking her wares down on the small table beside Guilhem's chair. The other chair was empty; Edward had disappeared. She heaved a sigh of relief.

Guilhem's keen eyes followed her movements, watched as she plunged a cloth into the bowl of steaming water, wringing it out. The drips shone in the firelight, falling like crystal tears.

'Should I be worried?' he murmured, as Alinor slapped the wet steaming cloth against the bleeding line of his wound, scrubbing vigorously.

'Not at all,' she replied brusquely. Bright flags of colour burned her cheeks, exaggerated by the leaping flames of the fire. A burning log fell sideways, sending up a shower of sparks. 'I'm perfectly capable.' But her fingers shook as she dipped them into foul-smelling unguent.

'Capable, but maybe not very forgiving.'

'Can you blame me? You carried me forcibly off that bridge. You wouldn't listen when I told you I could carry Edith.' Alinor shrugged her shoulders. 'This may hurt.' Pressing her palm to his shoulder, she smeared the thick paste across the wound. His bulging shoulder muscle moulded into her skin like warm marble: solid, strong. Her breath punched out, a short little gasp. She had tended to men before, certainly, but never a man like this, so...so beautiful. She smacked the earthenware pot of unguent down on the table with such violence that a faint crack appeared from base to top. *Remember who he is: a knight, tough and uncompromising, without an ounce of softness in his body.* But even as these thoughts ran through her mind, she knew she lied to herself. Beneath that harsh exterior was the man who had stayed by her side after Edward and his soldiers had left, the man who had carried Edith, with infinite gentleness, up the spiral staircase.

'I listened when you told me your father cursed you the day you were born.'

Her mouth dropped open. 'Please, don't speak of it. I meant nothing by it.' The words gushed out of her, tripping over each other.

He watched the stricken expression slip across her face. 'If you say so,' he said. There was no conviction in his tone.

Wiping her hands briskly on a cloth, she unrolled a length of bandage. 'You need to sit forward, with your arm held out,' Alinor ordered, cursing her own outspokenness. He had goaded her into blurting such a thing aloud and now his eyes were on her, on her face, scorching, bold. Curious.

'I thought all nuns had their heads shaved,' he said suddenly. His gaze was pinned to a spot beside her ear.

'Wh-what?' Alinor paused, the bandage hanging in the air, a flimsy barrier between them. She reeled back as he touched a single lock of hair sneaking out from beneath her wimple. Pure, white-gold hair. Hell's teeth! Why hadn't she checked on her appearance before she came in here? Furiously, she tucked the offending hair back beneath her wimple.

'Why isn't your head shaved?' Guilhem persisted. Her hair had been like silk: supple, vibrant. An unexpected longing gripped him; he wanted to rip the veil from her head, unwind that tightly wrapped wimple. What was the rest of her hair like? Was it long, curling, falling to her slender hips? He shook his head slightly, ridding himself of the tempting thought. He needed to stop indulging in these idle fantasies; he was intrigued, that was all.

'Stretch your arm out.' Impatient to finish the task, to run away from his probing questions, Alinor's voice was terse, strained. Dutifully, he extended his arm and she began to wrap the cloth around, beneath his armpit, over his shoulder, round and round.

'Why not?' Guilhem asked again.

'I choose not to.'

'And your God gives you that choice, does he? He seems particularly lenient.'

'He is.' She lowered her gaze to his shoulder, pretending to concentrate on finishing the task. Why was he asking so many questions?

'You're talking nonsense and you know it.'

Panic flashed across her delicate features. Ripping the end of the bandage into two halves, she tied it savagely into a knot. 'Look, we do things differently in this country; you're not used to our ways.'

He picked up his shirt, pulled it over his naked torso. 'Religion works the same in both our countries; don't try and fob me off. What are you hiding?'

'Nothing,' Alinor bit out. Apart from a poor, frightened girl in the cellars, but Bianca was none of his concern. 'I've finished,' she announced, swiftly gathering up the spare bandages, the unguent, clutching the bowl of water to her chest. The water slopped against her gown, splashing dark spots. 'I suggest you get some rest, like your men.' She glared pointedly at the curled bodies huddled in front of the fire, wrapped in their cloaks, her tone dismissive.

He tilted his chin, the brindled slash of his brow arching upwards. 'And stop bothering you.'

'And stop bothering me.' Alinor turned her back on him, flouncing away.

She returned to the large table in the middle of the infirmary, popping the unused bandages back into the shallow wicker baskets, looking around the beds to see if anyone else needed her help.

Every nerve-ending in her body seemed alert, highly strung, as if bracing themselves for some further onslaught; at any moment, she half-expected Guilhem to step beside her, asking more questions.

'Everything all right over there?' Maeve appeared at her side, tilting her head towards the fireplace. 'I had to find the Prince something to eat, but he's happy now; I've left him in the kitchens.'

'Everything's fine,' Alinor reassured her. 'I think most of them will sleep now.'

'Do you want to fetch some food for him?' She pointed at Guilhem, sprawled back in the chair, staring into the flames.

'No, I do not,' Alinor replied, scuffing at a mark on the floor with her leather boot. 'I'm sorry to say this, but he's not very pleasant. He's doing everything in his power to annoy me.' A bandage slipped from her grasp, unwinding down to the flagstones; she began to roll it up again, her movements precise and controlled, as if by performing the task perfectly she could take control of her thoughts and stop thinking about him.

'The Prince told me to look after him. Apparently he's his right-hand man, the Duc d'Attalens.'

Alinor jerked her head up, staring into Maeve's pale, lined features. 'Who?'

'The Duc d'Attalens? I think I've pronounced

his name correctly. Goodness, Alinor, you've become quite pale. Are you quite well?'

Alinor stared over at the man by the fire. Guilhem, Duc d'Attalens. Bianca's brother.

Chapter Five

How was it even remotely possible that the maid who huddled in the darkened cellar was related to such an inconsiderate oaf? Muttering something about fetching some food from the kitchens, Alinor stepped slowly towards the door, resisting the temptation to run out at full speed.

Grabbing a lighted torch, she plunged out into the night, striding purposefully towards the storehouse, the narrow doorway in the corner, the constricting stairs. Racing along the cellar corridor, her heart thudded half in terror, half in excitement. Bianca's brother was here! If that was the case, then the girl's predicament was solved; Guilhem could cross the Channel with her and escort her home. Who better, who *safer*, to take her than her own brother?

Bianca had been asleep, rolled up on the flagstones in the blanket. Now, blinking in the spitting light of the torch, she sat up, her loose hair cascading into her lap. 'What in Heaven's name are you gabbling on about, Alinor?' She rounded her eyes in puzzlement. 'What do you mean, 'he's here'?'

'Your brother,' Alinor gasped out. 'It's your brother, Guilhem! Upstairs!'

Bianca frowned. 'No, you must be mistaken. Guilhem isn't in this country. He's fighting in France, in Gascony with Prince Edward. '

Alinor forced herself to calm down, to slow her racing blood. Slinging the torch into an iron bracket, she took Bianca's slim hands between her own. 'Bianca, believe me, or at least, believe the Prioress who told me. Guilhem is sitting in our infirmary before the fire, with a wound to his shoulder.'

Bianca arched one eyebrow, her expression sceptical. 'What does he look like, then?' Her tone was challenging, brimming with disbelief.

'Look like? Well, he's…tall and well built.' Sensation licked over her, warm, treacherous. 'And… and his hair is exactly the same colour as yours… a tawny colour. His eyes are blue, a deep, deep blue, with long black eyelashes.' Alinor chewed on a nail. 'And he asks too many questions for my liking. He's too interested, too curious.'

'Oh, sweet Heaven.' A pallid greyness washed Bianca's face. 'He's really there, isn't he?'

'He is.' This was not the reaction Alinor had been expecting from Bianca. Why wasn't she pleased? 'What's the matter? I thought you'd be so happy to find out that he was here...'

'You haven't told him about me, have you?' Bianca plucked at Alinor's sleeve, openly agitated.

'Of course not,' Alinor replied promptly. 'But don't you see, Bianca, he's the solution to our problem; he can take you across the Channel and take you home.'

Bianca slumped to one side, her eyes wide and frightened. 'Guilhem is the last person I want to see. He cannot know I am here. He would make me go back. He would make me go back to Eustace and force me to marry him.'

'Surely he wouldn't do that, if he knew what my stepmother tried to do.'

'He wouldn't believe me, or us. He would say we're making it up, that we were being hysterical.'

'Oh, I'm sure we—'

'Alinor, stop it!' Bianca's voice was sharp, rattling out on a thread of anxiety. 'My mother told me that it was Guilhem who finally convinced her that marriage to Eustace was the best thing for me. With our father gone, she needed his approval, despite my own misgivings. Do you think I wanted to leave my home? I never wanted to come to England!' She sobbed, burying her face into her palms. 'I saw the letter Guilhem wrote to our mother from Gascony, giving his consent.' She hunched her shoulders forward into her chest. 'My mother was flattered that the Queen had arranged it for us, it was seen as a "good" marriage, uniting France with England, strengthening the ties between the two countries. I never wanted it. But what choice did I have when my brother had written the letter insisting that I go through with it?'

'Oh, Bianca, I'm so sorry,' Alinor whispered, dropping down beside her, hugging her. 'I didn't mean to upset you.' The cellar air clung to her skin, a slick of chill perspiration.

Bianca lifted her face. Tears tracked down her wan cheeks, glistening in the torchlight. 'I'm sorry, Alinor, you'll have to think of something else. Someone else. There is no way I am going anywhere with Guilhem.'

Something was banging away incessantly inside his head. Loud. Insistent. Hitching up into a seated position, Guilhem scrubbed at his face, trying to rub away the last vestiges of sleep, to clear the fog from his brain, and squinted towards the narrow window. Outside, it was still dark; the clanging noise continued. Throwing back the covers, he strode barefoot over to the window, linen undergarments clinging to his brawny thighs, and peered out into the blackness. The church bell tolling sonorously, summoning the nuns to early prayers. Veiled figures filed across the courtyard, heads bowed. Was she there, among them? His breath snagged. Alinor. She resented every last bit of his presence, and yet, the more hostile she was towards him, the more he was drawn to her. A woman who had taken her vows. An innocent. He should know better. And yet he couldn't forget the tempting jut of her hip as she brushed past him in that voluminous sack of a gown, the silken perfection of her skin when he had touched her face yesterday. The images tormented him. His gaze ran back and forth along the line of pale-coloured veils and swinging rosaries, but he failed to spot her. Disappointment carved through him; he frowned at the odd sensation.

He threw himself back on to the bed, bouncing against the sweet-smelling sheets, still warm from the press of his body. The ropes beneath the mattress creaked and strained with the movement. It seemed that the nuns spared no expense when it came to treating their guests. Although the room was small and sparsely furnished, the mattress was stuffed with horsehair, covered with sheets of woven flax and topped with feather pillows and furs. He stretched his long legs to the end of the bed, relishing the silken touch of the linen against his muscled limbs. After all those months of relentless fighting alongside Edward in Gascony at the behest of the King of France, desperate to reclaim his lands from the English, and after those awful months in captivity, this was sheer luxury.

It reminded him of his home: his mother, the lady of the manor, bustling about, firing off orders to the servants, making sure that everyone had everything they needed: food, warmth, a bed for the night. It reminded him of the happy, vibrant presence of his sister.

He closed his eyes, disquiet spiralling through him. After his release he had been reluctant to return home, the prospect of normal life jarring strongly with the ugly emotions coursing through him. He had wanted to fight, and fight hard, hoping to scour away the debilitating guilt that dragged him down like a lead-weighted cloak. He had known nothing of his mother's plans for Bianca, although she claimed to have sent a message to him, which he had never received. By the time Guilhem had finally returned home to inform his mother he was travelling to England with Prince Edward, Bianca had already made the treacherous journey to England herself. He had been so taken aback, annoyed even, by the way his mother had so easily acquiesced to the Queen's request. She had seen it as a wonderful match for her daughter. All he could do now was visit his sister and make sure that she was happy. He could do that at least.

'Fetch the rest of the bowls, please,' Alinor asked one of the novices, as she placed one dish after another along the vast length of the refectory table, the stack of earthenware teetering precariously against her chest. Her left arm ached incessantly today; she was having trouble carrying the crockery. Sunshine streamed down from the high windows, gleaming against the pewter mugs and spoons, brightening the glossy wood of the table. Ornate candlesticks studded its length, bundles of wax set in cold, hard dribbles spilling out from around the unlit wicks.

'How many?' asked the young nun.

'As many as you can find,' Alinor said, reaching the end of the table. 'We have to feed a lot of soldiers.'

'Thank you, Alinor, for staying to help.' Maeve emerged through a curtained opening in the corner of the refectory. 'I'm not sure how we would have coped without your capable hands. It isn't every day we receive such an influx of people.'

'You would have managed without me, Maeve,' Alinor assured her.

'Well, I am grateful.' Maeve narrowed her keen eyes, studying Alinor's face. 'But you look tired, my dear. Did you manage to sleep last night?'

'Not much,' Alinor replied truthfully. She had spent the night in the nuns' dormitory, tossing and turning in a pallet bed, worrying about Bianca, chased by a pair of sparkling blue eyes through her fitful night. What if Guilhem should find out that Bianca was hiding right beneath them?

'Ah, here they come now.' The Prioress glanced up at the main door. Soldiers began to file in, slotting themselves along the rickety wooden benches. The sisters moved amongst them in pairs, one holding a vast tureen of honeyed porridge, whilst the other ladled out the cooked oats. Steam rose, mingling with the shafts of sunlight. The men talked in low voices, murmuring their thanks, keeping their eyes lowered respectfully. 'At least it looks like they know how to behave themselves, thank the Lord,' Maeve added.

Alinor's heart sank as she spotted Guilhem, his tall, muscular frame covered by a close-fitting blue surcoat falling to mid-thigh, calf-length leather boots on his legs secured with crisscrossed laces. Beneath his surcoat, he wore a fine wool under-tunic, of which only the sleeves were visible. The material hugged his thick arms, emphasising the brawny curve of his biceps, the muscled sinew of his forearm. His hair shone like a bronze coin. Alinor swallowed hastily, turned away. 'At least some of them do,' she responded, waspishly.

Maeve noted the burn of colour sweep Alinor's cheeks. 'Has something happened?' Her voice sharpened.

'No, no,' Alinor replied vehemently. She grimaced at the floor, blood racing through her veins. How to explain the relentless beat of her heart that skipped and lurched at the smallest glimpse of Guilhem?

'I shouldn't worry, my dear.' Maeve placed one hand on Alinor's shoulder, placating her. 'They're leaving this morning. The Prince spoke to me last night. He's planning to stay at the Queen's palace at Knighton for a couple of days' rest and recuperation. It's only a few miles north from here. Some of the men are in no condition to fight.'

'Thank God.' Alinor smoothed her hands down the front of her apron; her palms were sweating.

'Alinor?' Sister Beatrice scurried up to her, lugging an empty cauldron of porridge between her two plump hands. 'You live at Claverstock, don't you?'

'Yes, you know I do.' Alinor smiled at her. 'Here, let me take that, it's too heavy for you.' She reached out for the cauldron, but Sister Beatrice shook her head, hanging on to the iron handles.

'No, I'll take it to the kitchens. You need to go and talk to him.' She nodded significantly over to the refectory table, her veil gathering lumpily behind her neck.

'Talk to whom?' A cold wash of panic shot through Alinor's veins. 'Who is asking you about Claverstock?' Her voice heightened, a shrill note.

'Him, that one over there, the handsome one with the blue tunic. Sitting next to the Prince.'

'What did you say to him?' Alinor blurted out, words juddering.

Beatrice laughed. 'Nothing really. He was asking if I knew the way to Claverstock, and I said I would ask you.'

'You didn't say that I lived there?'

'No, no, of course not!' Beatrice rounded her eyes at Alinor's reaction. 'What's the matter?' she asked in a small voice, then clamped her lips together, a dull flush washing over her dumpy cheeks. 'Have I done something wrong?'

'No. Don't worry.' Alinor grasped the iron pot from the nun's astounded hands. 'I'll take this now.'

'But...' Sister Beatrice's bottom lip sagged down '...aren't you going to talk to him?'

'Later!' Alinor turned away abruptly, heading for the refectory door, clasping the pot against her belly like a shield. Scampering down the wooden stairs, she walked swiftly along the open-sided cloister, the morning sun warming her left cheek. She cursed her own stupidity. How foolish she had been, sleeping the night away at the Priory. Why, in Heaven's name, had she not returned home last night to warn her stepmother? As Bianca's brother, Guilhem would naturally ask about Claverstock; it was where his sister was supposed to be, about to marry Alinor's stepbrother! And if Guilhem failed to gain directions to Claverstock

from her, then it wouldn't be long before someone else told him.

Abandoning the porridge pot against the cloister wall, Alinor spun on her heel and began to run,
linen veil flapping out. She had no time to change
out of her nun's garments; her only priority was to
reach Claverstock before Guilhem did. Skin puckering with terror, her mind toiled frantically on a
plan to leave the Priory as quickly and quietly as
possible. The refectory was situated on the first
floor of the west range; if Alinor cut through the
storerooms on the ground floor, she could slip out
towards the gatehouse unnoticed.

She almost made it.

A man came down the refectory stairs into the
cloister to block her path. A blue surcoat clung to
broad shoulders; silver embroidery winked and
glittered in the sunlight. A slight breeze lifted
strands of his hair, giving him a tousled look.
Bright blue eyes, the colour of the sea, gleamed
down at her as she skidded to a stop in front of
him.

He folded his arms slowly across his chest,
a human bulwark barricading her path. 'Where
are you going?' Guilhem's voice was stern, but
friendly.

Alinor angled her neat head towards him.
'Away from you,' she muttered grumpily.

He smiled, ignoring her rudeness. 'I think you can help me.'

'I doubt it.'

'Listen, the sisters tell me you know the way to Claverstock. I have asked the Prioress to give you leave to show me and she has granted her permission.'

'Oh, God, why?' she blurted out, without thinking. She clapped a hand over her mouth, as if to prevent further words from emerging. This whole situation was becoming worse and worse!

Guilhem laughed at her reaction. 'Because I am a knight with Prince Edward and therefore she trusts me? And because I was under the mistaken impression that most nuns like to help people?' he added scathingly. 'And, unfortunately for me, it seems that you are the only person who knows the way.' His voice held the hint of a question. 'Believe me, if there were anyone else, I would pick them instead.'

Maeve appeared at the top of the refectory stairs, her tall reed-thin figure framed by the thick oak doorposts. 'Ah, there you are.' Her calm, melodic tones drifted down. 'Can you take him, Alinor?'

She dipped her head slowly in agreement. The strength sapped from her limbs; a debilitating weakness creeping across her body. Halfway between her mouth and her lungs, her breath snared.

A horrible feeling of entrapment engulfed her, a tangled net from which she could not escape.

'Follow me,' said Guilhem. 'My horse is this way.'

A long open-fronted barn served as a makeshift stable at the Priory; a thatched roof tilted down to a low stone wall at the back, rough-cut posts supporting the roof at the front. Horses crammed into the shelter, rumps against rumps, wheeling their heads around as Guilhem and Alinor approached. The barn sat in shadow; thick dew daubed the long grass alongside, strings of diamonds in the limpid light.

Guilhem fetched his saddle and bridle from the storeroom and lowered them to the ground. Diving into the mass of horseflesh with the bridle swinging from his hand, he extracted his horse with ease, leading the glossy, black stallion out of the heaving, snorting mass.

'Where's yours?' He fastened the bridle with deft fingers around the horse's nose, settling the metal bit between the great yellow teeth, his eyebrow tipping upwards in question. The horse pawed at the cobbles with his great hooves, a hideous scraping sound, his forelocks feathered with an abundance of black hair. Alinor backed away, breath quickening in her lungs. Nausea trickled through her stomach, a faint queasiness. The fear hadn't gone away, then. Maybe it never would. Unconsciously, she rubbed at her arm, the twisted flesh hiding beneath the long sleeve of her nun's habit.

'My...what?' Her mind raced wildly. She had no intention of climbing on any horse! All she needed was to get ahead of him somehow so she could warn her stepmother, and give her time to think of a story to tell Guilhem about why Bianca wasn't there.

'Your horse, or donkey, or whatever it is that you sisters ride,' he replied tersely. Alinor's whole demeanour radiated such reluctance that it made him want to laugh. The delicate line of her jaw, her slender frame clad in that voluminous habit, belied a toughness of mind and spirit unusual in a woman. And yet she was a nun, trained to ig- nore all of life's pleasures and pastimes. Maybe that was why she showed such fortitude of will. Her eyes burned, green chips of emerald glow- ing out from pale-cream skin, and he thought: what a waste.

'I don't have anything to ride.' She raised one blonde eyebrow in his direction.

He screwed his mouth into a wry smile, as- sessing her coolly. 'Fine, then we'll take one of these.' Guilhem grabbed the mane of the nearest horse in the pack.

Alinor's heart plummeted. 'Put the horse back,

Guilhem, there's no point. I cannot ride,' she lied. 'I've never learned.'

Releasing the horse's mane, he walked over to the spot where she stood. The sun, inching out from behind the Priory's gable end, struck his hair into a mass of glistening strands, kindled flame. His big body stepped close, leaned over her, dominating her. 'Cannot, Alinor, or will not? I don't believe you. You seem to be able to do most things, so why do I think this is a stalling tactic to avoid showing me the way to Claverstock?'

She shrugged, maintaining a blank, calm expression. 'I'm telling the truth. I will walk to Claverstock and you can ride alongside.'

'How far is it?'

'Not above ten miles.'

'Ten miles! That will take all day!' He raked one hand through his hair, exasperated, then looked back at her. 'There's nothing for it. You'll have to ride with me.'

'But I can't!' Shock coursed through her veins. 'It's unseemly. The Prioress will never allow it!' Wild-eyed, she glanced at Guilhem's huge horse, chewing vigorously on his metal bit so it rattled between his teeth, shaking the long black fronds of his mane with impatience; the sickness in her stomach rolled, intensified. She hadn't ridden since…since the accident and she doubted very much she would be able to do it again.

'The Prioress will never know,' he said calmly. 'And I'm sure she will understand; you are helping me, after all.'

'But…!'

His arms circled her neat waist impatiently, swinging her light weight up into the space in front of the saddle. As her legs settled sideways over the horse and she squinted down over the bouncing mane, the smooth neck, her knuckles clenched white with fear, a sickening blackness prickling dangerously at the corners of her vision. Dizziness welled up, threatening to consume her; she fought against it, willing herself to remain upright; it's only a horse, she told herself, it's only a horse. She could not, would not, faint in front of this man! Her mind tacked back to that time before, her father's stern tones commanding her to ride Minstrel; the flick of fear as she clambered aboard the huge destrier's back. He had never forgiven her for not being born the strong, brave boy that he so desperately wanted. And she had wanted her father's approval. To show him she was good as any boy.

Holding on to Alinor's waist, Guilhem watched as all colour drained from the maid's cheeks, the healthy blush replaced by stark deathly white. Her long dark eyelashes shuttered down over her cheeks as she hunched forward, knuckles grey and stiff as they clenched into the horse's mane.

'Are you quite well?' His low voice held suspicion. He wouldn't be surprised if this was another of Alinor's little acts to hold up the process
of travelling to Claverstock.

A surge of panic rose within her. 'I can't do
this!' she gasped out, wriggling frantically against
his grip. 'Let me off, now! Please don't make
me do this!' Releasing the horse's mane, she attempted to jump down, but his strong hold prevented her, wedging her firmly on the animal.
Beneath his fingers, the muscles in her slim waist
tightened, then released.

'Let me off...now! I'm not riding!' Her voice
rose on a note of panic, shrill, desperate, her hands
flying to his shoulders for support. 'Please, let me
down!' Tears welled up in the corners of her ears;
tears of panic, of alarm.

'Alinor, stop this.' He tried to keep the note
of frustration out of his voice. God, he thought,
it was amazing how women would behave when
they didn't want to do something! Her tears and
panic appeared completely genuine, and yet, he
knew how stubborn, how wilful this maid could
be. Look how she had held her ground against the
soldiers on the bridge. It seemed she would stop
at nothing to achieve her own ends. 'You are riding with me and that is final.'

Chapter Six

Sticking his booted foot into the metal stirrup
that hung near Alinor's dangling legs, Guilhem
swung himself effortlessly into the saddle. Roped,
muscular arms settled around her slender frame to
gather up the reins that rested across the horse's
neck. Alinor was trembling, her white face a rigid
mask, her mouth set in a tight line. Doubt niggled
at him, a tiny thread. Had he misjudged her?

'Stop this now, Alinor,' he rapped out, jabbing
his heels decisively into the horse's rump. 'You
are not going to get your own way this time.'

She lifted her reddened eyes towards him.
Tears clung to her lashes like pearls. 'You have
no idea what you are talking about!' she hissed,
her right arm sweeping around to grab a bunch
of his tunic as the horse lurched forward. Her
clenched fist burrowed like a small knot against
his biceps, honed plates of muscle.

He ignored her. He was used to feminine dramatics; though he loved his family dearly, both his mother and his sister were not immune to emotional outbursts and fickle moods. And without his father's calm presence around, dead of a fever some years back, they seemed more prone to them, somehow. He had to congratulate Alinor, though, for she was doing an extremely convincing job. Tapping his heels against the animal's flanks, he steered the horse through the shadows of the deserted gatehouse. Beyond the Priory, the landscape stretched out over a flat expanse of water meadows that bordered a shallow river. A veil of mist hung low across the ground, drifting slowly upwards in the strengthening heat of the sun.

'Which way?'

Closing her eyes, her body like a wooden board as the horse moved forward, Alinor braced herself for the next onslaught of desperate panic. But to her surprise, a strange calmness cloaked her. Her muscles softened, losing their stiffness, the strain across her shoulders unclenching. Her horrible fear of the animal was beginning to inch away, by degrees.

'Alinor!' he barked at her. 'Which way is it?'

Pompous, arrogant oaf! The warmth of his skin through his sleeve percolated through her fingers. She snatched her hand away. 'That way!' She gestured roughly with a flick of her good arm. 'Follow the track along the river.'

He peered down at the top of her veil, tracing the fold of cloth to the point where it brushed her cheek, the skin imbued with a faint rose blush. He bent his head. What would it be like to kiss that skin, that soft silk? The smell of lavender lifted from her neck, the smell of summer, of long lazy afternoons. His heart lurched, oddly. 'If I find out you're about to lead me on a wild goose chase…' he muttered sharply, wrenching away, staring into the distance with narrowed eyes. What was he thinking? The woman was not only a harridan in her own right, she was also untouchable, married to God, and here he was, thinking about kissing her!

'I'm not!' she responded, curtly. 'Believe me, I have no wish to draw this out any longer than is necessary!'

'Agreed,' he responded, his tone mocking. Her tears were drying now; relief coursed through him at the return of her truculence. It was only natural to be frightened of horses if she had never ridden before. He was glad to see the tinge of colour seep back into her cheeks. 'Now, lean against me and hang on with both hands, otherwise we'll both be off.'

He waited for her to secure her position; with a jab of annoyance he realised that she only held on with one hand on the horse's mane, her other lying limply in her lap. 'I said "both hands", Alinor. Do you want to fall off?'

'This is fine,' she replied haughtily.

'No, this is not fine,' he growled at her. 'For God's sake, why are you making this so difficult?' Grabbing her fingers, he raised her left arm forcibly, dragging her reluctant fingers up to his chest. 'Hold on to me!' he ordered.

A sift of pain crossed her delicate features, quickly masked.

He saw it. Deft fingers wrapped about her left wrist; he pulled up her sagging sleeve. Beneath, another sleeve, fixed to her arm with buttons. He ripped violently at the material, the round buttons scattering like tiny hailstones down to the cobbles, revealing Alinor's slender forearm, the neat crook of her elbow. And on the inside of her forearm, her flesh, puckered and twisted, was laced with scars.

'No!' She tried to wrench her arm away, but his grip was unyielding.

'What is this?' he demanded. He stared at the ravaged skin, horrified at the damage, at the pain she must have endured. Guilt surged through him.

'How dare you!' she screeched at him, her green eyes round, aghast.

'What is this?' he said again. Beneath his thumb, the blood in her wrist pulsed, hot, racing. A blue trace of veins netted a little way up from her wrist, before disappearing into the scars, threads of purpling silver.

'It's nothing.' Her voice was clipped, terse.

'It doesn't look like nothing. How did you get it?'

She was silent for a moment. 'Would you even believe me if I told you?'

Her words stung. 'Try me.' A ruddy colour dusted the tops of his high cheekbones.

'My father wanted me to ride his destrier. A warhorse. I fell off and broke my arm. This is the result. There—are you happy now?'

The same father who had cursed the day she was born. God, what sort of childhood had she endured? She had probably been relieved to have been placed with the nuns. He shook his head, sticking one hand through his thick tawny hair. She had been telling the truth all along. Her fear of horses was genuine. 'Look, Alinor—' He searched for the words to apologise.

'Don't bother,' she interrupted, her voice bitter. 'It was a long time ago.' The expression on her face was shuttered, closed, her eyes blank as she fixed her gaze on the graceful willows in the distance, her mind working quickly. She hated the fact that he'd seen her injury, but maybe, just maybe, it would work to her advantage. 'Now do you see why I don't want to ride? Will you let me down now?'

Her chin jutted out defiantly, defining the haughty tilt of her mouth. Her fear had dissipated:

Guilhem sensed it in the softness of her body against him. He was not about to let her walk. Or win, for that matter. 'No, Alinor, we will ride.' His voice was stern, a command. 'Nothing is going to happen to you. My horse is safe and so are you.'

Damn him! Seething with resentment, Alinor fumed as Guilhem clamped her against him and urged the horse into a fast trot. She hated that her physical weakness had been exposed and to him, of all people! Her weakened arm was something she had successfully hidden from most people and now this man, this man who had barrelled into her life with all the grace of a wild boar, had exposed it! Biting her lips, she frowned, acutely aware of how close his body was to hers, his inner thighs knocking into her with the horse's movement. Heat rose in her cheeks; thank goodness he couldn't see her face! The plated muscles of his chest bumped intimately against her shoulder. One solid arm wrapped around the slim column of her upper back, corded biceps burning through the thin weave of her habit. She tried to shift her position, to create some space between their bodies, but he tightened his grip as she attempted to pull away. A flicker of movement vibrated in her belly, blossoming, newborn. She needed to get away from him.

As the rising heat from sun slowly lifted the

early morning mist, they rode along the wide chalk path that meandered loosely alongside the river. As the mist vanished, the landscape began to be revealed: huge domed willows, branches trailing down into the river's flow; gnarled, twisted alders poking out this way and that from the shallow banks. A sleek head with a whiskered nose broke the smooth surface of the water: an otter. Round-topped hills, interspersed with dry, narrow valleys, rose up on either side of the water meadows, the grass still lush and green despite the lateness of the year. Here and there, a few sheep grazed, white dots against the verdant pasture.

For some miles, they moved swiftly at a bouncing canter, a gait which knocked Alinor continually backwards into Guilhem. But with one of his arms braced against her shoulder, the other secure around her belly, it was unlikely that she would fall off. Hating to admit it, she couldn't remember the last time she had felt so safe. Since her mother's death, since Wilhelma and her son had come to live at Claverstock, she was constantly on her guard, especially with Eustace. On several occasions he had walked into her chamber, unannounced, and she had taken to carrying the short knife in her belt as protection.

Narrowing her eyes to the horizon, she realised that they would soon turn up into the vast forests that skirted the Claverstock estate. Too soon! She needed to take Guilhem on a small detour, one where he would be completely lost, and she could extract herself, quickly, back to Claverstock. As they cantered along the path, the belt of trees gradually building to their right, she watched out for the track she knew that would take them up into the trees.

'Guilhem, we need to stop!'

He groaned. 'Why? What now?'

She tipped her head up to him, then wished she hadn't. His lean, square-cut jaw, the sensuous curve of his upper lip, loomed inches from her eyes. 'I…er…' Her confidence wavered. 'I…er…need to go…up there.' Gesturing towards the wooded slope, the enormous beech trees, she hoped he would understand her meaning.

He squinted at her suspiciously, eyes blue chips of sapphire. 'Really? We've only just left the Priory.'

'No, we haven't, we've been riding for hours!' she protested.

'Can't you wait? Surely we're almost there?'

'No, another hour at least.' Her lie hung between them, quivering in the limpid air. She squirmed uncomfortably, hip knocking against the saddle's pommel.

Guilhem sighed, then leaned forward, dismounting with a swift jump. 'I'll come with you.'

Sliding haphazardly down from the horse before he had time to help her, she arched one well-defined eyebrow at him. 'I don't think so.'

'All right then, I'll stay here. But don't go too far.' A gust of wind blew through the trees, dislodging a volley of leaves, drifting lazily downwards.

'I'll go up there, behind that rock.' She indicated a mossy outcrop of limestone, a little way up the slope. Her heart sat in her mouth. The Claverstock estate was only a mile to the north; if she could gain the top of this wooded escarpment, she could cut through the fields and reach her home before he did. And hopefully he would lose his way, delaying him even further. 'But you have to give me time, Guilhem. Women have a lot of layers.'

His lips curved into a wry smile, grudging. 'Go on, then. Be as quick as you can.' Unbuckling the leather bottle secured to his horse's rump, he pulled the stopper and drank. Water spilled down the sides of his mouth, down the strong, hollowed column of his neck.

Alinor hesitated. Could she really do this?

'Go on,' he urged, wiping the trickles of liquid away with the back of his sleeve. 'Hurry up, otherwise I will come up and fetch you.'

She didn't doubt it. It was now or never. Her heart thudded wildly as she picked her way around a bramble-infested thicket, then lifted her skirts clear as she climbed the hill towards the stony outcrop, pushing through the ferns and scrubby bushes. She was physically fit, unusual in a woman of her nobility, her body honed from walking and helping out with all the jobs in the Priory and at Claverstock. With her father and stepbrother away, it fell to her to run the estate. Her stepmother did nothing. Her breath accelerated as she reached the rock and vanished from Guilhem's view, darting around the back. Then she increased her pace, almost running, air bursting out from her lungs in short, fierce gusts, her quick, agile steps hampered by the steepness of the ground, the spongy fallen leaves, the slick patches of bare mud. If she could just reach the stone wall at the top, she would be almost home.

'Alinor?' Guilhem's voice floated up to her. 'Are you ready yet?'

If she called down to him, he would realise immediately that she wasn't in the place where she had promised to be. She continued to climb steadily, as fast as the muscles in her legs could carry her. Her knees ached with the effort. Sweat gathered beneath her arms, trickled down her spine. She was strong, but did she have enough strength to outrun him? She…

'Alinor! You little wretch…' Guilhem's voice, closer now.

The slope angled upwards in gradient, becoming almost vertical; she fell on to her hands and knees to clamber her way up. The wall wavered high above her, chunks of stone delineated against clear, blue sky. Her goal, if only she could reach it before he caught her! Her fingers dug frenziedly into the loose crumbly soil, laced with a mess of ferns and exposed tree roots. Holly leaves scratched at her palms, at her forearm exposed by the torn, flapping sleeve, drawing blood. Soggy leaves spilled across her sleeves as she dislodged them, clumps pulling free unhelpfully beneath her grasp. Frustrated by her lack of progress, she stretched up, scrabbling for purchase, towards a thicker tree root so she could haul herself up.

Caught up in her frantic attempt to run away, she never even heard him.

'Got you!' A large hand fastened around the heel of her leather boot, fingers digging into the cracked, well-worn leather. Kicking down, she clung with desperation to the tree root above her head.

'Enough, Alinor,' he said sternly. 'Come down now.'

A sob rose in her chest and she resisted the temptation to bury her forehead into the dank vegetation, the crush of ferns. Her arm ached from the effort of holding on to the tree root, but she hung on, her mouth set in a stubborn line.

'So be it. I gave you a chance.' Her other foot dangled in mid-air; seizing it, he yanked violently, easily loosening her grip on the tree root. She slithered haphazardly down, elbows and knees bashing painfully against razor-edged flints and knotty roots until her feet touched the ground.

Guilhem flipped her around, pushing her back into the earthy bank so that she was forced to look at him, one hand planted on each of her shoulders, trapping her securely within the cage of his arms. His lean features, stern and forbidding, swam before her eyes.

'What is going on, Alinor? Why are you so reluctant to take me to Claverstock?' Her eyes were like those of a cat, he thought, huge and green, shining with resentment.

'Why are you treating me like this?' she snapped up at him. 'You've no right!' Wriggling her shoulders in annoyance, she tried to break his fearsome grip.

'Stop avoiding the question, Alinor,' he replied, calmly. His voice held a thread of steel. 'Why are you running away?'

'Because it's improper!' she stuttered back at him. 'A nun shouldn't be seen riding, alone, with a man.'

'You're no nun.' Whipping the veil from her head, he plucked at the close-fitting wimple beneath, flinging both to the ground in temper.

He swallowed, mouth suddenly dry. Irritation drained away.

In the filtered sunlight, her hair was revealed, gleaming like spun silk, silver-gold, the long tresses caught into a plaited bundle at the base of her neck. Wings of hair framed the delicate oval of her face, curving low over her ears from a central parting. Framed by the earthy slope, she was like an angel fallen from the heavens, bright and luminous against the brown soil, emerald eyes glittering fiercely from her angry face, the pale fragility of her skin emphasised by the astonishing colour of her hair. He wanted to touch, to feel.

'I am!' she whispered, defiantly. The lie echoed in the still air.

Time stretched, lengthened between them, the quiet beneath the trees broken only by the excited call of a blackbird, the trilling of a wren as it hopped out from beneath a haze of brambles. A light wind floated through the branches above, stirring the jointed twigs, making them creak.

His mind emptied of conscious thought, logic sprinting away. The slow, measured rate of his blood picked up speed, pumping faster, harder, around his massive frame. My God, she was beautiful. Stunning. His eyes travelled down over her face, tracing the sensual curve of her upper lip, the obstinate tilt of her small chin.

'Guilhem?' she said again. What was he doing?

A dangerous wildness had entered his eyes, blue fire kindled. 'Guilhem, I told you, I am a nun! I am!' His body closed in on her, warm breath grazing her cheeks. He smelled of leather, of honey.

'I don't believe you,' he murmured. Big hands cupped her face, holding her steady; his head lowered towards hers. She squeezed her eyes shut, as if bracing herself for an impact. But the touch of his mouth was surprisingly gentle. Delight zig-zagged straight to the pit of her belly. A delicious rush of feeling, treacherous, overwhelming, surged through her, unstoppable. His body crushed against hers, chest to chest, thigh to thigh. Her mind clawed for normality, for restraint, screeching at her to run away, to hit out, anything to free herself from him, but her heart forbade her. Hands that had been about to push him away hung limply by her sides.

She sighed, a fleeting sound, a whisper of yearning.

He groaned. Hunger gripped his loins, a relentless craving, and he shifted closer, melding his body to hers, arms cradling her slim shoulders, broad chest crushing her soft breasts. His tongue played along her closed lips, questing, insistent. Spirals of desire ricocheted through her slender frame, buffeting her. Instinctively, she parted her mouth. Her hands crept upwards, hesitant at first, over the fine wool of his tunic to the powerful column of his neck. His hair tickled her fingers, tendrils of rough silk.

And then it was over.

Guilhem tore his lips away, breathing heavily. Backing away abruptly, he stuck one hand through his thatch of tawny hair. His hand shook; he turned away in disgust at his own behaviour. What was he thinking? He wasn't one of those men, those coarse soldiers, who took their pleasure without thought, or conscience! Since his time in prison, after Fremont, he hadn't been with a woman, his body too numb with grief, too...no, he couldn't think of that now.

'We need to get going,' he said gruffly, his voice grim. He began to walk down towards the horse, expecting her to follow him.

Alinor sagged back, shocked and trembling, reeling from the devastating impact of his kiss. Her knees were weak, barely holding her upright. How dare he do this to her! Tears shimmered in the corners of her eyes; why hadn't she shoved him away when she first suspected what might happen? She had seen his eyes darken, had felt the tension shift between them. Why had she been so feeble-minded, so foolish?

Because I wanted him to kiss me. She closed her eyes in shame. She was no better than a common harlot on the streets. And here she was, dressed as a sister of God. What a fool she was.

Realising she wasn't moving, he turned impatiently. 'Are you coming?'

With quick, aggressive movements, she wrapped her wimple back around her head; jammed her veil on. 'You can't treat me like this!' she responded, furiously.

Her words drove into him; no, he shouldn't be treating her like this. He had overstepped the boundaries of his own self-restraint, completely unable to resist her. When he had ripped away that veil and wimple, exposing her astounding beauty, he had lost all composure, all control, his mind and body surrendering to the sensation of the moment. Her mouth had been so sweet, so delectable, that even to think of it now sent excitement jittering through his groin. But he did not deserve to take such pleasure; he was not worthy of such feelings, not after what he had done. It would be easier, for both of them, if he maintained an air of complete indifference, and behave as if the kiss had not affected him in the least.

'Like what?'

A flag of embarrassment deepened the colour on her cheeks. 'You can't....kiss me like that and then just walk away!' She hitched one shoulder up, an awkward gesture.

Guilhem raised one eyebrow, his eyes cold, impenetrable. 'What do you want me to do, marry you? It was only a kiss, Alinor, it didn't mean anything.' Each word was like a frozen stone.

'But I'm a—'

He held up a hand. 'Spare me the "nun" story, Alinor,' he said, bitterly. 'I don't know who you are, but you are most definitely not a nun.'

'You could apologise, at least!' she hissed at him, changing tack.

'Sorry,' he said, but there was no hint of regret in his tone. 'Now, can we get a move on?'

Chapter Seven

Embarrassed by her lack of self-restraint, Alinor
marched up through the forest, Guilhem following, leading his horse. The path had not been
used in a while and she pushed her way through
small thickets of scrub and brambles, the ragged
hem of her habit dragging through the wet leaves,
snagging on the low vegetation. Thank God, she
thought, that the trees were too thick, too impenetrable for them to ride together. She couldn't face
that again, not after what had just happened.

Her limbs thrummed from the devastating po-
tency of his kiss. Acutely conscious of his eyes
on her back, she stumbled along, her gait awkward, contrived. Her face was hot. In order for
her to regain any sense of dignity, she would have
to show that the kiss had not affected her in the
slightest, that his behaviour had been deplorable,
a complete betrayal of trust; anything, *anything*,
but the truth: that she hadn't wanted him to stop.

At the top of the slope, the oaks gave way to pines and the path became drier, covered with a bed of rust-coloured needles. A wooden gate was set into the stone wall, giving access to the flat meadowland beyond. In the shaded places where the sun's rays hadn't yet touched, the fields glittered with a sparkling coat of heavy dew.

'There,' she said truculently, placing one hand on the damp wood of the gate. Beyond the trees, beyond the rich pasture fields, at the apex of two wide valleys, sat Claverstock Castle. Her home.

'A fine castle, from the looks of it,' Guilhem said, coming to stand beside her.

'Yes, it is,' she said, her eyes bright with annoyance.

'You know it, then?'

'I...er...' She tailed off lamely as she realised her mistake, picking at a loose splinter of wood on the gate. Of course, why would he think that she had any connection to Claverstock at all?

His hand covered hers. 'Tell me.'

'Don't....don't touch me!' she said, furiously, wrenching her hand away. She folded her arms tightly across her chest, her small chin jutting out, combative.

'Oh, come on, Alinor.' He brought his palms up in front of her face, a gesture of surrender. 'There's no need to be quite so outraged with me. It was only a kiss. I'm sure it isn't the first!'

He was wrong. It had been her first. She stared at him, mutinously, knowing she had to calm down, to forget. Her whole frame wilted slightly and she clung to the gate.

'Tell me how you know Claverstock,' he urged.

Air shuddered in her lungs, a huge shiver seizing her slender frame. 'I'm not sure I can explain...' She cleared her throat.

'Try me.' Mud streaked her cheek, giving her the appearance of a ragged urchin, a waif.

'I live at Claverstock.'

'I see.' A small crease appeared between his thick eyebrows. 'So what were you doing, living at the Priory? Did your parents put you there?' Over his shoulder, the destrier lowered his head, nudging at Guilhem's tunic; he stroked the animal's nose, cradling it for a moment.

'I don't live there; I stay there sometimes and help out when the nuns need me,' Alinor explained. 'A lot of the sisters are old; they need help with tasks, taking goods to market, that sort of thing.'

'But why would you do that?' he asked, curious.

It keeps me out of the way of my stepmother and her awful son, thought Alinor, but she couldn't tell him that. It sounded so pathetic, so mean-spirited. 'I like to do it.' Her answer sounded lame, even to her own ears.

His brilliant blue eyes bore into her, keen, perceptive. She shuffled beneath the intensity of his gaze. 'If Claverstock is your home,' he said slowly, 'then you'll have met my sister, Bianca.'

Her stomach flipped; she shook her head violently. 'No, no, I haven't been back for some time.' The false note in her speech clanged in her ears. 'I've never met her.'

Within the massive bailey walls, the castle sat alone on a grassy mound. The only way in was over a drawbridge that crossed a moat. The water appeared bottomless, choked with green trailing weeds, blooms of algae. Eyeing her burly companion with interest, guards stood to attention in the stone gatehouse as Alinor passed through into the inner bailey. Skirting the well in the middle of the courtyard, she headed for the wooden steps that led up to the great hall, slipping through an archway that led to a curtained opening. Pushing through the unwieldy velvet fabric, she held back the thick material with a half-hearted gesture so that Guilhem was able to follow.

He ducked his head beneath the low stone lintel, mouth quirking into a half-smile. Alinor looked as though she wanted to strangle him, he thought. No doubt he deserved it. But her whole manner radiated such hostility, such awkwardness, that he wasn't convinced it was solely to do with the fact that he had kissed her. She resented his presence, quite obviously not wanting him at Claverstock. And he wanted to know why.

The raftered chamber was deserted, a limited fire burning fitfully beneath the carved stone fireplace. Smoke trailed listlessly out into the room. A substantial table covered with a white cloth dominated the high dais, pewter plates and goblets gleaming along its length. Colourful woollen tapestries decorated the wall behind, softening the rough stone.

'Why don't you wait here—' Alinor gestured to an oak chair beside the fire '—and I will go and find my stepmother.' And hopefully warn her before she comes face to face with this unexpected guest, she thought. 'I shan't be long.' Flicking her skirts to one side, she turned away abruptly, not waiting to see if he would do as he was bid. She disappeared, her stride quick and decisive.

Scuttling along the dim corridor, Alinor made for the circular stairwell at the far end. If Wilhelma was anywhere, it would be in the ladies' solar, one floor higher up. She had to warn her, so that her stepmother was prepared; they had to think up a story, quickly, as to the reason why Bianca wasn't here. Her hands trembled as she climbed up and up the narrow stairs, spiralling round, her brain darting this way and that to pos-

sible solutions. Wilhelma thought that Bianca was
dead; it was only due to Alinor's interference, her
refusal to carry out Wilhelma's wishes, that Bianca was safe and well.

Rounding the last step to climb on to the landing, she ran straight into her stepmother.

'Alinor!' Wilhelma screeched. 'How many
times have I told you, watch where you're going!'
Her stepmother was tall, taller than her, her expensive garments hanging from her thin, elegant
frame. She wore a barbette, a length of white
linen that wrapped tightly around her face and
chin, secured on the top of her head. A cloth-
covered circlet, heavily embroidered with gold
thread, further secured the barbette and also held
her veil, which fell to a point beyond her shoulders.

'Sorry!' Alinor gasped. 'But...'

'Where have you been? Helping out those
crusty old sisters again? Really, Alinor, I—'

'Stop, Wilhelma, listen to me!' Alinor's voice
took on a deadly urgency. She clutched her stepmother's stick-like arm and shook it slightly. 'I
had to bring someone with me, he's in the great
hall...'

'I saw him. Who is he?' Outside the arrow slit,
a pigeon cooed softly, then flapped away.

'Bianca's brother, Guilhem, Duc d'Attalens.'

In the shadows, Wilhelma's face sagged visibly. The dark grooves beneath her eyes became suddenly more pronounced. 'Wh-what?'

'Bianca's brother!' Alinor hissed. 'He's come to see her. What are we going to tell him?'

'Oh, Lord!' Wilhelma staggered slightly, clutching on to the curved metal banister.

'You should have thought of this before you asked me to poison her! Did you know she had a brother?'

'Her family are all in France. I never thought we would see any of them here.' Wilhelma's voice took on a frantic edge. 'The Queen arranged it all.' She poked Alinor in the arm, narrowing her eyes. 'None of this would have happened, my girl, if you had agreed to marry Eustace. That way the Queen could never have interfered, could never have sent such an—such an inappropriate girl to marry my son! It's all your fault, Alinor.'

Alinor reeled backwards beneath her stepmother's vindictive words. Was this the way it was going to go? Her stepmother had been extremely careful to avoid any implication of being involved in killing Bianca. If they were ever questioned, only Alinor was to blame. Only Alinor had Bianca's supposed blood on her hands. Would Wilhelma openly denounce her for Bianca's death? At least the girl was still alive, she thought miserably.

'She is dead, isn't she?' Wilhelma said sharply. 'You did do what I asked of you?'

'Yes,' Alinor lied, a sense of dread coiling around her heart.

'Oh, don't worry, I'm not about to reveal what you have done.' Wilhelma's voice grew in strength, the colour returning to her cheeks. 'We'll simply say that we haven't seen her, that she never arrived. He'll believe that, surely?'

Alinor bit her lip. For all their sakes, she hoped so.

'Duc D'Attalens! My lord!' Wilhelma slid gracefully into the hall, her skirts slipping across the flagstone floor, Alinor following nervously in her wake. The servants had spread clean rushes; loose strands caught on the embroidered hem of Wilhelma's dress as she moved forward, her arms outstretched in greeting towards Guilhem. 'Welcome to our humble abode!' She tossed her head back and gave a small, tinkling laugh; she didn't believe anything of the sort. Claverstock was a vast, wealthy estate and Wilhelma knew it.

Pushing upright out of his chair, Guilhem bowed low to his hostess. 'My lady,' he said, straightening up. 'No doubt Alinor has told you of the reason for my visit.'

A tiny frown crinkled Wilhelma's brow, creasing the thin, dry skin on her forehead. 'Yes, but I don't quite understand…'

'She is here, isn't she?' Guilhem rapped out,

suspiciously. He took one step forward, towering over Wilhelma.

'She is not.' Wilhelma's voice was abrupt, final. 'I'm sorry, my lord, but she never arrived. When the Queen suggested the marriage, we all thought it was an excellent idea, so did Eustace, but when she never appeared, we assumed that she, or the Queen, had changed their minds.'

'Did you ask anyone?' Guilhem's blue eyes darkened dangerously. 'Did you send a message back to my mother, or to Queen Eleanor, asking where she was?'

'Of course!' Wilhelma protested, but it was a lie. She had done nothing of the sort. Bianca had arrived and that very night Wilhelma had asked Alinor to use her most dangerous plants to poison Bianca. 'Maybe, maybe, your sister decided that marriage was not for her.'

'But why would she do that?' said Guilhem, his tone threaded with steel. He turned towards the fireplace, resting one hand on the stone mantel. 'My mother certainly believes she is here. Where else would she be?'

Alinor watched the rigid line of his back as he stared into the flames, the strong swathe of muscle at his neck. A thread of meanness crept through her; withholding the truth about Bianca made her feel cruel. But if she told him, would he drag Bianca back to Claverstock and force her to go through with the marriage? Doubt coiled in her heart.

'She must have changed her mind,' Wilhelma stated, with an air of closure. 'Now, can I interest you in any food? The kitchens will be preparing for the evening meal quite soon, but there is always something...'

'Where is she, then?' A taut muscle jumped in Guilhem's jawline. 'Where is she?'

Wilhelma shrugged her shoulders, apparently indifferent. 'My lord, I haven't the faintest idea.'

Irritated by the woman's evasive answers, Guilhem glanced over at Alinor, hanging back in the shadows. Her arms banded tightly across her chest, as if warding him off, her whole body taut, like a harp string under tension. Catching his eye, she shrank back visibly, her expression stricken, white.

She knew something.

'Yes, I'll stay,' he answered slowly, keeping his gaze pinned to Alinor. A look of dismay, swiftly masked, crossed her face at his reply. Oh, yes, the chit was definitely hiding something, and he aimed to find out what it was.

Yanking off her veil and wimple, shedding her nun's habit, stained and dirty from the day's exertions, Alinor stood miserably in front of a bowl of steaming water. One of the servants had brought it to her chamber after she had fled the great hall. Clad in her underdress, she lifted her left arm, staring at the ruined material of her sleeve, the broken buttons, recalling Guilhem's horrified expression as he viewed her mangled arm. Why was he staying? Why hadn't he left when he discovered that Bianca wasn't here? Releasing her side-lacings, Alinor pulled the fabric over her head, adding the gown to the pile beside her.

Shivering slightly in her gauzy linen shift, her feet bare against the polished elm floorboards, Alinor dipped her fingers into the warm water, splashing her face. She knew why. She had caught the gleam of interest in Guilhem's face earlier, when they were in the great hall. He was not convinced by their flimsy story. Such a man would not give up easily in discovering the truth.

Drying her face and hands on a fine linen towel, she drew out the pins securing the plaited bun at the back of her head, scattering them on the coffer. The long braid snaked down over her shoulders. A leather lace secured the plait; she undid it, shaking out her hair, running her fingers through the golden tresses. A comb, fashioned from horn, lay on the oak chest beside the earthenware bowl of water. She picked it up, pulling the comb through the shining filaments of her hair, half-closing her eyes with the rhythmic action. Exhaustion flowed through her, her limbs aching from the awkward, tortuous ride with Guilhem, her fall from the slope in the forest. His mouth on hers.

She ran her tongue tentatively across the plush skin of her bottom lip, remembering. The hush of his breath, ragged against her cheek. Solid thighs grinding into her soft curves. Her belly hollowed out, jolting with sweet anticipation.

'Alinor! Are you in there?' A sharp rap at the door, followed by a thump.

The comb slipped from her nerveless fingers, clattering across the floorboards. Sweet Jesu! She had forgotten to secure the door! Alinor darted across the chamber, her arms reaching for the iron bolt.

Too late! The door burst open, thudding back against the plastered wall. Guilhem filled the doorframe, stooping beneath the thick, oak lintel.

'No! Go away!' Alinor shouted, backing away. His eyes shone over her, ruthless, determined, tawny hair falling in haphazard strands across his forehead. She hopped from one cold foot to the other, acutely conscious of her bare legs, the scant covering of her chemise. 'Get out!'

Guilhem slammed the door behind him. 'Not until I get some answers!' he said. The words died in his throat.

Her hair. Glistening filaments of pure gold cascaded past her neat waist, the curling ends tickling her hips. Like rippling water. His fingers tingled, desperate to touch each shining strand and press it to his face, to savour its soft caress against his bare skin. Her chemise was of a sheer gauzy stuff, hanging to mid-thigh, exposing slim calves, dainty ankles. Beneath the diaphanous cloth, he glimpsed the shadow of her breasts rounding delectably, nipples dark and rosy. She stood before him like something magical, a goddess from another world: luminous, enchanting.

Desire clawed his solar plexus; his muscles tightened ominously. His loins gripped with longing, ripping like wildfire through the dry kindling of his soul. He drove his fingernails into the calloused flesh of his palm. He averted his gaze, staring hard at the window, the bowl of water, the pile of her clothes on the floor, anything to distract him from the magnificent beauty who stood before him. Skipping across to the bed, Alinor hoisted up a blanket, revealing a veiled glimpse of her hip, a tantalising thigh. Jerking the blanket around her shoulders, she shook the folds out over her chemise, covering her semi-nakedness.

Thank God. He let out a long, tremulous breath. He had to leave. He couldn't trust himself.

'You shouldn't be here, Guilhem.' Her eyes leapt with emerald flames. Her feet were blue with cold, the small half-moons of her toenails pearly, like the insides of seashells. 'What do you want?'

I want you.

Self-control teetered on the edge of an abyss, lust galloping through him unchecked, driving away the numbness around his heart, chasing away the demons that plagued him. If he stayed much longer, he would fall. His hands balled into fists at his side.

'No, I shouldn't,' Guilhem agreed. His voice was gruff, oddly disjointed. 'I'll speak to you later.' He turned on his heel, slamming the door behind him.

Chapter Eight

'Where did you find that old rag?' Wilhelma glanced critically at her step-daughter, her small eyes a curious colour: a pale wash of brown and olive. 'Is it one of your mother's?' Her tone was scathing, judgemental. As she leaned forward, her loose, bony fingers gripped the stem of her pewter goblet, brimming with red wine. She lifted it to her narrow lips and took a restrained sip, dabbing fastidiously at her mouth with a linen napkin.

'Yes, it was my mother's,' replied Alinor, her tone neutral. Wilhelma's cutting remarks had little effect on her; she had endured so many years of them since her mother had died. She smoothed her palms down the faded violet-coloured wool across her thighs. Her lovely mother, who had striven to soften her father's harsh treatment towards her, who had fussed and spoiled and loved her. How Alinor missed her.

'Are you listening to me, Alinor?' Wilhelma

dug sharp nails into Alinor's forearm, plucking at her sleeve.

'Sorry, what did you say?'

Wilhelma tutted with irritation, clicking her fingers at one of the servants to come and pour her some more wine. 'Do you think that man is going to join us for dinner?' she asked. 'I've sent one of the servants to tell him the food is ready.'

'He will,' replied Alinor hollowly. Guilhem wanted answers, hence the reason he had appeared in her chamber at full tilt. But why had he disappeared so quickly? His behaviour seemed inexplicable, meekly following her request for him to leave. In the short time that she had known him, it seemed completely out of character.

Wilhelma moved her plate to the left slightly, adjusted the position of her eating knife, then her goblet on the pristine white tablecloth. 'I cannot believe you brought that man here, Alinor, how stupid…how completely foolish of you after what you did!'

'I didn't have much choice,' she responded bleakly. A shudder rippled through her veins as she remembered Guilhem's firm hands on her waist, the rush of air as he threw her up on to his horse. The broad frame of his chest nudging her spine.

'Oh, really.' Wilhelma's response was scathing. 'It's not like he dragged you here by your hair!'

If she had put up any more resistance, it might have come to that. 'It would have looked suspicious if I had put up too much of a protest,' Alinor replied. A servant placed a steaming platter of freshly baked rolls in front of the two women; the warm yeasty smell rose up to join the hazy fug emitted by the smoky fire.

'Knowing you, you probably didn't try hard enough.' Wilhelma's eyes flicked upwards, towards the curtained doorway. 'Here he comes.'

Guilhem strode past the trestle tables, heading towards the high dais on which Alinor sat with her stepmother. The few peasants who were eating in the lower part of the hall glanced at his tall imposing figure with interest. He climbed the wooden steps to the dais two at a time. Instinctively, Alinor shrank back into her chair, wanting suddenly to be invisible. Her heart knocked at her ribs with…what? Was it fear of this man? The way he erupted into a room, a powerful, dynamic force filling the space with light and energy—how could she possible contend with such a person? But she had to, if only for Bianca's sake. She had made the girl a promise not to tell her brother where she was and it was a promise she intended to keep.

Guilhem halted beside Wilhelma's chair, bowing from the waist, the blue material of his surcoat stretching across the rounded bulk of his shoulders.

'Please, my lord, sit.' Wilhelma twisted a smile at him.

He slid into the chair next to Alinor, his arm bumping companionably against hers. She hitched away at the unexpected contact, the movement agitated, jerky. Her lungs contracted, breath squeezing. She was afraid, afraid of what he was going to say, of what he was going to do next.

Keen and predatory, his blue eyes mocked her, drifting over her flushed cheek, the silk veil across her shoulder. How could he ever have mistaken her for a nun? Spine pulled rigid, her nose in the air as she fixed her gaze on some indefinable spot in the lower hall, Alinor was every inch the noble lady: costly pearl buttons fastened the tight sleeves of her underdress; her sleeveless over-gown was constructed from fine, supple wool, the colour of lavender, embroidered around the neckline and hem with silver thread. The scent of roses percolated from her skin. He sensed the agitation rippling beneath her brittle, unyielding stance, the dance of fear that widened her beautiful eyes and made her hands shake.

Wilhelma clicked her fingers; in moments, platters of steaming fish, roast meats and vegetables had been placed before them by the servants. 'Please, help yourself, my lord,' She swept one hand, knobbly-fingered, over the food.

'Should we not wait for your menfolk? Will they not be joining us?' Guilhem enquired.

'All away, fighting on behalf of the King in Wales,' Wilhelma replied. 'My husband, the Earl of Claverstock, is Alinor's father, of course, and my son, Eustace, is with him.' She waggled her empty goblet impatiently until a servant scuttled forward to fill it. 'Try some of the beef, my lord,' she suggested. 'Alinor, lift this platter over to Guilhem, it's too heavy for me.'

Alinor stretched her arms out, only to feel Guilhem reach across her and brush her hands away. 'Let me,' he said, as his upper arm grazed her chest, intimate, sensual. Her face flared at the brief touch. 'It's too heavy for you, too.' He raised the oval plate easily, setting it down in front of him.

His stomach growled. The porridge at the Priory seemed a long time ago now. 'This looks good,' he said, beginning to fill his plate. Beside him Alinor was silent. He glanced at her. 'Are you not hungry?'

'Not really,' she replied woodenly. She reached out for her wine, nerveless fingers fumbling against the ornate stem, knocking it. The goblet tipped, red wine flowing out on to the tablecloth into a wide, spreading stain. She watched in dismay, wanting to weep. Guilhem's knowing gaze was hot upon her, a touch of fire searing along her neck. Her blood thudded, treacherously.

'Oh, Alinor! You clumsy girl!' Wilhema shrieked at her. She turned to a servant, firing orders.

Guilhem inclined his head towards Alinor. Flickering candlelight burnished his thick, springing hair. 'I know you know.' His sculptured cheekbone was inches from her veil, the soft bloom of her cheek. The silver thread decorating her cloth-covered circlet winked in the candlelight.

'Wh-what?' Sweat prickled in her palms, and she laid them flat on the cool tablecloth, then picked them up and placed them in her lap.

'Where is she, Alinor?' Spearing a lump of cooked fish with his eating knife, he popped it into his mouth.

Her heart quailed at his menacing tone. 'I don't know what you mean. I've told you, we've told you, Bianca never arrived here. Your constant suspicion of us is irritating.'

'It's nothing compared to your constant evasiveness,' he growled back at her. The iridescent blue of his gaze flashed over her. 'Nothing about this situation makes sense. How can a fully grown woman completely disappear?'

Her neck ached from the continual strain of lying to him, the continual avoidance of the truth.

She picked miserably at a loose thread on her gown. Beside her, Wilhema hiccoughed loudly, then giggled. She had taken too much to drink, as usual.

'I...' Her mind cast around desperately for a way out, an escape from his searching questions. She shifted around, recognised the hazy look in her stepmother's eyes. It wouldn't be long before she became loud and voluble, drinking at the speed she was going. 'I...need to take Wilhelma upstairs.'

Guilhem studied the drooping figure behind Alinor. He laughed. 'Running away from me won't help you. I will get the information I need, one way or another.' He sprawled back in the chair, raising his goblet to his lips. 'Take her.'

Alinor hesitated. 'Are you going back to Prince Edward tonight?'

'What do you think?'

Her stomach plummeted. She shrugged her shoulders, feigning indifference. 'It makes no difference to us; your chamber is prepared for the night.' Standing up, she turned so abruptly that the outer curve of her thigh banged against the table-edge. Her eyes watered as pain seared up the muscle: a cruel bite. Guilhem's hand was around her arm, his grip like an iron manacle, crushing her fine bones.

'Get some sleep; we'll talk in the morning. I'm not finished with you.'

* * *

I'm not finished with you. Guilhem's threatening words flew after her, tormenting her as she bundled Wilhema out of the great hall with the help of Mary, her stepmother's maidservant. They helped her up the narrow circular stairs and on to the first floor where her stepmother's bedchamber was situated. Every few moments, Wilhema stopped, bracing one hand against the white-plastered walls, catching her breath, her gaunt face slick with sweat. Then she would stagger onwards, supported on both sides by Alinor and Mary until, after what seemed like an eternity, they reached her chamber. Wilhelma's slippered feet dragged across the polished floorboards as they manhandled her over to the bed.

Mary removed Wilhema's shoes, lifting her legs on to the bed furs.

'Why does she do this?' Alinor said, almost to herself. 'Why does she insist on drinking so much?'

'It happens most nights, my lady,' Mary replied. 'But more so since the men left to fight in Wales.' Tucking the blanket more securely around Wilhelma, she straightened up. 'Oh, I almost forgot, my lady.' She dug around in the large pocket of her apron. 'I found this the other day in the stairwell. I thought it belonged to you.'

Mary's outstretched palm held a circle of gleaming silver. A ring.

Her heart knocked in her throat. On the outside of the ring, the crest of an eagle, the crest of d'Attalens, and on the inside, a name. Bianca. Aghast, she snatched it out of Mary's palm, closing her fingers around it, hiding it.

'Yes, it is mine,' she replied shakily. 'Thank you, Mary. I will leave you to take care of my stepmother now.' Forcing her numb legs to move, she darted out of the chamber, racing for the sanctity of her own room. Once inside, she shut the door, placing the chunky wooden bar across so no one else could enter, and opened her palm.

Bianca's ring winked up at her. Proof that Guilhem's sister had been to Claverstock. Thank God the maid had found it. Digging beneath the folds of her wimple and gown, Alinor extricated the leather lace that hung down on the inside of her dress, on which her mother's ring had been secured. Undoing the simple knot at the nape of her neck, she slipped Bianca's ring on to join it. The delicately wrought silver clinked down against her mother's ring. She would return it to Bianca when she saw her, which, owing to Guilhem's presence, would be sooner, rather than later.

Tying the leather lace securely, she tucked both rings down so they sat against her skin. Her mind worked quickly. She would wait in her chamber until she knew Guilhem had gone to bed, then she would slip down, and out, heading for the village where Ralph lived. She needed to persuade Ralph to take Bianca to the coast, this very night, before Guilhem came too close to the truth. If she stayed here, it would only be a matter of time before he prised the truth from her. A vague sense of guilt swam over her as she sat on the bed to wait, her cloak gathered at her side; guilt that she was unable to tell Guilhem that his sister was safe, at least. He was worried; she could see that from the look in his eyes when he talked about her, but still, a promise was a promise, and it was not something she would give up lightly.

Alinor lay back on her bed, resting her head against the feather pillow, kneading her weak arm. Exhaustion dragged at her eyelids. She could not, would not, fall asleep. Bianca's freedom depended on her. Her eyelids drifted down. A pair of sparkling midnight eyes barged into her mind, the firm, delineated curve of a bottom lip. The race of her blood increased. What was the matter with her? Ever since that man had barged into her life, her perspective seemed altered, tilted oddly with the norm. He had done this. Her body felt different, flesh tingling, aware, laced with the bubbling heat of expectation. It didn't make sense; Guilhem was an utter torment, tough and intimidating, yet she couldn't stop thinking about his big body pressed into hers. She sat up, frowning. There was something about Bianca's description of her brother that did not add up.

The chapel bell had tolled the hours and she had counted. She waited until the chapel bell rang ten times. Guilhem would have gone to his chamber by now. Rising from the bed, she swung her cloak around her shoulders, fastening it across her chest, and sticking her arms through the slits cut into the fabric in front. Opening her door, she moved swiftly along the corridor, looking neither left, nor right, her slippered tread silent. Her trailing gown and cloak slipped down behind her as she descended the stairs.

The great hall was in darkness, save for one flickering torch by the main entrance and the dying embers in the fireplace, softly glowing. Alinor's forehead creased; she made a mental note to speak to the servants about leaving a torch alight after everyone had retired to their chambers. The smell of wax from the spent candles hung in the air.

From the inky gloom of the high dais, a voice spoke. 'Good evening, Alinor.'

Chapter Nine

Alinor turned in shock. 'Eustace?' she croaked out, recognising the voice.

At the top table, held in the shadows, a shape moved. As her eyes became accustomed to the gloom, she picked out the corpulent outline of her stepbrother, slumped in his mother's chair, the glint of pewter as he raised a goblet to his lips.

'Eustace!' She breathed out, astounded. 'What in Heaven's name are you doing here? I thought you were fighting in Wales for the King…and Father? Is Father here too?' She scanned the length of the table, but Eustace was the only person there.

'No, Alinor, your father isn't here. But I decided to come home. I wanted to sleep in a proper bed for a few days.'

She moved lightly over to the steps of the high dais. 'Eustace…we have someone else staying at the moment. You know what happened with Bianca d'Attalens…?'

'Mother sent a message. The marriage was arranged before I left for Wales; I knew what she was planning.' He grinned nastily. 'Well done, Alinor. At least you can do something right, for once.'

She licked her lips, the delicate flesh suddenly devoid of moisture. 'Well, her brother sleeps upstairs.'

'Sweet Jesu!' Eustace banged the goblet down on the table. He wiped his mouth with the back of his sleeve, an agitated gesture. Thrusting himself out of the chair, he made his way down the steps into the hall, glancing towards the stairwell, as if expecting Guilhem to come pounding down at any moment. In the half-light, spots of grease gleamed on his tunic. His hair was flat, limp, plastered to his oddly shaped head with dirt, a couple of strands stuck to his wide forehead. He was only a couple of inches taller than Alinor, but what he lacked in height, he made up for in girth. His tunic strained against his rounded belly, fleshy folds gathering beneath his jawline. 'What if he finds out what you have done?' he demanded grimly. 'We'll lose everything! If only you had done as you were told in the first place! If I had been married to you, the Queen wouldn't have sent that stupid girl in the first place!'

Alinor sighed. 'Eustace, you know I'm never going to marry you. Even with Bianca gone. Why can't you accept that?'

Her stepbrother's face darkened, angry patches of colour appearing beneath his pale-brown eyes. 'No, Alinor, I can't. I want Claverstock. And marrying you is the only way that will happen.' He grinned suddenly, showing a row of grimy, uneven teeth. 'But you know, I don't even have to marry you,' he said. 'Just have you.'

'Don't be ridiculous, Eustace.' Alinor pivoted smartly on her heel, intending to head for the main door. 'You're being a fool.' Her cloak swirled around her. Eustace was a revolting person, snide and secretive, a bully, and she wanted nothing to do with him.

'Don't mock me, Alinor.' His hand snaked out, grabbed at her forearm, dragging her back towards him. He was surprisingly strong.

'Stop this! Let go of me!' she hissed, wrenching downwards, trying to release her arm. 'I will tell my father!'

Eustace smirked, his face looming close to hers. An unpleasant whiff of foetid, wine-fuelled breath, of unwashed body, filled her nostrils. 'Your father doesn't care about you, Alinor; all he cares about is his bloodline, you inheriting Claverstock and pleasing his darling Wilhelma: whatever she wants. And she wants me to have you. And frankly, I am bored of waiting.'

He shoved at her so violently that her hips bumped against the edge of a trestle table. The

spindly wooden legs skittered back along the flagstone floor with a discordant, scraping sound. One
hand was around her throat, the other against her
midriff, pushing her down so that her spine arched
painfully backwards. Panic scythed through her,
replacing irritation; sweet Jesu, was this truly his
intention? To rape her and then claim her as his
bride?

'You can't do this! Eustace, stop, please!' Nausea swept through her as she read the determination in his round, greedy eyes, in the globules
of sweat on his forehead. The hard wood of the
table pressed into her shoulder blades; his fingers
gripped into her painfully as he whipped up the
hem of her skirts. She kicked out forcefully, her
slippers falling from her stockinged feet, struggled wildly, trying to make contact with something, anything that would disable him enough
for her to break free, but his heavy weight was
upon her and she cried out, in fear and desperation. Her arms were pinned beneath her; his hand
moved, closing so forcibly around her throat that
he began to choke her windpipe. If only she could
reach her knife in her belt! This couldn't happen!
She couldn't let it happen!

Flinging off his tunic and shirt, throwing
them down on to the wooden floorboards, Guilhem lifted the jug from the oak coffer and poured

the water out into the earthenware bowl. Using one of the linen flannels folded neatly on a low wooden stool beside the coffer, he scrubbed at the bare skin of his torso, his neck, his arms. He ran wet hands through his hair, dampening it slightly. Avoiding his bandaged shoulder, he moved his arm forward in a circular motion, trying to relieve the sore skin around his wound. Drying his upper body briskly with a towel, he looked around the guest chamber. Whilst he had been eating, someone had been in to light the charcoal brazier in the corner and draw the plush velvet curtains across the wide window apertures. Candles had been set in niches around the walls, bathing the whole room in a golden glow. The large horsehair mattress on the four-poster bed was heaped with woven blankets and furs.

A restlessness plagued his mind; it jumped like a stuttering candle as he thought about Alinor, about her stepmother. The way Alinor shifted uncomfortably, her green eyes wide and huge, when he asked her about Bianca; the dismayed expression on her pale, beautiful face when he announced he was staying the night. Was he such an ogre that she could not trust him with the truth? He realised that he wanted her to confide in him. She knew where Bianca was, he was certain of it. Pulling his shirt over his head, fawn-coloured braies hugging his lean waist, he strode towards the window, thrust back the curtain. Kneeling on to the windowsill, he opened the catch on the diamond-paned window, pushed it open. He looked down into the darkness of the inner bailey; the chill air brushed against his hair. Lit by a single torch, a guard was on duty at the gatehouse, his head lolling forward on to his chest. Guilhem picked out the low roof of the stables on the right-hand side, built into the substantial curtain wall, and the faint outline of a well, outside what must be the door to the kitchens.

He drew back, about to close the window. And then he heard it. A woman's shriek, bursting through the silence. Flooding the night air.

Alinor.

The screams went on and on. Guilhem wrenched open his door and ran, the desperate sound driving into his chest like a knife. Down the spiral staircase, his long legs jumped down the narrow steps five at a time until he burst out through the archway into the hall. He saw Alinor, arms flailing wildly, skirts bunched up around her hips, bent backwards over a trestle table and a man, pinning her down with one meaty fist, fiddling with his belt. A murderous anger broke over him, a boiling wave of fury, and he sprang forward, grabbing Alinor's attacker by his collar, wrenching him back and shoving one heavy fist into his face. The man flailed backwards, dropping, sprawling on to the floor, head knocking back against the flagstones. His eyes rolled back as he lost consciousness.

'Oh, my God, my God!' Alinor was struggling to sit up. Tears streamed down her face, bleached white with fear. She touched her dishevelled hair with trembling fingers, her expression lost, vulnerable. Like a wraith, a ghost of her former self.

Guilhem came towards her, folding her quaking body into his chest, his big arms tight around her shoulders, her back. The thought that she hid something from him, that she knew what had happened to Bianca, vanished, blown away by her cries for help. All he wanted to do was help her, comfort her. 'It's over, Alinor. He's out cold.'

'I can't believe he would do such a thing,' she sobbed against his chest. Her tears soaked through the fine linen of his shirt, wetting his skin.

Above the silken brightness of her hair, shimmering beneath her gauzy veil, Guilhem frowned. For some insane reason he hoped, he prayed that he had reached Alinor in time. 'Did he hurt you?' he asked gruffly, latent anger licking along his veins, a rope of fire.

She lifted her chin up, face stricken. Patches of exhaustion stained the delicate skin beneath her eyes. 'No!' she replied vehemently. 'No, he didn't!' Her speech was jerky, blunt. One of her braids had come adrift, coiling down in a loose, glossy rope across the slope of her breast, tickling his wrist. Her cloak spread out from her neat shoulders, voluminous folds gathering softly on the table behind her.

Relief coursed through him at her stuttered words. 'Thank God.' He touched her cheek, an unconscious gesture. Her skin slid beneath his fingers, a touch of downy feather. Like silk. 'Who is he?' He moved his hand away abruptly.

'My stepbrother, Eustace,' she whispered.

He stepped back, hands on her upper arms, disgusted. 'Are you serious?'

'I never thought he would go this far.' Alinor raised her head listlessly, meeting Guilhem's piercing blue eyes 'I thought at least that I was safe from that.'

'God, what sort of family do you belong to?' he bellowed at her. He pushed his fingers through his hair, jawline rigid, strained taut.

Alinor blinked at him, stunned by his reaction. 'It's not that bad,' she ventured in a small voice.

'Not that bad?' he said, his heart squeezing at the forlorn look crossing her face. 'I don't understand, Alinor. Why would your own stepbrother do such a thing to you?'

She pressed her palms to her eyes, hard, trying to stop the well of tears. 'Before…before the Queen decided Eustace should marry your sister, he was intent on marrying me.' Her shoulders hunched inwards, shaking from the effort of holding the tears back. 'But I kept refusing.' Her trembling hands dropped from her face, her voice toneless, bleak. 'He wants Claverstock and all its wealth, you see. I am my father's only heir.'

'My God...' breathed Guilhem. 'So he thought by raping you, he could claim you as his bride?'

She nodded dully.

'The man who is supposed to be marrying Bianca,' announced Guilhem slowly, tilting his head to assess her, a lone muscle quirking in his jaw. 'Maybe she's had a lucky escape. Wherever she is.'

She flinched at his pointed remark. A pall of guilt swept over her, a darkening cloak. Her conscience nibbled at her, fraying the edges of her nerves, and she shoved the thought away. 'Do you think Eustace cares about a Queen's demands?' she replied bitterly. 'He does exactly as he pleases.'

He glanced down, then wished he hadn't. Her gown was rucked up around her hips. Gossamer-light stockings encased the silky length of her legs as they swung down from the table. The fine indent of her knee, the push of lean muscle in her pearly-white thighs peeked out from beneath the bunched hemline. Breath snared in his chest, a surge of desire pulsing through him. For one blind, insane moment all he wanted to do was lay

Alinor gently back upon the table and made long, sweet love to her. God, what was he thinking? He was no better than the man who lay out cold on the flagstones! Harnessing every last ounce of self-control, he plucked her skirts down over her knees, allowing them to fall.

Alinor scrubbed at her eyes. 'I thought I was safe here,' she whispered. 'But now...'

He caught her quaking hands, held them against his chest. His eyes sparkled, not blue, but black, predatory, the lean handsome lines of his face inches away from hers. A musky scent rose from him, reminding her of rugged moorland, of tumbling, churning rivers. He smelled of danger, of a wildness; her body cleaved towards him even as she shook in the aftermath of Eustace's attack. She longed to collapse against him, have his strong arms at her back once more; to draw on that strength, his solidity. She had been battling alone for such a long, long time; it felt good to rely on someone else, if only for a fraction of a moment.

With her eyes, she traced the sculptured hollow of his neck, the dusting of bronze hairs exposed by the unlaced collar of his shirt. What would it be like to run her hands across his skin? To touch, to explore? Would his skin feel warm, velvety, or cold and smooth, like marble? Her fingers tingled treacherously.

'I need to get out of here,' Alinor gasped, appalled at the wayward direction of her thoughts, and she hopped down, swaying a little as she slid haphazardly into the miniscule gap between Guilhem and the table. Pulling her hands from his loose hold, she bunched small fists by her side. 'Guilhem, I need to go. Before he wakes up.'

He grasped her arm. 'You shouldn't have to run away, Alinor,' he said softly.

She scowled at him, at the rugged column of his neck, the muscled sling of collarbone beneath his shirt. 'What would you have me do?' she hissed. 'Wait around here until he tries that again? I'm not safe here!'

'But this is your home, Alinor,' he replied, calmly. 'He should be brought to account for what he has tried to do. Surely there is someone who can help you, some relation? Maybe your father can be persuaded...?'

'No.' Her voice was ragged. 'Father blames me for not being the boy I should have been, because then the bloodline of inheritance would have been easy. He has always said that Eustace and I should marry.' She laughed hollowly. 'And then the Queen came along and scuppered all their plans.'

She had no one. Not one person to look after her, or look out for her. Guilhem's mouth tightened. 'He should be brought to account for his actions.'

'Don't you think I haven't tried? she replied bitterly. 'My father, my stepmother—they laugh in my face when I protest. But I will never marry that man.' She tipped her chin up, her mouth a stubborn line. 'Or any man for that matter.'

In the flickering half-light of the great hall, her skin took on a pearly sheen; her mouth, tipping up at the corners, was plush, full. If he bent his head now, he could kiss her, Guilhem thought, just brush his mouth against hers: a fragile, sensual touch.

'That would be a shame,' he murmured.

Her green eyes widened. 'Do you think I want to be locked into a loveless marriage where I have to do as I'm told by a man, day after day? As opposed to now, where I can make my own choices, where I can be free?'

'Are you free, Alinor? Are you really?'

She tracked the shadowed line of his cheekbone, the burnished skin pulled taut across the bone. A hollowness punched into her stomach, a horrible realisation at his words. 'No,' she whispered. 'No, I'm not.'

'A loving husband at your side would give you far more power, far more freedom than you have now, Alinor, for all your hiding behind your nun's disguise, or your prowess with a knife.' He glanced pointedly at the blade hanging from her girdle.

'Loving husband?' she hurled back at him. 'Where do you suggest I find one of those? Marriages are forged as contracts, tying up land and money, especially for women like me. We are like cattle, common goods, traded at the market. Love never comes into it.' She flushed suddenly, biting down hard on her lip; she had never, ever spoken like this to anyone about her situation, so why now, to this man? 'Anyway—' she forged onwards, pushing back a glossy tendril of hair that had fallen across her forehead '—these are family matters, of no interest to you. Eustace, my stepmother, they're my problems to sort out, not yours.' She threw him a bright, false smile, signalling an end to their conversation. 'Now, will you let me pass?'

She was fighting the system, he thought suddenly. So stubborn, digging in her heels to retain her dignity. Her fortitude was admirable, if misguided, he thought grudgingly. Lesser women would have given into the inevitable situation months ago, but Alinor? Nay, she was cut of a better, more determined cloth than that.

She took a step to the right, intending to go around him, but he moved to stand in front of her, blocking her path.

'Where are you going?'

'To friends in the village.' Ralph, she thought. If she kept her wits about her she would still be able to carry out her plan with Bianca.

'Then I'll come with you.'

'There's no need,' she cut in sharply. 'I am perfectly familiar with the route.'

Guilhem crossed his arms over his chest, as if challenging her to continue with her line of argument. 'And what do you think the first thing your stepbrother will do when he realises you have gone?'

A feeling of despair washed over Alinor; biting her lip, she toed the uneven flagstones. 'He'll come after me,' she replied woodenly.

'Aye, he will. And try the same thing again, Alinor. And again and again, until...'

She screwed up her eyes in horror, placing her hands over her ears. 'Guilhem, stop it, please! Stop saying such awful things.'

'You are vulnerable, Alinor,' he announced bluntly. 'Who do you have to protect you?'

Despair washed over her. She stared at the stone floor, tears pricking at the side of her eyes.

'There's no one, is there?' he rapped out at her. 'You're on your own.'

Her head jerked back at his harsh words; she wound her arms across her stomach. 'Thank you for pointing that out to me,' she responded grimly. 'Now, will you let me pass?'

'I'm coming with you.'

'Why would you want to do that? Why are you even remotely interested?'

His gaze flicked down over her, over her trim, fragile figure, across huge eyes sparkling with tears. Because I don't want to let you go just yet, he thought with surprise. And I want to protect you.

'Because you know something about my sister Bianca. You are wearing your cloak already — were you planning to give me the slip?

Alinor's heart sank.

Striding to the main entrance, Guilhem grabbed the flaring, spitting brand out of the iron holder, the only light in the hall. 'I need to fetch my tunic,' he said. 'Come with me.' Alinor dropped her gaze, toeing the uneven flagstones uncomfortably. 'Or you can wait here,' he suggested, a mocking light entering his eyes as he glanced at Eustace's prone figure, 'but I can't guarantee that he won't wake up.'

'I'll come,' she mumbled, following him to the stairwell, annoyed with her own acquiescence. She should have stayed in the great hall, to demonstrate to Guilhem that she wasn't frightened of Eustace and what he could do. But that would be a lie. She was scared of Eustace; she had seen a side to him this evening that had terrified her and made her realise the danger she was in.

Lifting her skirts so she wouldn't trip on the narrow steps, she trailed after Guilhem as he climbed the stairs. 'Here, hold this,' he said, placing the brand in her hand. She stood in the doorway of his chamber, her weak arm braced against the thick oak frame, her other arm holding on to the light, shining the spitting torch into Guilhem's chamber. He yanked his blue tunic over his head, down over his lean hips, moulded thighs snug in woollen braies. A traitorous heat coiled in her belly, gathering slowly.

'Let's go,' he said, strapping on his sword belt around his tunic, and fastening his cloak around his shoulders. 'You lead the way.'

'The only way out is through the great hall.' She fought hard to keep the fear from her voice.

'I doubt he'll mess with you if I'm at your side.'

Glancing at the strapping man in the doorway, his gathered cloak swinging from his broad shoulders, Alinor doubted it, too, and for a single moment she luxuriated in the feeling of having someone who would stand up for her, who would fight her corner. Was this what it was like? To be with someone who truly loved you? She grimaced, the corners of her mouth turning down. *Take a hold of yourself, Alinor,* she told herself sternly. *He's only doing this because he wants information about Bianca, not because he feels any sense of duty, or loyalty towards you.*

She stopped, the flaming brand shedding sparks into the confined space. The jewelled brooch holding the sides of her cloak together winked and sparkled in the light. 'I'm not scared of Eustace.'

He raised his eyebrows, recalling her trembling body against his chest in the aftermath of Eustace's attack. 'After what he just tried to do? You should be.' He paused. 'It's not a crime to admit you're frightened of something, Alinor. In fact, in your case, I think you should admit it more often. It might make you less foolhardy, rushing into situations...

'I didn't rush into this one, did I?' she whispered sadly. The brand drooped in her hands and he reached for it.

Remorse pushed through him at the defeated sag of her shoulders. He was being cruel, goading her to admit her fear. 'No,' he said. 'No, you didn't.'

Chapter Ten

Outside, ominous grey clouds billowed across the moon, a smoky haze obscuring the silvery light. A spatter of raindrops hit the cobbles, pushed by a fierce little breeze. The guard at the gatehouse lifted his head, regarding the couple dully as they emerged from the castle, then dropped his chin to his chest once more. Alinor shivered as she followed Guilhem down the steps and into the courtyard, the stone cobbles unexpectedly chill against the soles of her feet.

'My slippers!' she gasped, remembering.

Guilhem turned. 'Where are they?'

Alinor squirmed uncomfortably. 'They're... they're...in there.' She jerked her head in the direction of the great hall. 'They fell off when... when...' Her speech faded; she stared hopelessly at the ground.

He saw the panic sift across her face. 'I will fetch them.'

He loped back across the courtyard. Alinor grimaced. Why had she not fetched the shoes herself? She should have scooped them up as they had passed through the great hall, not stood here quavering like a candle flame, pathetic and weak, too ashamed of what had happened with Eustace to go back in. Too frightened of him. A sense of entrapment surged over her; she felt caught, hobbled, too weak to run away from Guilhem, too scared to go back into the castle and face the wrath of Eustace. Her whole frame drooped with fatigue; the urge to sink down and lay her forehead on the cool, damp cobbles flooded over her. But she couldn't do that. She had never done such a thing in her life; she would not give in.

Guihem came towards her, red leather slippers crushed within his tanned fingers. They looked incongruous, clasped in his sinewy grip, and she held out her hands for them. He thrust them into her outstretched hands. Bending over, she stuck her toes quickly into the pliable leather.

She straightened up. 'Is he dead?' she whispered. 'Did you see him move at all?'

Guilhem smiled grimly. 'Still unconscious, but very much alive, unfortunately. He won't wake up for a long time, though.' He rubbed his thumb across the knuckles of his hand. 'There's a lump the size of an egg on his head.'

'My God, he'll be so angry,' Alinor said, turning away and stepping through the wide open arch in the centre of the stables, breathing in the scent of hay, and leather. She increased her pace; it was imperative that she left Claverstock before he woke up.

'Nothing more than he deserved,' Guilhem ground out. A rivulet of pure fury coursed through him at the memory of Alinor pinned beneath that man. 'In fact, I probably should have killed him.'

She paused, stunned by the stab of sudden anger in Guilhem's tone. Did he really care about Eustace's behaviour towards her that much? 'Guilhem... I...er...' she murmured, her voice hesitant, 'thank you for what you did.'

He cocked his head to one side, forcing his breathing to slow, to calm down. The light from the gatehouse torch glittered over the embroidery on his tunic front. 'It was nothing, Alinor. I would have done the same for anyone.'

Self-pity wormed its way into her heart, a tiny kernel of misery. Of course. He would have done the same for anyone. Why would she think anything different? Had she believed that, in some way, she was special to him? His kiss had sent her senses awry, a kiss that held little substance for him, yet had made a powerful impact on her. She peeked up at his stern face from the shadows. Guilhem was a soldier, a battle-hardened knight, familiar with fists and sword alike. Knocking Eustace to the ground meant nothing to him. Just like she was nothing to him. She would do well to remember that and preserve her own sanity.

Alinor walked through the stables, searching for the small, dove-grey palfrey. At her approach, her horse nickered gently, recognising her mistress. She leaned into the soft velvety nose. Warm air gusted from the horse's nostrils; the animal swung its great head from side to side in pleasure.

Guilhem approached, ran one hand over the palfrey's grey head. 'Is she yours?' he asked.

'She was. I rode her before my accident.'

'Will you ride her again?'

She remembered the rush of air, the sickening crunch in her arm as she hit the hard ground falling from her father's horse. She shook her head. 'I don't know.'

'Why not now?'

'I… I'm not sure.' Uncertainty clouded her face.

'You can ride with me, or ride on your own. Either way, we need to leave now.' He tilted his head to one side, brilliant eyes gently assessing her.

Alinor paddled her fingertips into the close-cropped pelt; the horse nudged her shoulder.

'You can do this, Alinor. I know you can. You weren't frightened when you rode with me, were you? Not after the first few minutes.'

No, she hadn't been. A sense of confidence, of a growing belief in her own ability rippled through her; she drew strength from his words. Strange to think that a man who exerted such a physical effect on her could also imbue her with such a feeling of self-confidence. After her accident, in those long, painful days of recovery, she had truly believed she would never have the courage to ride again, and yet, here she was, actively considering it.

He opened the door to the stall, leading out her palfrey. 'Where's the saddle?' The animal's hooves slipped and scraped on the cobbles.

Wordlessly, she pointed to the far wall, the saddle slung over a low wooden bar, the bridles hanging from wooden pegs. He settled the heavy leather on her horse, tightening the girth straps, adjusting the stirrups. A nub of excitement burned low in her belly, excitement coupled with a thread of fear—could she really do this? Unconsciously, her fingers dug into the weakened ligaments of her arm, willing it to work properly for her, to be strong.

Her knees shook.

Guilhem laced his fingers together, stooping slightly beside her horse. 'Hands on my shoulders, foot in my hands,' he instructed her. 'You remember how to do this, don't you?' His eyes were bright, encouraging, long eyelashes shadowing the hollows in his cheeks.

'I do. I learned when I was small.' Her hands rested against his neck and she lifted her foot, slipping it across his interlinked fingers. In a trice, he had thrown her slight weight up into the saddle and she turned in the air, settling herself expertly, as if she had ridden only yesterday, one leg dangling down on each side. Her skirts bunched around her knees. Pure joy leaped through her body and she laughed, gathering up the reins.

Guilhem watched the smile tipping up the corners of her beautiful mouth, desire looping through him. He strode away, seeing to his own horse, sticking one booted foot into the shining stirrup, and mounted up.

'Move towards me,' he said, hitching around to look at Alinor. She was still smiling. Despite all that had happened to her, she was smiling. His heart jumped with gladness, with the fact that he had been able to help her. He had known she could do it; he had seen as much determination and fortitude in this one diminutive bundle of femininity as he had seen in a whole army. Alinor touched her heels to her palfrey, her grin widening as the horse moved, edging the animal alongside Guilhem.

'How do you feel?' he asked, noting the way she held her reins with her good arm, whilst her weak arm rested at the front of the saddle. He frowned. 'Will you be able to hold on all right?'

'Of course I can hold on!' she said. 'Guilhem, this is amazing, I never thought I would ride again, and yet now… I can't believe it!'

He grinned back at her, at the sheer pleasure flooding her delicate features. 'Then let's get a move on, Alinor, before your stepbrother comes to his senses!'

As they clattered out through the gatehouse, a squall of rain hit them, large, freezing drops spattering their cloaks with dark patches. Alinor screwed up her eyes, trying to discern the track through the relentless drizzle.

'How far is the village where your friends live?' asked Guilhem, slowing his horse so she could move alongside him.

'Coombe Bissett? Not above five miles.' She waved airily up into the darkness, indicating a vague direction. The wind was rising, sighing through the trees that circled Claverstock, jostling branches, spinning leaves furiously to the ground.

'Good, because this weather is not going to improve,' he said. 'You lead.' Alinor pulled up the wide hood of her cloak against the rain, obscuring her veil, the silver circlet on her head, a row of pleats gathering the back of her cloak. She squeezed her knees gently into the palfrey's flanks, her heart surging with happiness as the animal responded immediately to her slight touch. Why had she never possessed the courage to ride earlier, to climb back into the saddle after her accident? She knew why. Guilhem had spurred her on, almost as if he had handed her a piece of his own fearlessness, his courage. She had to thank him for that, at least. If he hadn't been there, in the stables with her, talking to her in his calm, low tone, inspiring her, she would never have done such a thing.

The constant slanting rain made it difficult to see, but she had travelled this route a hundred times, the village lying mid-way between Claverstock Castle and the Priory. Despite the rain, the moon shed a greyish light from behind the thin cloud, enough light for them to be able to pick out the track rising to the ridge. They plodded upwards, through the shelter of the trees, until they emerged at the top, the white chalk of the track shining eastwards.

Up here, the wind was fiercer, catching at her hood, at the ends of her cloak, blowing the fabric about wildly. Her palfrey's mane blew up straight in the breeze as she pressed her right knee into the mare's rounded side, urging the animal to turn on to the track. The rain splattered against her cheeks, sluiced across her chin.

'We need to keep going!' Guilhem appeared beside her, one side of his cloak thrown over his shoulder; it wrapped around his neck like a make-shift scarf emphasising the lean, raw toughness of his jaw. He shook his head, wet droplets spinning out from his thick hair. 'Let's pick up the pace,' he said, kicking his heels into the destrier's flanks, taking off down the track.

Alinor was thrown back as her own horse sprang excitedly to follow Guilhem's as it cantered off, hooves flying up in the darkness; she clutched at the reins, hoping, praying that she would stay in her seat. Had he forgotten that she only had one good arm to ride with? Her leg muscles clenched and strained with the effort of staying in the saddle, her whole body hunching forward so she could keep her balance. Her hood collapsed back on her shoulders, veil spinning out, unravelling out behind her like a white wing. She clung on desperately, teeth gritted as she focused on Guilhem's broad outline. Finally, he reined his animal in at a point where the pathway forked, one track leading down into the valley, one track remaining on the high level.

Her palfrey skidded to a halt beside him and she dropped the reins instantly, flexing the tight fingers of her right hand. Every muscle ached, her weak arm throbbed painfully even though it had done nothing, and she wanted to cry.

'Which way?' he shouted at her. The roar of the wind threatened to take his words away. The rain coursed down thickly, washing across the sculptured contours of his face.

She hunkered down miserably, wet cloak dragging like a stone against her shoulders. Water seeped down her neck, creeping with icy fingers down her spine. Her veil clung to her cheek like a limp rag, her circlet digging uncomfortably into her forehead, cold metal against damp, warm skin.

'What's the matter?' he asked, taking in the forlorn wilt of her figure, the bowed head. She looked like a wraith, he thought suddenly, pressed down into her saddle, slim shoulders pulled down by her sodden clothes.

Her eyes sparked at him, furiously. 'You shouldn't have taken off like that! I can't ride as fast as you! I'm not one of your soldiers!'

No, she was not. She was fragile and beautiful and he should have taken more care with her. A pang of guilt seared through him; her weak arm lay across the saddle in front of her, chiding him. He had forgotten. 'I am sorry,' he said, 'my only thought was to get out of this rain as fast as possible.' He cocked his head on one side. 'You did well though, keeping up. You're a good horsewoman.'

Alinor lifted her head, raised her shoulders, her heart warming at his apology, his compliments. She schooled her features into a stern, blank mask, careful not to show how much his words affected her. 'You'd better follow me,' she said, steering her horse towards the track leading down from the ridge.

Ralph's cottage was one of the larger homes in the village. The grubby lime-washed walls showed up pale in the gloom, the wattle and daub bumpy, pitted. The rain cascaded down relentlessly from the thatched roof, pooling into a sea of mud beneath. Round pillows of moss clung to the straw thatch, given it a spotty, uneven look. The external shutters were closed; no smoke rose from the inverted V-shaped chimney.

'Whose house is this?' said Guilhem, springing down from his horse and looping the reins over the low picket fence that ran around the property. A row of browning foxgloves, seed-heads spent and crinkled after the long, dry summer, sagged crazily under the continual onslaught of the rain.

Alinor sat on her horse, a miserable, cold lump. Her clothes were so saturated and heavy with water that she wondered if she could even move. 'It belongs to Ralph.' She shivered, teeth knocking together violently.

'The man who was with you on the cart at the river.'

She raised her eyebrows, diamond raindrops clinging to her lashes. 'I'm surprised you remember. You only saw him briefly.'

'I remember,' he said, his voice husky. I remember you. How could he forget her luminous, angry face, the shining blade waggling precariously near his chest, the hurled-out Latin curses? He would never forget.

Summoning up every last reserve of strength, Alinor kicked her right foot out of the stirrup, leaning her weight on the horse's neck so she could swing her leg around. Clutching at the saddle with her good hand, she managed to slide haphazardly down until her slippers touched the ground, then disappeared into thick, gooey mud. Puddles swilled around her ankles, soaking her stockings.

Guilhem came around to her side of the horse. 'Why didn't you wait for me?' he asked. 'I would have helped you dismount.' He reached out his hand; she seized his fingers gratefully, pulling her feet out from the mud with a dismal sucking sound. He tied her horse to the fence as they walked through. Her clothes trailed in the mud: her cloak, the flowing hem on her gown. She blinked continually, trying to keep the rain out of her eyes as she blundered forward.

The edge of the thatch overhung the low lintel, lengths of straw poking out, a haphazard fringe. Ducking his head, Guilhem thumped on the door with a heavy fist.

'Shh!' Alinor moved in front of him, nudging him aside. 'Don't wake the children!' Raising the wooden latch, she pushed the cottage door inwards. 'Ralph?' she called softly. 'Ralph, are you there? It's me, Alinor.' There was a grunt, then the sound of someone moving, a rustle of a straw. A man in a loose shirt, unfastened at the collar, appeared in the small gap. Ralph.

'Lady Alinor?' he said. 'What's going on?' He peered out in the gloom, eyes resting on Guilhem's tall figure, standing close behind Alinor. A hostile scowl crossed his face. 'And what's he doing here?'

'I can explain everything,' Alinor stuttered out. Her teeth chattered uncontrollably, her jaw wobbling violently with the movement. Shivers ricocheted up and down her spine. Gripping her arms across her stomach, she attempted to still her quaking body. She couldn't seem to concentrate on why she was here, her mind flying off in all directions, flitting chaotically.

'Are you all right, mistress?' Ralph asked suddenly, eyeing Alinor's wet, pale face.

'No, she's not,' Guilhem said, his voice booming in her ear. 'Light a fire, Ralph. And fetch some spare clothes. For a start, we can take this off.' His hands came across her shoulders to undo the cloak at her neck, lifting the rain-soaked garment away. His knuckles brushed her damp chin. 'God, this material weighs a ton! How on earth did you manage to stay on the horse wearing this?' His hands cupped her shoulders, testing the fabric of her gown. 'You're wet through, Alinor, you need to change.' His voice was a low rumble, authoritative.

Shivering, she stumbled into the cottage. Her slippers squelched noisily across the earth floor. Bertha, Ralph's wife, appeared, holding a pile of dry clothes. Her face was flushed, embarrassed. 'This is all I have, mistress, not quite what you're used to.'

'Thank you Bertha,' she murmured gratefully. 'You know all that doesn't matter to me. I am so sorry for disturbing you at such a late hour.'

'I'll wait outside,' said Guilhem, his broad frame dominating the cramped interior of the cottage. There were only two rooms on the ground floor: one for the animals, the cow and the goats, and one for the humans, a fireplace set into the back wall over which they cooked, a rickety table and a set of chairs where they ate. A ladder led up to a higher level, where the whole family slept and where the children slept now. Turning smartly on his heel, Guilhem disappeared outside.

'I'll go, too,' Ralph said.

Alinor touched his arm. 'Ralph,' she whispered urgently, her eyes lifting meaningfully towards the door through which Guilhem had recently departed. 'I need your help. I need to talk to you… alone. Without him.'

He nodded. 'Later,' he said.

* * *

Bertha lifted off Alinor's silver circlet, removing her veil and wimple at the same time, placing them on the table in a sodden, wet heap. Her deft fingers worked at the knot on Alinor's girdle, releasing the plaited cord, unbuckling her separate knife belt so that her long, sleeveless tunic could be removed. Next came her underdress, Alinor lifting her arms so the gown could be pulled over her head. The rings on the leather lace around her neck chinked together: a metallic, ringing sound.

'I'll drape these over the stools in front of the fire, mistress, so they can dry.' Bertha handed her a rough linen towel. 'Here, my lady, use this.'

Although her hair was heavy with water and cold against her scalp, her plaits were still pinned into place at the nape of her neck. They would dry eventually. She rubbed the towel briskly around her neck and shoulders, realising with relief that her linen chemise was not as soaked through as her outer garments. Removing her mud-splashed stockings and slippers, she ran the towel up and down her chill legs and feet. Bertha poked the still-glowing ashes and stoked up the fire with more wood.

'I'm sorry about all this,' Alinor said, the warmth beginning to return to her body. 'I really didn't know where else to go.'

Bertha came towards her, a short plump little woman, her brown eyes kind, concerned. She placed a hand on Alinor's forearm. 'Think nothing of it, my lady. It's a pleasure to be able to do something for you for a change. You have done so much for us, for the village.' She cocked her head, almost as if she were about to ask another question, then took in Alinor's pale exhausted face and clamped her lips tight shut.

Alinor picked up the simple gown that Bertha had brought for her and slipped it over her head, using her own girdle to gather the dress in at the waist. She fastened the leather knife belt securely. Her wimple and veil steamed gently before the fire, so she left her face and neck uncovered. She was simply too tired to care.

'Are you ready yet?' Guilhem rapped on the door from outside. 'It's horrible out here!'

'Yes,' Bertha called out. 'You can come back in now!'

As Alinor sat down on one of the low, three-legged stools by the fire, her hand flew suddenly to the leather lace at her throat, to her mother's ring. To Bianca's ring! Shock trickled through her. It wasn't there! The leather lace must have fallen off, or become loose somehow when she was changing. As Guilhem came back into the cottage, she was scanning the ground, frantically, searching for a glimmer of silver.

'What are you looking for?' he said, pleased

to see a delicate flush back in the creamy alabaster of her cheeks. 'Have you lost something?' The pure gold of her hair, darkened to burnished bronze by the rain, was bound into plaits coiled neatly at the back of her head. A single droplet of water, glistening, ran down her bare neck, travelling over her graceful collarbone and disappearing beneath the rough fabric of her gown.

'No, it's nothing really,' she muttered hurriedly, eyes pinned to the earth floor. 'I'll find it in a moment.'

'Is this it?' he said, swooping down and picking up the leather lace wrapped around the foot of a stool. As he straightened up, the necklace hung down from his lean fingers, the two rings clicking together, spinning slowly, glimmering treacherously in the firelight.

'Yes, thank you!' she gasped, relieved, grabbing hurriedly for the lace. 'It must have fallen from my neck when I took my gown off.'

'I see.' Guilhem seized one of the rings between his fingers, staring closely at it. 'Alinor,' he said slowly, reading the letters on the inside of the ring, 'this ring belongs to my sister.'

'How could it be?' she cried out, unable to keep the edge of desperation from her voice. 'That's impossible!'

Guilhem came close to her, almost stepping on her bare toes, and bent down so that his gaze, fierce and penetrating, met hers, and she stumbled back from the sheer force of it, knocking clumsily into the stool. He gripped her shoulders, face set in a ruthless mask. 'Is it?' he ground out.

Chapter Eleven

'Yes, of course it is!' Alinor declared hotly. Fear slopped through her, a rolling viscous tide of sickening nausea. Her palms were clammy. How long could she keep this up for? How long could she keep lying to him so that Bianca could be free? 'I've never met your sister!'

Guilhem moved closer, the rings dangling ominously from the lace around his fingers, and she backed away until her hips and spine pressed back into the cold cottage wall. 'Tell me where you got this ring,' he said, his voice low, threatening, as he hulked over her, trapping her in the corner.

'Er... I think that maybe you should leave?' Ralph said, eyeing Guilhem's broad back doubtfully, the lethal sword hanging from his belt. Bertha huddled at his side, lines of worry carved into her face.

Guilhem turned, his eyes glinting, rapier sharp. 'Get up there, both of you, now!' He jabbed his finger towards the ladder. Mouths gaping in shock, they scuttled up the makeshift rungs to the sleeping platform, dragging their wide-eyed children away from the open edge and into the shadows at the back.

'Tell me how you got this ring.' His eyes were on her again.

Alinor's tongue moved woodenly against the roof of her mouth. 'I found it,' she replied, tipping her chin in the air, trying to inject a shred of confidence into her voice.

A muscle contracted in his jaw, a tiny movement below the sculptured hollow of his cheek. 'Stop lying to me,' Guilhem said. 'I will have the truth eventually, one way or the other.'

'If you kill me, I won't be able to tell you anything!' she thrust back at him. Her eyes were huge, sparkling, green shards of light.

'Oh, I'm not going to kill you, Alinor, don't worry. There are far better ways of extracting information than that.'

What in Heaven's name was he talking about? Some kind of torture? Her breath emerged in short, truncated gasps as he loomed over her, big and tall and dangerous, his handsome face inches from her own. His breath sifted across her face, warming her cheek, stirring the damp fronds of hair curling around her earlobe. A vibrant masculine scent rolled from his skin; he smelt of rain, soil, an earthy sweetness. Her heart leaped, not with fright, but with something else, a peculiar skipping excitement, an exquisite anticipation of what might happen. What was the matter with her? He was quite obviously about to throttle her, yet she was not afraid. She wanted him to be close to her, welcomed it.

He leaned into her, solid thighs pressing against hers, hard muscle against pliable curves. She couldn't concentrate, her mind dancing off in all directions; she should be battling at his shoulders with her fists, trying to free herself, but all she wanted to do was sink into his arms and crush her body to his. Her conscious brain instructed her to resist, to push him away, but her heart sang at his closeness; she wanted more, so much more of him.

His mouth scuffed against hers, a butterfly touch, light, sensual. 'Tell me where you got the ring,' he murmured.

Shock raced through her at his intimate caress. 'You can't do this!' she managed to choke out against his lips, astounded. Liquid heat tracked through her body, pooling in her belly, in the very core of her, gathering, building.

'Oh, yes, I can,' Guilhem replied, his mouth sketching the delicate cushion of her cheek. 'I will keep going until you tell me what you know.' His skilful hands moved up the slim flanks of her waist, stalling beneath her armpits. He rubbed his thumbs along the side of her breasts, slowly, carefully, testing the full roundness of her bosom, grazing the nipples.

She gasped with pleasure, staggering back against the rough cob wall. Sweet Jesu, what was happening? He was supposed to be punishing her and yet her body had turned into a quivering mass beneath his hands. He was no doubt experienced in the ways of lovemaking; she was an innocent. And up above them, Ralph, Bertha and their children, listening to everything. Her face suffused with colour at the thought, her senses reeling with embarrassment. Breathing heavily, she shoved at Guilhem's chest, a ridge of unyielding muscle beneath her fingers. 'Stop this!' she panted, her belly flip-flopping insanely. 'You must stop!

He wrenched his lips away at her cry, desire spinning in the blue depths of his eyes. Blood hurtled through his veins. The curving neckline of her borrowed dress gaped dangerously, revealing the fragile arc of her collarbone; a pulse beat frantically in the shadowed hollow of her throat. Her skin was luminous, with a pearl-like sheen. Distracted, he stuck one hand through his thick hair, sending the strands skywards.

This wasn't supposed to happen. The moment his lips had touched hers a strange recklessness had possessed him, driving away the main reason for kissing her, forcing it to skitter, as if a dog snapped at its heels. His intention had been to threaten, to pressurise her into telling him the truth about Bianca. But instead, he had only succeeded in desiring her more, wanting her. He stepped away, face stricken, troubled.

'I'm sorry,' he murmured, his voice hoarse. He folded his arms across his chest, puckering the fine blue wool of his tunic. He backed away into the middle of the chamber, as if to prevent himself from touching her again. 'I just want to know that Bianca is safe,' he said. To Alinor's surprise, his voice trembled slightly. 'Tell me that, at least. Please.'

Alinor clasped her hands together, twisting her fingers anxiously, her skin hot, throbbing from his touch. Shame washed over her; his intimate touch was only half to blame. What gave her the right to withhold such information from him? He was concerned and worried about his sister as any brother would be; that much was obvious.

'Bianca is safe,' she whispered into the tense, flickering silence between them. 'She is safe.'

Relief flooded his features, the stern set of his mouth relaxing slightly. 'Thank God...' he breathed. He sat down heavily on a stool, resting his elbows on his knees. 'Did the marriage to your stepbrother even take place?'

She shook her head, fiddling with a loose thread on her girdle.

'Why not? Did Bianca run away?'

'No, nothing like that.' Alinor sighed. How much could she tell him, without compromising Bianca's position? 'It...it was complicated. All I can tell you is that she had to leave Claverstock and I helped her.'

'God, what in Hell's name happened?' he muttered, almost to himself. 'Where is she now?' His voice was quiet, grimly persistent.

Alinor bit her lips to keep the tears from her eyes. 'She made me promise not to tell you.' She hung her head, staring blankly at the floor, at the wisps of straw scattered randomly across the hard-packed earth.

Guilhem raised one eyebrow, a thick, dark-brown arch. 'Why on earth would she do that? Why does she not want me to know?' He clasped his hands together, knuckles white against his tanned fingers.

'Because you would force her to go through with the marriage to Eustace,' she replied bitterly. 'And you've seen for yourself what sort of man he is.'

Guilhem frowned. 'I would do no such thing.'

'But I thought you arranged the whole thing. You, your mother and Queen Eleanor.'

'You're mistaken. I had nothing to do with it. I was away at the time.' Fighting with Edward. Always fighting.

'But why would she say such things, if they aren't true?' A sense of fluttering hope, of relief, seeped through her veins. She had never wanted to believe the dark, ruthless picture that Bianca had drawn of her brother.

Guilhem rested his eyes on her for a moment, thinking. 'I have no idea, Alinor. I can't explain it. I haven't seen Bianca for such a long time.' A raft of sadness crossed his face, his expression bereft.

Emotion lurched within her. Pushing herself away from the wall, Alinor stepped over to him, wanting to comfort him, to smooth the look of raw hurt from his face. He had nothing to do with Bianca's marriage. She knew it. Suddenly she realised she had known it all along. Yes, he was a soldier and friends with the notorious Prince Edward, but there was something about him, something beneath that huge, muscle-bound exterior, those trappings of war, that reached out and plucked at the strings of her heart. She placed one hand on his shoulder. 'I have misjudged you.'

Guilhem brought his own hand up, tangled his fingers with hers. He shook his head. 'No, you have stood by Bianca and held your promise.' His eyes were bleak, sparkling sapphires. 'And I have treated you abominably.'

'Not without good reason,' she replied. 'It doesn't matter.' Soft colour flooded her face. How could she tell him that her body still hummed in his presence, her innards fluid and vulnerable, flaring treacherously at his nearness? That his supposed punishment, his lips on hers, had been sweet torture for her? And yet for him, it must have meant so little, merely a useful method of prising information from her. She was a complete innocent, docile and compliant beneath his experienced touch, nothing more. She must show restraint and hide her desire, for he would surely laugh in her face if he knew the truth.

'It does matter, Alinor.' He spread his fingers across her forearm. Beneath the thin fabric of Bertha's shift, her skin burned. 'I scared you and for that I am sorry.' He absorbed the fine details of her face: the translucent skin, sheened with a faint pink blush, her eyes twinkling green. Guilt churned in his gut; he had behaved exactly like her stepbrother, throwing his weight across her, pinning her to the wall, pawing at her like some lecherous brute. 'It won't happen again.'

Her heart throbbed with the sincerity of his apology and she nodded jerkily, schooling her features into a blank, unreadable mask. She tugged at her arm; he released her immediately and she folded her arms tightly across her bosom, creating a barrier between them. A fragment of hope wondered if he might break his promise, but she dashed the thought down, annoyed that she was even considering such an outrageous idea.

'Where is my sister? Will you take me to her?'

'I will.' Purple shadows patched the hollow beneath her eyes; she was exhausted. Her shoulders hunched forward slightly with the thought of going out in all that rain and darkness again, of clambering awkwardly on to her horse. She ran an experimental hand across her clothes, steaming gently in front of the fire. 'They're not quite dry yet, but they will do,' she ventured brightly. 'If you allow me to change…' Her slender frame drooped with fatigue, but she forced her spine upwards, pulling her ligaments into a straight line.

He smiled. 'Even I am not such a tyrant, Alinor, to make you travel any further tonight. It's been a long day and we're both tired. Let's sleep here tonight and ride in the morning.'

Guilhem jumped down from his glossy destrier on to the cobbled courtyard of the Priory. He rested his hand on the saddle. 'So you hid Bianca under my very nose!' he said, with an edge of disbelief. His leather boots and fawn braies were spattered with mud from the ride; the ground had been spongy, saturated with rain from the night before, the tracks strewn with broken branches, a mess of leaves. This morning, the day was bright and breezy, white fluffy clouds scudding merrily across the sky, with not a hint of the wild storm from the previous night. 'Did anyone else know she was here?'

'No one.' Alinor leaned down, patting the warm neck of her palfrey. 'It was safer that way.' A shiver gripped her spine; her gown had only been partially dry this morning, dampness clinging within the thicker folds of fabric, and now that dampness irritated her skin.

Guilhem came around to her horse's side. 'Come, let me help you.' Clasping strong hands about her waist, he swung her down to the ground. 'All right?' he asked.

'Fine,' she replied briskly. A shudder rippled through her at the touch of his hands. All night, she had tossed and turned on the sleeping platform alongside Bertha, Ralph and the children, acutely aware that Guilhem slept below, his broad frame rolled in his cloak in front of the fire. *Forget! Forget!* she reminded herself. *Forget the brush of his lips, the graze of his big thumbs against sensitive skin. Forget it all, otherwise it will be the undoing of you!*

Guilhem led both horses into the stables, their big hooves slipping and sliding on the greasy cobbles, securing the reins on the wooden bar that ran around the back wall. He emerged, blinking in a sudden ray of strong sunlight. 'Where is she, then?' he said.

'This way.' Alinor inclined her head. 'The

place will be deserted…the nuns are at prayer in the chapel.'

Guilhem followed her through the silent refectory, twirling dust motes caught in the shafts of sunlight and then outside, along the cloisters, through into the storeroom. She picked her way around the wooden crates and barrels, and pulled open the narrow-arched door.

'I have forgotten to bring a light.' Alinor grimaced. 'But it will be easy to find our way.' She slipped beneath the arch, stepping carefully down the narrow stairs into the gaping blackness.

Guilhem poked his head through the doorway, squeezing his big shoulders into the small space. His large feet negotiated the steps down into the blackness, then on the level, he stopped, his palm sweating against the damp stone. The air in his lungs constricted. He couldn't see a thing.

'Alinor?' he called, closing his eyes tight. His scalp prickled. He could have been back there. Locked in a dark, filthy dungeon, infested with vermin, for defying the order of his commander, Prince Edward's brother. Solitary confinement for days and days on end. After what he had done, he had welcomed the punishment, but it had done nothing to absolve the guilt. Even after Edward had freed him, shame clung like a leg-shackle, hobbling his soul.

'I'm right here,' Alinor said, laughing out of the

blackness. 'What's the matter, don't tell me you're scared of the dark? Bianca is just along there, around the corner. It's not far.' Her face swam up close to him, luminous, vivid. His bright star. He was silent, tracing the familiar delicate outlines of her cheek, her jaw, in the gloom. Clung to them.

'Are you?' she said again. The teasing drained from her voice.

His eyes were savage, bleak.

'Guilhem, what's the matter?' Alinor placed one hand against his chest. His heart thudded rapidly beneath her fingers. 'What is it?'

'I was locked away once. In prison.' His voice was raw. 'This place reminded me of it, for a moment.' He stuck his hand through his hair, keeping his eyes pinned to her face. The dry, chill air covered them like a cloak.

She took his fingers in hers, gripped them. 'Guilhem, I am sorry. I had no idea. What happened?'

He glared down into the sweetness of her face. How could he tell why he had been locked up? The awful things he had done? He couldn't speak of it. 'I'm all right now,' he said gruffly. His throat was tight, as if someone held an iron fist around it.

'Tell me,' she whispered.

'No. Not now.' *Not ever.* 'Where is Bianca?'

Alinor eyed him doubtfully. He was fobbing her off and they both knew it. His skin was pinched, grey, and she wanted to wind her arms about him to drive the devastating hollowness from his eyes. 'I was going to suggest that you stay here for a moment, whilst I go and tell Bianca. I'm not sure how she is going to take the news; she will feel that I have betrayed her. But maybe you should come with me...' She chewed worriedly on her bottom lip.

He clasped her fingers, holding them against the thick band of muscle across his ribs. 'No, you go on,' he said. 'I will wait here until you come for me.'

'Are you sure?'

'Yes, I'm fine.' He smiled, the corners of his mouth angled awkwardly. 'Go on.' He nudged the indent of her waist, giving her a little push.

She squeezed his fingers, then flicked her skirts around to disappear into the darkness. He heard her feet scuffle against the flagstone floor, the trailing sift of her lavender-coloured gown. Lifting one hand, he wiped the sheen of sweat from his brow.

'Where have you been?' Bianca screeched up at her with a half-sob, as Alinor entered the vault. 'Oh, my Lord, I am so relieved to see you!' Staggering up from her seated position, she threw herself forward into Alinor's arms. 'You've been gone for so long, I thought something had happened to you!' The torch in the vault was still burning, thankfully, throwing its flickering, spitting light across walls constructed of large, rough-cut stone. Alinor had made sure that Bianca was well stocked with fresh torches, so she could transfer the flame from one to the other when the light became low.

'Something did happen to me, Bianca. You best sit back down, while I explain.'

'Oh, my God, what is it?' The girl sank down to the pile of blankets, her skirts spreading around her: rustling blue folds of expensive silk. 'You haven't met those soldiers again, have you?'

'Your brother is here.'

'I know that!' Bianca scoffed. 'You told me before. But you didn't tell him about me though, did you? I told you not to do that. '

Alinor's heart squeezed, a loose thread of betrayal, unravelling.

'Your brother... Guilhem...he came with me to Claverstock, he wanted to see you. And then... then he found your ring; it was a mistake, I had it hidden but it came loose from my neck. So he knew you'd been with me.' Her explanation emerged in a hollow rush, the words stumbling over each other. She stretched out her hand, a gesture of reassurance, placating.

'Alinor,' Bianca moaned, 'please tell me this isn't true!' Her skin adopted a grey, ashy sheen.

'Bianca, listen to me, I think you have him wrong. He had nothing to do with the marriage to Eustace, he told me so himself!'

Bianca stared at her wide-eyed with disbelief. 'I can't believe what you're telling me; I can't take it in!' She sank back down on to the tumbled blankets. 'Does he know where I am?'

'Yes. He wants to see you. He's worried about you.'

'And you believe him, you silly chump!' Bianca lashed back at her. She knocked at her own head, fingers scrunched into a fist, a dramatic gesture. 'What a fool you are, Alinor! Fallen in love with him, have you? Fallen for those handsome looks? The Devil take him!' Her tone was bitter, scathing. 'How did he make you tell him where I was? What did he do to you?'

A hot wave of embarrassment swept Alinor's cheeks as she remembered his hands upon her body, his mouth roaming over hers; she turned away, fiddling with the torch in its holder. Her whole frame wilted with fatigue as if stretched in a mangle, strung between two people who…my God, she thought in a rush…two people who she had come to care about. Bianca…and Guilhem.

'He'll come for me and drag me back to Eustace. He'll force me!' Bianca leapt to her feet, began to pace the flagstone floor of the vault, the pearls in her silver circlet swinging violently. 'I trusted you, Alinor!' she said, with a sob of despair. 'How could you do this?'

'Because I made her tell me.' Guilhem leaned one shoulder against the open arch of the vault, his low voice flooding the space, calm, quietly compelling. 'If you're going to berate anyone, Bianca, then berate me. Alinor's not the one at fault here. She held your secret.'

'Guilhem?' Bianca breathed out, blue eyes huge with shock. 'You're really here?' Her eyes roamed across the tall shadowy figure of her brother. Alinor moved quickly across the cellar, her skirts rustling across the flagstones, and wrapped her arms about Bianca.

'Aye, Sister.' He crossed his arms across his chest. 'And I think we need to sort a few things out.'

Huddled back against the stone wall, Bianca sank down, clasping her knees and eyed him warily. 'Are you going to make me go back to Eustace?'

'No, absolutely not. I was shocked when I found out you had gone to England to marry him.'

'Shocked?' squeaked Bianca, astonished. 'But you knew about it. You gave your consent. In the letter!'

Guilhem shook his head. 'I never sent a letter.'

'Mother showed me,' Bianca said slowly. 'I read it. You said how happy you were for me to go through with the marriage.'

'It's not true,' Guilhem replied. 'I would not have given my consent without coming home and speaking to you about it. And Mother knew that if I had found out that you were unwilling, I would not have agreed to such a marriage. With or without a queen's command.'

'Then...' Bianca slumped sideways into Alinor's arms, placing her palm flat upon her forehead in consternation '...did she lie to me? To make me go through with it? I was reluctant; I didn't want to leave France.'

'Perhaps. Maybe she thought that if she showed you some proof that I was happy for the marriage to go ahead then that would change your mind, persuade you.'

Bianca buried her face in her hands. 'Oh, God, what a mess! She must have forged the letter, your signature. Why would she do such a thing?'

'Because marriage to an English lord bestowed a high honour on our family, Bianca. And arranged by the Queen, as well.' A muscle quirked in his jaw. 'I should have been there for you,' he said slowly. Where had he been? Fighting his demons, raging against the enemy, when all along the enemy was inside him, battling from within. He had been so selfish.

Bianca lifted her face from her hands. 'Has Alinor told you what happened at Claverstock?'

Guilhem pushed himself away from the wall,

moved slowly towards her and knelt down, taking his sister's hands within his own. 'You tell me.' Pulling her fingers from his, Bianca threw her arms about her brother, burying her face in the crook of his neck. Over his sister's shoulder, Guilhem smiled at Alinor.

Her heart gave a small leap of pleasure. She had done the right thing. Brother and sister were reunited. Whatever had made him stop in the corridor seemed to have dissipated, vanished. But she knew it was there. She could see it lurking in his eyes: a sense of a man destroyed. What in Heaven's name had happened to him?

'I will leave you,' Alinor said.

'Don't go,' he murmured. 'Stay, please.'

Lifting her head from Guilhem's shoulder, Bianca turned, reached her hand out to snare Alinor's fingers. 'Yes, please stay. I need you to help me explain.'

The three of them sat in the pile of blankets at the back of the vault, Guilhem propping his back against the cold stone wall, one knee drawn up. Bianca huddled into his side; he wrapped one arm around her shoulders. Alinor sat away from them, aloof, her spine rigid. What was she doing here? They didn't need her any more. She was certain Guilhem would make the right decisions concerning Bianca, make sure she was safe.

She shifted uncomfortably on the blanket, un-curling her legs so they stretched out in front of her. Bianca's accusations seared into her brain: *'How did he make you tell him where I was? What did he do to you?'*...*'Fallen in love with him, have you?'* A tide of misery swept over her; she wanted to go, to run away and hide in some dark, secret place, away from him, away from his searching eyes, his devastating looks. All she could think about was what he had done to her, what he could do to her. She was undone, her whole world spin-ning at the briefest touch of his lips. He had tum-bled her from her perch of self-control, mired her with his kiss. And yet her heart sang with the memory. What in Heaven's name was happening to her? Dull, sensible Alinor. The one everyone relied on. Where had she gone?

'...didn't you, Alinor?'

Alinor glanced up to find two pairs of identical blue eyes staring at her. 'Sorry... I didn't hear...' she stuttered out.

'Oh, Alinor.' Bianca laughed. 'I was telling Guilhem what you did, how you...'

'How you saved Bianca's life,' Guilhem said. Admiration laced his tone. 'My God, Alinor, I can't believe what your stepmother asked you to do, what a risk you took!'

'There was no other way,' she said quietly. 'Wilhelma asked me to...to poison Bianca, to get rid of her. If I had refused, then Wilhelma would have taken matters into her own hands, would have found some other way.'

'She must be brought before the sheriff's court and tried for what she has done, for what she had attempted to do,' Guilhem said.

'Where's your proof? It's my word against hers; there's no blood on her hands.'

He grinned savagely. 'Oh, I'm sure I can find some way of bringing her in.'

'She's so desperate that Claverstock should go to Eustace, she'll do anything. I've told my father so many times that I don't want the estate; I've told him to disinherit me, that I'll make my own way in the world, but he simply refuses to listen!' Desperation clawed at her voice.

'But... Alinor,' Bianca said, worry creasing the space between her tawny brows, 'if you do that, if you renounce your home, then you will have nothing. You will be penniless, without support.'

'Unless I find...' Alinor stopped. What had she been about to say? Unless I find someone to love me, to support me? But that was a ridiculous notion. Who would marry her? 'I don't care,' she said, finally. 'I don't want Claverstock if I have to marry Eustace! I would rather be destitute and work the land for someone else. I would give it all up in a moment.' She stood up abruptly. 'And I am so sorry, Bianca that you have become caught up in all this family stupidity and my stubbornness. I do realise that if I had done as my father told me, then the Queen would never have arranged your own marriage! This is all my fault!'

Guilhem saw the flash of determination, of despair, in Alinor's eyes, and recognised it. Lord, but she was brave. Lesser women would have bowed to their fate months ago, but not Alinor. She refused to conform to her father's wishes, despite the consequences. Thank God she hadn't married her stepbrother, he thought with relief. Her life would have been a living hell.

'Alinor, stop blaming yourself. You made the right decision,' Guilhem said. 'Bianca is safe now.' He thought for a moment. 'I will tell the Queen what happened; she can write to our mother and dissolve the marriage contract.'

'Do you think that would work?'

'Yes,' Guilhem said. He glanced over at Alinor, her shuttered expression. A sense of something ending flooded over him. But a protesting, gnawing feeling in his belly told him that he didn't want it to end. Alinor looked exhausted, sagging forward with fatigue, her lavender-coloured gown spread upon the flagstones around her. The urge to hold her in his arms, to comfort her, to tell her everything would be all right, surged over him. But how could he even begin to offer her comfort when his own mind and body were still ravaged by the demons from the past? How could he subject her to what he had done? Tell her the truth? She would be horrified, hate him for ever. He couldn't risk that. He had no wish for her to hate him, no, he wanted her to…to what? Love him? Despair, black and coruscating, stumbled through him. How could he contemplate such a thing? He was not worthy of her.

Chapter Twelve

Beneath covert glances, heads ducking quickly down to study their porridge bowls lest they be caught staring too much, the nuns surveyed their unexpected guests at the end of the table. Alinor they knew, of course, but not this Alinor, dressed in her noble lady's finery: the elaborately decorated gown, the silver embroidery and rows of tiny pearl buttons, her flowing silk veil. And the knight with his devilish eyes and hard-cut features was the same man who had been with Prince Edward. But the other lady, tall and elegant—who was she?

'My Lord Guilhem!' The Prioress swept down the refectory to the spot where Guilhem sat with Alinor and Bianca. Brown wooden beads, a rosary, hung around her neck; a cross bounced gently against her chest. 'I certainly did not expect to see you again so soon! It's a pleasure, of course!' Guilhem rose, bowing courteously. Maeve settled herself in her chair beside them. 'How's the arm?' she asked. 'Not paining you too much, I hope?'

Guilhem rolled his shoulder, testing the muscles beneath. 'In truth, I had almost forgotten about it.' He laughed. 'Almost as good as new, thanks to Alinor.'

'It was nothing,' murmured Alinor. Perspiration prickled in her hollowed palms as she remembered. The sleekness of his bare flesh beneath her fingers as she worked on the wound. She fidgeted with her linen napkin, shaking out the creases, smoothing the fabric flat across her lap, chewed distractedly on her bottom lip.

'Too modest, as usual,' the Prioress boomed at her, her manner jovial. 'Your skill in healing is renowned, yet you go out of your way to hide it.' A young novice placed a bowl of porridge before her, the steam rising from the hot oats like a white mist. 'Sister Edith is up and about again, thanks to your care. '

'That is good news,' Alinor said. 'Although I'm sure she would have improved eventually even if I had done nothing.'

'No, Alinor, that is not true,' said Maeve, her keen eyes swivelling to Bianca sitting quietly beside Guilhem. Her gaze trailed slowly over the young girl's face.

Guilhem followed her glance. 'My apologies, allow me to present my sister, Lady Bianca d'Attalens,' he said, smiling. Scraping out the last remnants of his bowl, eating with obvious appreciation, he threw the spoon in with a clatter.

Maeve smiled at the blonde-haired maid. 'I'm honoured to meet you, Bianca. You are welcome.' Her brow creased. 'But why are you all here? I thought you would stay at home once you had taken Lord Guilhem there, Alinor?'

'It's a long story,' said Alinor, placing her wooden spoon down on the table, a precise careful movement. Hunger evaded her; her mouth was claggy, devoid of moisture, as if stuffed with wool. 'One that I promise to tell you as soon as I can. But Bianca must go home as soon as possible, to France...?' She trailed off, unsure, folding her hands in front of her. She wouldn't be going anywhere.

Guilhem shook his head, the light streaming down from the high windows catching his eyes, turning the irises a brilliant blue: a flash of pure colour, shocking, intense. 'No, not yet. Bianca needs to come with me and talk to the Queen. Tell her what has happened in her own words.'

'And what will you do, my dear?' Maeve turned to Alinor, her manner shrewd, solicitous.

'I'll return to Claverstock,' said Alinor, attempting to keep her tone brisk, level. A boulder of sadness lodged in her chest, huge, unwieldy. The thought of going back, of having to face Eustace again...but what other choice did she have? She had nowhere left to turn. Guilhem and Bianca would go and she would never see them again; the thought left her surprisingly bereft, forlorn.

'Don't be ridiculous!' Guilhem growled, thumping the table with one fist. He stood up abruptly, his muscled thigh knocking into the table so that all the pewter rattled; the Prioress jerked back in her seat, banging her head on the carved chair-back. Her sparse eyelashes flew up in surprise.

Guilhem thrust one hand through his hair. 'I can't believe you would even suggest such a thing!'

'What is it? What have I said?' Surely returning to Claverstock was her only option, despite what the consequences might be. Her slim shoulders hunched forward. She had caused enough trouble already; maybe now it was time to accept her fate, give in.

He bent over her, his head close to hers, warm breath tickling the side of her cheek, a strand of burnished hair brushing her earlobe. He braced his body weight against the table, his tanned fingers splayed on the pale oak planks. 'Have you forgotten what happened, Alinor? What nearly happened to you back there?'

'Don't say it out loud,' she whispered, turning fractionally. The jut of his cheekbone, dusted with sunburn, was inches from her face. Her eyes flicked up, pleading silently with him. 'Please.'

He inclined his head, acknowledging her request. 'You cannot go back there,' he said, more calmly. His breath stirred the fine silk of her veil, pressing the gauzy fabric against her hair.

'It's my home.' She smiled up at him tremulously. 'I have no other.'

Maeve leaned over, placed her hand on Alinor's forearm. 'You can stay here, with us, Alinor. The Priory is your home, too.'

'Thank you, Maeve, it would certainly help—'

'Out of the question.' Guilhem interrupted. 'I'm sorry, Maeve, but this is the first place that Eustace will look. And with the greatest respect, I don't think a group of nuns will be able to stop him dragging Alinor away.'

'Oh,' said Maeve, quietly, surveying Alinor with worried eyes. 'I didn't realise it was quite that bad.'

'Worse,' said Guilhem. His voice was grim. 'You can come with us, Alinor, at least until Eustace and your stepmother have been dealt with.' He tried to keep the sense of relief from his voice; under the guise of protecting her, he could keep her by his side. He told himself it was a simple matter of chivalry: it was clear that Alinor had no one else to whom she could turn—she needed his help.

Alinor peered at him closely, a trace of suspicion in her gaze. Her mind, confused, darted this way and that, skittering haphazardly in search of answers. Why was he doing this? He was not responsible for her. She had given him what he wanted in the form of Bianca. 'Can I speak to you in private, please?' she said, her voice awkward, truncated. Rising from the bench, she hoisted her skirts to step back over it, not waiting for his answer. She swept out of the refectory and into the storeroom next door. Shelves stacked with bulging sacks lined the dim chamber; small windows covered with slatted boards allowed cool air to filter in and keep the produce from spoiling. A smell of strong cheese permeated the air.

'What is it?' Guilhem said, immediately behind her. Pivoting on her heel, she turned to face him, reeling back suddenly. He was too close! His blue eyes gleamed down, radiant, intense.

'Why are you doing this?' she hissed. 'You know Bianca will be safe; I am no concern of yours now.'

Oh, but you are, he thought suddenly, his gaze roaming across her sweet, enchanting face, the plushness of her mouth. He couldn't explain his reluctance to let her go; all he knew was that she couldn't leave him, not just yet. She was so vulnerable, so alone, and yet she didn't seem to recognise the danger she was in. 'If you go back to

Claverstock, that man will rape you, Alinor,' he said harshly. 'And that will be it. You will have to be his wife, for the courts will not accept the word of a woman over a man.'

She flinched at his cruel words, hunching her shoulders forward, folding her arms across her chest. Guilt surged through him as if he himself had physically attacked her, as if he had punched her in the stomach, causing her slim, willowy frame to flex inward on itself. But she had to realise, had to understand the perilousness of her situation.

'I've always been able to take care of myself,' she replied, her voice mutinous, sticking her chin into the air. 'You're trying to scare me.' She touched the short knife hanging from the belt at her side, as if it were a talisman.

He followed the movement, mouth curling down, half-mocking. 'Maybe you've just been lucky up to now,' he said.

'Maybe.' Alinor shrugged her shoulders. 'Or maybe now is the time to accept my fate,' she replied dully. 'I've fought against it for so long, but now I have nowhere left to run.'

God, no!

'I've told you, Alinor, come with us to Knighton Palace. It's your only solution. I will tell the Queen what happened to you. Your so-called family can be brought to justice.' Placing his big hands on her shoulders, he traced her fragile collarbone beneath the thin silk of her gown. 'You have to trust me.'

Her eyes were questioning as she glanced up at him, bewildered. 'I don't understand,' she whispered. 'I don't understand why you are doing this for me.'

Because I...

Stunned, Guilhem dropped his hands, aghast at what his mind had been about to say. A muscle jumped in the shadowed hollow of his cheek. Something had sneaked beneath the armour-plated cladding of his soul, inching through the layers of horror and isolation, and had struck a flint against his cold, numb heart. And that something came from her: Alinor, hopping from one foot to another in front of him, her manner fierce and yet oddly defenceless, uncertainty eddying from her in waves. A sense of connection, an unspoken bond, flowed between them, like a thread of tangling yarn.

He cleared his throat, raised one hefty shoulder as if it didn't matter one way or the other. 'You'd be doing me a favour. Bianca's had a horrible time; she needs you more than ever at the moment. She values your friendship, surely you can see that. Come with us to Knighton, if only to keep her company.' His suggestion was flimsy and he knew it, but it was all he could think of to keep her by his side.

With a surge of relief, she tipped her head shakily in agreement, grasping at his proposal like a lifeline. He had given her a reason for staying, a platonic, viable reason; nothing to do with him, but to do with Bianca, to support her as her friend. 'I will come,' she agreed tentatively, 'if you think it would help.'

The chalk track was dry, white dust flying up, caking the horses' legs; heat saturated the air. A haze of mosquitoes danced in a cloud before the trio of riders. Bianca reached across with a gloved hand, seizing Alinor's fingers; squeezed them. 'I'm so glad you're here,' she said, her knees nudging against Alinor as she rode alongside.

Alinor smiled at her. She was happy, too, and not just for Bianca's sake. She studied the tall, broad figure riding up ahead of them, tracing the muscled rope of spine beneath the blue tunic, the wayward curl of hair. Her heart fluttered, treacherous. She was beginning to rely on him, rely on his solid, implacable presence; her sense of relief told her so. It was good of him to offer to sort out the problems with her family, but she had to remember that that was all it was; he was helping her, and nothing more. She had to remain stern, aloof around him.

Bianca followed her glance. 'Alinor... I am

sorry for all those awful things I said to you; you
did the right thing by bringing Guilhem to me.'

Alinor smiled tersely. 'I'm not sure "bringing"
is the right word. After he found your ring, he
made me tell him where you were.' His mouth on
hers in Ralph's cottage, every sinew, every muscle
in his body vibrant and alive, pressing into her
delicate flesh. She shivered.

'Oh, I know he can be an oaf with his sol-
dierly ways.' Bianca laughed, a tinkling sound,
hitching forward in her saddle to adjust her seat.
The piebald mare tossed her head up, fringed
mane frothing sideways. 'He spends most of his
time with Edward's army, so his manners can be
tough, brutal sometimes. You mustn't be frightened of him.'

I'm not frightened of him.

A pair of magpies stalked across the rough
grass beside the path, wings blue-black, glossy,
then flew away, chattering wildly as the horses
drew level.

'Oh, and, Alinor,' Bianca chattered on, sweeping back her veil from her shoulder, 'I am so sorry
for what I said. Back at the Priory.'

Alinor frowned. What on earth was Bianca
talking about?

'I accused you of being in love with him. Remember?' Bianca snorted with amusement. 'The
very thought of it! I was confused and angry...

I thought you had betrayed me; that's why such foolish words came out of my mouth! I am sorry. To think that you are in love with him! The very notion.'

I am in love with him. A stupid, ridiculous infatuation.

Alinor's heart folded in on itself, again and again, until all that remained was the tiniest piece of emotion, of tenderness. He couldn't know. He mustn't know. She couldn't stand to see the look of polite shock on his face if he ever found out. His mockery. She would die of shame. She glared fiercely at the rugged back, his stance easy in the saddle as he canted sideways to avoid a low-hanging branch.

Bianca laughed at her. 'My God, Alinor. You look like you want to kill him! Spare him the lash of your acerbic tongue, will you? He's been through so much.' Her voice lowered, a significant layer of meaning cloaking her simple speech. The sun, filtering through the trees, cast dappled shadows across her face.

'What do you mean?' Alinor asked carefully. Guilhem's heart had beat rapidly beneath her fingers in the dark of the cellars. Sweat had slicked his brow. Did Bianca know the full story of what had happened to him? Anything, anything, to know more about this man, with his bronze-coloured hair and eyes of sapphire, who had burst into her world with such passion, such energy, and turned her whole life upside down.

'Well, I don't know exactly,' Bianca continued slowly. 'But there have been rumours. All I know is that he was fighting in Gascony with Prince Edward and then we received messages that he had been captured, thrown in a dungeon somewhere.'

Her mouth tightened. She had witnessed the utter despair in his face, their bodies caught together in the stairwell. 'Who did it to him?' Alinor said. Her speech pushed out in a violent burst of sound. 'What reason did they have for putting him there?'

Bianca looked at her, her gaze curious. 'Goodness, Alinor, you look quite scary! Remind me not to meet you on a dark night.' She flicked her reins idly against the horse's neck as they plodded along, twitching the flies away. 'I don't know any more details. Guilhem has never spoken of what happened, to this day.'

Alinor kicked her horse on ahead, moving out from the trees and into a patch of open pasture: an uneven slope, the ground ridged and bumpy. Tussocks of stiff moor grass clumped along the edges of a stream, sides deep-cut, raw earth exposed. Her hands trembled; she gripped the reins, imagining what Guilhem might have been through, how he had suffered.

Up ahead, Guilhem had reined in his horse, springing to the ground where the stream ran shallow and lapped a narrow semi-circle of small stones. He led his horse to the water; the animal's head dropped down, bridle jangling. The women approached, pulling in the bridles on their horses. Guilhem moved around to Alinor, hands clamping around her slim waist to lift her out of the saddle. She clutched at his upper arms as he swung her light weight through the air, embroidered hemline flying out in the breeze. He caught a tantalising glimpse of small red slippers before settling her firmly on the ground. He did the same for Bianca, taking both their horses to the stream.

'Oh, I can't tell you how good this feels!' Bianca said with delight, lifting her pale, beautiful face to the sun, shaking back her veil. The pearls in her circlet glowed, a luminous light. The creases in her wimple pulled out smoothly with the movement. 'After being stuck in that cellar. How long was I there for, Alinor?'

Alinor counted in her head, remembering their scurried escape from Claverstock, hand in hand; the ragged panic, the rapid breaths of fear. She had taken such a risk, for if Wilhelma had caught them...what would have happened? Would she have killed them both? 'Not above a few days, Bianca.'

Bianca laughed, nodding. 'Well, it seemed like

for ever!' Lifting her skirts, she twirled about the loose gravel, revealing trim ankles in fine silk stockings. Her silk veil flew out, spinning in the gentle breeze. Her slim height made her movements elegant, graceful, the stones crunching softly beneath her feet. Her skirts billowed out, threatening to dip into the stream. 'And now I'm free!'

Eyes sparkling, Guilhem caught his sister by the elbow before she made herself giddy and ended up in the water. They made a handsome pair, Alinor thought, with their intense blue eyes and vigorous, burnished hair; their height.

Hanging on to Bianca, Guilhem glanced over at Alinor, to where she stood staring down into the gurgling water, her expression pensive. Behind her, a heat haze shimmered, casting her slender silhouette in a dazzling surround, making her seem magical, from another world. To think how much she had done for Bianca was almost inconceivable given her size and strength, but she had managed it; she had saved his sister, yet she seemed incapable of realising her own danger. His heart surged, mouth tightening, jaw rigid. How could he do this? There was no denying the connection between them; it reared up every time he went near her, raw and primal, flaring in the air between them. He wanted to protect her, to keep her safe, but he had to draw on self-restraint to keep his emotions under control. He hoped and prayed he would be able to do it, for both their sakes.

Heading north-east, with Guilhem up front, they rode through the villages of Nunton and Alderbury, attracting scant attention. At this hour of the day, the flinty track was deserted, cottage doors closed; few people were about. The villagers would be working hard in the fields, gathering in the last harvests for their lord. After all the rain and wind yestereve, the worry would be that inclement autumn weather would be setting in for good.

They skirted to the south of Standlynch, the half-built cathedral spire dominating the jumble of roofs in the distance, reaching high up into the blue sky. Wooden scaffolding embraced the building, men like tiny black insects hauling buckets of stone up to the highest level with ropes and pulleys. Here, across an area of rich pastureland, the river flowing down from the city split and divided: an elongated web of bisecting channels, running shallow through the undulating grassland. Huge willows draped into the glassy water, green tresses sketching the surface, creating ripples of disturbance, dapples of shade. Water lapped and gurgled over stony riverbeds. The track to Knighton took them through several man-made fording points, where the river ran, inch-deep, over large flat stones.

As they trotted through the last of the fords, water splashed up, flicked by the horses' hooves. Sparkling droplets landed on Alinor's skirts, trickling down over the napped wool like tears. They were nearing the palace at Knighton; her mind began to focus and think forward, attempting to form some sort of plan. She couldn't stay with Guilhem and Bianca for ever; they had their own separate lives to lead. Her heart curled into a miserable lump in her chest, but she squashed down the feeling, stamped hard on it. Now was not the time to wallow in self-pity; she was stronger than that. If the Queen brought her stepmother and brother to justice, then she would be able to go home, and carry on with her life as before. It would be as if she had never met Guilhem.

But how could it be? Would she ever be able to forget him? The searing touch of his mouth that turned her innards to liquid fire; the strong hand at her back, supporting her; his vivid, caring glance? He had given her enough memories to fill a lifetime. Would it be enough for her to live on, to continue? She allowed her mind to roam, desperate to gather every memory of the blistering heat of his touch, his rugged, musky smell.

The afternoon sun warmed her back. Her muscles sagged with inertia, a lack of energy. She tracked a black moorhen skirting the riverbank, dipping and diving, its beak stark orange against chestnut feathers. As she stretched her spine out, her ligaments pulled, straining with the movement. Thinking about Guilhem made her soft, dull-witted, she realised, lulling her into a sensual, dream-like state. And that was all it was, she told herself sternly: a dream. She would do well to remember the bitter reality of her situation and not indulge in the fleeting idealised nonsense of her thoughts. What was wrong with her? Her eyelids kept fluttering downwards; once or twice she had to pull herself sharply upright to stop herself falling sideways. She screwed up her eyes to focus on Guilhem trotting in front of her, attempting to rid her brain of its drowsy befuddlement. The horse's glossy rump, smooth-haired, flashed in the sunlight, leather saddlebags bouncing behind, gold buckles glinting.

Before her rode a man who had suffered, thought Alinor, and only God knew how much. And yet to look at him, to view his sheer stature and physique, it seemed beyond belief to think that someone would have been able to capture him, to trap that wild, vital spirit and shut him away in darkness. Inconceivable. Her eyelids drifted downwards, mind troubled with thoughts of Guilhem's captivity, worrying at her. Her horse plodded onwards, gait rhythmic, soporific, up the gentle slope on the other side of the river crossing. Alinor's head drooped forward to her chest.

'Oh, Guilhem, help me!' Bianca called out to her brother. She moved her horse tight in beside Alinor, propping the lolling figure upright. 'Goodness, Alinor, you weigh a ton!' she gasped out.

'I have her.' An arm scooped about Alinor's waist and she was pulled straight up into the saddle from the other side. Her head reeled; she was only vaguely aware that she had slipped and that someone had caught her. Through the layers of sleep and thought, she heard Guilhem's voice. But he was in the dungeon, he was trapped!

'What happened to you?' Her voice sprang out, sharp and accusatory. Her head whipped round to meet the brief puzzlement in his smiling eyes. The thick muscles in his upper arm nudged her spine, his arm curling around her.

'Nothing.' He laughed, his grin spreading wide. 'But you fell asleep!'

She clapped her hands across her mouth in horror, as if to stop any further incriminating words from emerging. What had she said? Hectic colour crossed her cheeks. She had been thinking about him, about his imprisonment, and then, she had asked the question out loud, the question that had been rolling around in her head before she dozed off! 'Oh, God, I'm sorry!' Mortified,

Alinor pressed her palms flat over her eyes, scrubbing briskly. 'I don't know what happened...'

'You fell asleep,' Guilhem said again, bright eyes roving across her face. 'It's nothing to look so shocked about.' His reins fell slack about his horse's neck. His arm embraced her: an iron-clad brace against her spine; his knee and upper thigh crushed against hers as the animals rode close. 'You're exhausted, Alinor.' Purple half-moons of tiredness patched beneath her eyes. 'Which is not really surprising, considering all that has happened in the past few days.'

'She needs to sleep, Guilhem,' Bianca said, tapping her heels into her horse's rump to move alongside them.

'Absolutely,' he agreed. 'Knighton is not far now, not above a few miles.' He sent her a soft smile, teeth white and even in his tanned face. 'Do you think you can make it? Or do you want to ride with me?'

'I can make it alone!' she blurted out hotly. The last thing she wanted was to be closer to this man than she had to. She was not about to make a fool of herself again.

Knighton Palace stood on a high point above the city of Standlynch, its position dominating the surrounding countryside. A vast deer park surrounded the palace, a landscape of undulating pasture, trees cleared so that deer and sheep could graze. Clusters of fallow deer, pale brown with white spots along their backs, took fright at their horses passing, flying off on spindly legs up the slope, tails whisking. The park's outer edges were bounded by a man-made bank and topped with a palisade fence, higher than a man's head. The palace itself was a succession of white-plastered buildings, strung out along the ridge like square beads on a string.

'I'm not sure…' Alinor said doubtfully as they approached the western gatehouse. She eyed the magnificent buildings, the carved stone gargoyles cresting the roof lines, the expensive hand-blown glass glinting in the latticed windows. 'I'm not sure I should be here at all.'

'Nonsense!' replied Bianca. 'You're here to keep me company. I'm so nervous that the Queen won't agree to dissolve this marriage contract with your stepbrother. What have you got to worry about?'

Him, she thought, glancing at the breadth of Guilhem's shoulders beneath his surcoat, taut blue wool. He jumped from his horse, striding forward at the moment his boots hit the ground to greet an older woman emerging from a large double-height building. He obviously knew her, reaching out and clasping both her hands. He turned, pointing at Bianca and Alinor, and the woman tilted her head to look over his shoulder at them.

'Hannah will take you to the guest chambers.' He walked over to Alinor, rested his hand on the pommel of her saddle. His fingers were sinewy, strong, a net of veins across his tanned hand, blond hairs fringing his wrist. 'You can rest before we go and meet Queen Eleanor.'

Anxiety fluttered in her stomach at the prospect. 'What do you think she will do?' she whispered, folding her arms tight across her middle.

He saw the panic shift across her delicate features, the haunting look in her eyes. 'You mustn't be frightened, Alinor. Eustace has no power at Knighton. You are safe. Once we tell the Queen what has happened, I suspect she will send her soldiers to bring him and your stepmother here to answer the accusations face to face.'

'And will I have to be there?'

'Maybe.' But I will be there too, he thought. He would make sure of it.

Chapter Thirteen

The water was hot, fragrant and delicious. Plumes of steam rose up from the circular wooden bathtub, wreathing around Alinor's head. Shifting her hips, she wriggled down into the water, the linen cloth that lined the tub soft against her bare skin, protecting her from splinters. Heated liquid lapped against her neck. The accumulated tension in her body eased, the worries about Bianca, about Eustace; all temporarily flew away and her mind emptied gradually until all she was left with was… Guilhem.

Bianca's words still haunted her. What had happened to him in France? To be locked up and left to die; why, she couldn't even begin to imagine how horrific that must have been. Would she ever be brave enough to ask him about it? She bit her lip, doubt crawling through her heart. She might ask, but he would surely never tell her; why would he? He scarcely knew her.

Beneath the water, she moved the flannel slowly across her breasts, down over her flat stomach. Silky dark lashes fluttered downwards, touching her cheek. Why did her flesh respond in such a way to him, why did the briefest touch of his hand, or the faintest glimpse of his smile, send her heart racing to a pitch that was almost intolerable? She had never lain with a man, she was an innocent, but she wasn't totally clueless. Even at the very thought of him, her loins gripped with an unbearable longing; she sank down below the waterline, soaking her hair, trying to rid herself of such wayward thoughts, wash them away. She desired him, she wanted him, and there wasn't a damned thing she could do about it.

Spluttering upwards, she pushed her wet hair out of her eyes, blinking rapidly, scrubbing ferociously at her arms, her neck. Lifting one leg, she rubbed the flannel down her calf, over her foot. She would do well to cast such thoughts from her mind. It was obvious he held no such desire for her; he had laughed off his kiss as if it had been a trifle and had left her chamber so abruptly at Claverstock when she was in a state of undress, it was obvious that he couldn't stand the sight of her. Aye, he was kind, and had helped her after Eustace's attack, but, as he had rightly stated, any man, any knight in his situation would have done the same for her, out of chivalric duty.

She would present her predicament to the Queen; she didn't need him nursemaiding her all the while. Up to now, she had managed perfectly well alone, priding herself on her own reliance. Wilhelma's behaviour with Bianca, the episode with Eustace—both had shocked her, set her back temporarily, but now...now she felt stronger, more able to deal confidently with her stepmother and brother again. Guilhem's quiet, laid-back energy drew her, his sheer physicality supported her, but she had begun to rely on him too much. It would make it far harder for her when they inevitably parted.

Her heart squeezed and she shoved the odd feeling of loss right to the back of her mind. Clambering to her feet, she stood up out of the tub, water sluicing down her slim, elegant limbs, and grabbed the towel that had been placed on a stool next to the bath. She could fight her own battles. Stepping out of the tub, she rubbed the woven linen briskly over her body, bending her head so her wet hair trailed forward, the curling ends touching the rug beneath her bare toes. She rubbed the towel through her hair, soaking up the moisture. Throwing her hair back, she wrapped herself in the towel's rough folds, tucking it securely in the shadowed hollow between her breasts.

Outside the lattice window, the sun crested the low horizon. Padding over to the deep-set glass, polished floorboards cool against her feet, she peered out to the western gatehouse, a red-roofed building, walls white-plastered like the rest of the palace. Through a pointed archway, a steady stream of carts, horsemen, knights and peasants made their way in and out of the inner bailey: carts laden with felled oak, peasants carrying fierce-looking scythes across their shoulders, silver blades flashing in the sunlight; children, dogs, weaving in and out of people's legs.

The days were shortening now, readying themselves for the dark days of winter. And yet it would be hours until the evening feasting, when Guilhem would present Bianca and herself to the Queen. Her eyes strayed to the four-poster bed, made up with fresh linens and furs. A charcoal brazier crackled merrily in one corner, filling the chamber with a glorious heat. She yawned, wriggling her shoulders, shaking out her towel-dried hair down her back. Should she dress and visit Bianca in the next chamber? But the mattress was substantial, inviting, stuffed tight and full with horsehair, the pillows plumped with downy goose feathers. Guilhem had said they should rest. Clad in the towel, her shoulders bare, Alinor rolled on to the bed, and closed her eyes. Slept.

'Guilhem, you are telling me the truth, aren't you?' Sitting by the fire in her private chambers,

Queen Eleanor narrowed her eyes at her favourite knight, sprawling languidly in the chair opposite her. He had been a good friend to her son for a long time, ever since they had trained as knights together; Guilhem was as much a part of her household as Prince Edward. 'It sounds so unbelievable that Wilhelma of Claverstock would attempt to murder your sister, so that her own stepdaughter could marry her son.' Lines of concern creased her smooth, white forehead.

Guilhem surveyed the veining in the marble column on one side of the fireplace, the intricate over-mantel with tiny figures carved along its length to represent the twelve months of the year. He stuck one leg out, flexing his foot towards Eleanor's russet gown, the flowing hem decorated with delicate flowers worked in gold thread. 'Unfortunately, I believe it all to be true. Bianca wouldn't lie about something like this.' And neither would Alinor, he thought, a pair of huge green eyes moving vividly across his vision.

He sprung from the chair, striding over to the window, a pair of narrow panes bisected by a fluted stone column. The glass between the lead latticing was etched with silver, a trailing pattern of ivy leaves and honeysuckle. From here, he could see the great hall with its red-glazed coxcomb ridge tiles, the conical roof of the kitchens and, closer by, the building that housed the guest chambers, where

Bianca and Alinor were. He hoped they were resting. Alinor's head had drooped once or twice since she had almost fallen off her horse with tiredness. But to insist that she rode with him would have placed her delicious body against him, and, in truth, he wasn't sure he could bear such temptation. Far safer that she rode her own horse, even if there was a danger of her crashing to the ground.

'Guilhem, I am so sorry; I never realised when I arranged this marriage for Bianca that I was putting her in so much danger. Wilhelma and her son came to me on a good, reliable recommendation.' Eleanor plucked at a loose thread, floating adrift on the lustrous silk of her gown.

'How could you have known?' Guilhem replied. 'You mustn't blame yourself. Thank God Alinor was there; it was her quick wit that saved my sister.'

'Alinor?' The Queen raised pale, wispy brows, faint arcs above her hazel eyes at his use of her first name. 'I didn't realise you were on such familiar terms with the girl.'

'Apologies.' A ruddy colour dusted the tops of his cheekbones. 'I mean, Lady Alinor.'

The Queen stared hard at him for a moment. 'I will send for Wilhelma and her son and have them brought before me directly.' She inclined her head towards a lady-in-waiting standing by the door. 'Margaret, fetch me John de Plessis and John Fitz Geoffrey. They can ride over to Claverstock and bring them back to me.' She glanced at Guilhem's tall figure, braced against the window frame. 'I would send you, but I need you here for the nonce. With Henry in captivity...' her mouth drooped slightly '... I...that is, Edward and I, we need your advice. Edward will be very pleased to see you. He was most put out that you decided to ride to Claverstock with...this Lady Alinor.'

'But I went to visit my sister; he knew that.'

The Queen extracted a silk kerchief from the brocade pouch that dangled from her woven girdle; sniffed into it delicately. 'You know how he values your company. But, your visit to Claverstock was a good decision. If you hadn't gone there, then none of this subterfuge with your sister's marriage or, rather, non-marriage, would have been discovered.'

If I hadn't gone there, my heart would still be my own. Would he have preferred it that way?

'Where is Edward?' he managed to croak out, shifting away from the window.

'Out.' Eleanor rolled her eyes. 'He rode out with a few knights this morning towards Marlborough—not to fight, but to try to find where de Montfort has gone. Where they have taken my good husband. I can only hope and pray that he is in good health.' She stared into the fire, momentarily distracted. 'Edward will be back before nightfall, God willing.'

Guilhem nodded. He would go and check on the horses, make sure they were properly stabled before going to his own allocated chamber; he needed a wash, a change of clothes.

The Queen hitched forward, contemplating the flames of the fire, clasping her milk-white hands together. 'Guilhem... I think it might be better if you fetch your sister and this...this Alinor to me now; I would like to meet them and hear their story from their own lips; it will be too chaotic at the feasting tonight.'

Standing beside the chair he had recently vacated, Guilhem placed one hand on the carved back. 'Would you mind waiting an hour or two? They are both exhausted; I told them to rest.'

Eleanor pursed her lips; she wasn't used to being contradicted. She hesitated, frowning, then a smile broke across her face and she waggled her fingers at him, the gemstones adorning her hand sparking in the firelight. 'Goodness, only you, Guilhem, only you, would get away with such a request. Be gone with you and bring them to me later, but before the feasting. Understood?'

He lifted her hand, bending low, touching his lips to her jewelled fingers. 'Understood, my lady.'

The stables were enormous at Knighton, big enough to house one-hundred-and-twenty horses comfortably, so it was some time before Guilhem managed to locate his own destrier and the two palfreys ridden by Bianca and Alinor. Their saddles removed, all three had been secured in a stall each, rubbed down and given a net of sweet-smelling hay to eat. His hand smoothed over the nose of the grey palfrey, Alinor's horse, and the animal nibbled at his shoulder, whinnying softly. Satisfied, Guilhem followed the direction of one of the stable lads to find his allocated guest chamber and hopefully, his leather packs that had been removed from his horse.

Reaching the room, he was pleased to see that his saddlebags were stacked by the bed, alongside the other leather bags containing his chainmail hauberk and chausses, his helmet. His armour had been carried from the Priory on one of the carts that travelled with Edward's army: the carts that transported anything that the Prince and his knights couldn't take with them on horseback. In the middle of the chamber, a wooden tub had been filled with hot water; he stripped off his tunic and braies, kicked off his dusty boots and climbed in, his hard, aching muscles revelling in the luxury.

He emerged from the chamber an hour or so later, refreshed, revived and wearing clean garments extracted from his pack. A passing servant in the corridor indicated the chambers allocated to

Bianca and Alinor: two doors next to each other at the end of the passageway.

'Bianca?' he called through the wooden slats of the door, knocking gently. 'Are you awake?'

'What?' His sister's voice emerged, shrill and befuddled. 'Is that you, Guilhem?'

'Aye, it's me. Can I come in?'

'Yes. The door is open.'

He pushed into the bright room. Bianca was beneath the bedclothes, but sitting up, two long tawny braids snaking down from each side of her head. With her circlet, veil and wimple removed, she appeared so much younger, her skin smooth and flushed from sleep.

'The Queen wants to see you,' he said. 'You and Alinor, before the feasting. She asked me to bring you to her. You'd better put some clothes on.'

'Oh, Guilhem,' Bianca moaned, the hint of a whine marring her voice. 'I don't want to go yet; I'm having such a lovely rest. I thought we would see her later, in the evening.'

'She wants to see you now,' Guilhem replied tersely. 'Surely it's better that we sort out this muddle sooner rather than later.'

'I suppose so.' Bianca's mouth drooped. 'You'd better wake Alinor then; she's next door.'

His heart skipped, blood picking up speed at the mention of her name.

'I'll come back for you in a little while,' he said. 'Be ready. And make sure you bar this door; anyone could walk in.'

Sun filtered through a series of tall narrow windows, casting stripes of diagonal light across the corridor as he moved along to Alinor's door. Outside, a pigeon on the tiles cawed softly. He rapped lightly, calling her name.

No answer.

'Alinor!' he hissed again. 'You need to wake up now!'

Silence.

He lifted the latch, pushed inwards, remembering an earlier time, an earlier day, when he had barged into her chamber at Claverstock, to discover her clad only in a flimsy chemise, slender legs silhouetted beneath the gauzy fabric. Tiny pink toenails gleaming up at him from the dark floorboards. His breath hitched.

The door refused to budge, barred from the inside. 'God, Alinor,' he bellowed, frustrated, annoyed that she had protected herself with the very thing which he had asked his sister to do. He thumped at the thick, solid planks with one massive fist, shaking the hinges. 'Wake up! You need to open this door!'

He heard a sound from within, the faintest scuffling. Wood scraped against wood as the bar was lifted; the iron latch clicked up and the door creaked inwards, only by an inch or so. Alinor's face appeared in the narrow gap, flushed, sleep-soft.

His heart creased; he clenched one fist at his side, digging his nails into the base of his palm. 'The Queen wants to see you. Are you dressed?' he asked brusquely. But even through the restricted aperture he knew the answer. Knuckles white, her hand gripped into a bunch of linen towel at a spot just above her bosom; her glorious hair was loose, falling about her face in curling, pale gold tresses.

Her eyes were like green fire. 'No,' she whispered, her throat parched from her disturbed sleep.

'Put something on,' he ordered sternly. 'I'll fetch you in a little while. And bar the door behind you again.'

Alinor nodded, closing the door softly. He wondered if she had heard him correctly; she seemed so befuddled with sleep. Hesitating, he waited for the sound of the wooden bar to be fitted back in place. He wanted her to be secure.

The sound failed to materialise. He waited a few more moments. 'Alinor, put the bar across,' he called.

No response.

Impatient, he opened the door, meaning to chastise her for her complete lack of security.

His eyes flew to the bed. She was there, lashes

cast down across her cheeks, sleeping soundly, as if she had never opened the door to him. Stretched out on top of the bed furs, she lay on her side towards him, golden head resting on the pillow, slender figure wrapped in the linen towel. The hand that had gripped the towel so tightly now lay, palm upwards on the coverlet and the towel itself, sweet Jesu, was now untethered, slipping treacherously, revealing the enticing shadow between her breasts.

He couldn't move, every muscle in his body clenched in delicious anticipation, his feet rooted to the spot as he drank in the sight of her, like a man in the desert who has at last found water. Nerve endings quivered with awareness. He swallowed, moisture deserting his mouth. How could he have let this happen? To him of all people? He could command whole armies, march for days on end, fight with a skill and physical strength superior to most of his peers and yet, here he was, brought to his knees by a golden-haired maid who floored him with a single glance, the scant touch of her hand.

He needed to wake her and get out of here. Flames licked at the base of his belly, stirring dangerously. Propelling himself forward, legs flabby like wet rope, he crouched down by the bed, his face on a level with hers. Her breath sifted over his cheek, stirred his hair. Just breathing in her delicate scent transported him to a different place: an exquisite, magical world, far away from the horrors of war, the horrors of that dark, confined space that had been his home for months. Shake her awake, his reason told him. Shake her by the shoulder and have done with it! Strands of white-gold hair straggled across her bare shoulder, pooling down on to the coverlet in a silky mass. His eye traced the delicate ridge of her collarbone, the shadowed hollow of her throat; the patina of her skin gleamed like a lustrous pearl. As if guided by an invisible hand, his fingers lifted, trailed along her temple, down one side of her cheek, testing the downy softness below her ear.

At his touch, Alinor sighed, lips parting, rolling on to her back. The edges of the towel gaped apart perilously, fell away from her body. Her naked body. The full rounded beauty of her breasts was exposed, the flat pearly expanse of her stomach, the entrancing dip of her belly button, the flare of her hips. Desire ripped through him, incandescent, uncontrollable, devouring his self-control.

Behind him the door opened. 'Are you coming?' Bianca poked her head into the chamber. 'You've been ages...is Alinor there?'

Guilhem sprang to his feet as if stabbed, scowling darkly, and turned the bulk of his body to hide the half-covered figure on the bed. 'Out!' he said, pointing his finger at Bianca. 'Get out, now!'

'Is Alinor all right?' Bianca asked, frowning. 'She's not ill or anything?'

'Just get out!' he yelled at her, flushing darkly. 'I'll come and fetch you in a moment!'

Widening her eyes suspiciously at her brother, Bianca withdrew. The door clicked behind her.

Blood racing, Guilhem grabbed Alinor's cloak from a chair and slung it over her haphazardly, covering her from neck to toe. Shame coursed through him, black and coruscating. His behaviour had been despicable: like that of a voyeur, debauched and immoral, feasting his lewd eyes upon her delectable curves whilst she slept on in blithe innocence, unaware of his lecherous sneaking scrutiny. He couldn't have her, and yet, God in Heaven, how he wanted her, those sweet limbs wrapped around his own, her mouth on his.

'Alinor, wake up!' he bellowed hoarsely, pulling at her shoulder roughly, then stepped back decisively into the middle of the room when her eyes opened softly.

'Oh!' she said, smiling, her hair rustling on the pillow as she turned her face towards him. 'What are you doing here?'

Guilt swept over him, like dirty smoke. 'I'll fetch Bianca.' His voice was ragged. 'She can help you to dress. Queen Eleanor wants to see you now.'

Chapter Fourteen

In the Queen's solar, Prince Edward sprawled in the high-backed armchair opposite his mother, long legs stretched out before him, his face flushed and grubby, red tunic speckled with dust. He still wore his chainmail, the metallic hood pushed back from his limp blond hair, matted to his scalp by cooling sweat. The low evening sun, pooling to a spot of light on the tiled floor, wavered as one of the Queen's ladies closed the narrow window.

'He's here, you say?' Edward said to Eleanor, draining the contents of his silver goblet. Wiping his mouth with his bare hand, he held the empty vessel out to be refilled. A dimpled serving maid moved forward with an earthenware jug and carefully poured more wine into the shining cup hanging from the Prince's hand.

The Queen drew herself upright in her chair and smiled. 'Yes, Edward, Guilhem is here. He's brought his sister, with another lady in attendance—there have been some problems with Bianca's marriage and I promised I would sort them out for him.'

Edward hunched down in his seat, his mouth petulant. 'Then sort it out quickly, will you? I need him for my campaign, with no domestic distractions.'

'It's hardly a "domestic distraction", as you call it,' the Queen replied waspishly. Her mouth tightened, tiny lines wrinkling the skin beneath her bottom lip. 'I will not allow you to belittle such a thing. The mother of the man Bianca was supposed to marry tried to kill her. And would have succeeded if it hadn't been for this other girl, her stepdaughter.'

Edward yawned, then leaned forward, swirling the red wine in his goblet, deliberately sending the level nearer and nearer to the brim. His fingers were bony, gripping like claws around the gleaming silver. 'I hope you haven't forgotten about my campaign, Mother? To free Father from Simon de Montfort's clutches and overthrow his army in the process. My father,' he repeated. 'Your husband.' His sarcastic emphasis on the final two words was unmistakable.

Eleanor rose in an elegant rustle of skirts. 'No, my son, I have not forgotten.' She laid one hand on Edward's shoulder. 'And I thank you for everything you are doing. But that doesn't mean I cannot help others whilst your campaign is ongoing.'

Her son shook his head: a sharp, irritable movement. 'You mistake me, Mother. I have no quarrel with you helping others, but I need Guilhem at my side.'

'No one commands Guilhem. He's a free agent.'

Edward rolled his eyes ruefully. 'Aye, more's the pity.' He grimaced at the flames, spitting fitfully in the hearth. 'What a shame he has enough money not to be beholden to any lord, or prince, for that matter.'

'And yet he is still loyal to you, Edward,' Eleanor replied, hitching forward slightly. 'And a good friend. You cannot buy trust like that with coin.'

'As usual, Mother, you are right.' Edward lifted his goblet to take another gulp of wine.

There was a knock at the door and the maidservant opened it. Alinor and Bianca stood on the threshold, hesitating, Alinor in her lavender-coloured gown, Bianca wearing blue silk, both women like bright flowers hovering in the shadows beneath the pointed arch.

'Come forward, ladies, please.' The Queen smiled graciously and beckoned them in. 'You are in a predicament, I understand; I am anxious to hear your story.'

Guilhem stepped into the room behind the women, ducking his head beneath the low doorway. Seeing him, Edward placed his goblet down on a small side table and sprang from his seat, moving across the polished, tiled floor with a grin, blatantly ignoring the two ladies. 'My God, Guilhem!' He slapped his friend on the back. 'Am I glad to see you!'

Guilhem laughed. 'I've only been away for one night.' And yet, he thought, glancing at Alinor's neat head, the graceful fall of her veil, it seemed like a lifetime. Something had altered within him, eased, nudged at the tough icy lump that had been his heart. He was different.

'Long enough, Guilhem. Come, come and have a drink and tell me what's been happening. It sounds like you've become caught up in some boring domestic tangle!' He clutched at Guilhem's bulky upper arm, intending to take him over to the fire. 'Another chair, here!' he snapped at the maidservant.

'Stop a moment, Edward!' Guilhem held his ground. 'Forgive me, but my sister must speak to the Queen; let the ladies sit around the fire. We can stand.'

'Oh, all right, if we must!' grouched Edward. For the first time, he glanced over at the women, watching them curtsy before his mother. With a gracious wave of her hand, the Queen indicated that they settle themselves in the chairs opposite her. He ran a finger around the inside of the neck of his chainmail; the iron links chafed against his skin, irritating him.

'Who is the lady with your sister?' he muttered to Guilhem. 'God, she's beautiful; where did you find her?'

Right under your nose, thought Guilhem. How could he explain to Edward that the woman with skin like silver, with her eyes of emerald fire, was the same diminutive nun who had given them so much trouble at the river crossing?

'She is the stepsister of the man Bianca was supposed to marry,' he explained. 'It was she who helped my sister to safety after the threat on her life.'

'Brave woman,' Edward acknowledged. 'She doesn't look that strong.'

Don't be fooled, thought Guilhem. Hidden beneath that sylphlike frame was a courage to match a dozen of his foot soldiers. 'She might not look strong,' he agreed, 'but she possesses a formidable strength of purpose.'

Edward peered at him suspiciously. Spidery red lines clustered in the inner corners of his watery blue eyes. 'Are you acquainted with the lady? You sound like you know her.'

'No, I don't. I'm judging her on her actions. She helped my sister escape at night and hid her so that Bianca was safe. Doesn't that seem strong to you?' He struggled to keep the colour from rising in his face; why, even speaking about her turned him into some shambling, lovesick puppy!

Edward nodded. 'My mother will make sure that those responsible for what happened will be brought before the courts. Who is the girl's father? Where is he in all of this? What's their family name?'

'Claverstock. Her name is Lady Alinor of Claverstock. I never discovered her father's Christian name.' He frowned. Edward's mouth hung open in surprise, cheeks slack.

'Surely you jest?' Edward croaked out. 'Alinor of Claverstock, that chit over there? Are you sure?'

An icy chill crawled up Guilhem's spine. 'What is it?'

'Her blessed father has changed his allegiance. I thought he was heading up a campaign in Wales for us and then I find out that he's sneaked off to join with de Montfort, along with his blasted stepson! Her father is a traitor to the King, Guilhem. '

'My God.' Guilhem shook his head sharply, as if to clear his head. 'Alinor has no idea.'

Edward squinted to the women gathered in front of the fire, his top lip twisted into a sneer. 'How can you be so sure, Guilhem? These women are wily creatures at the best of times. Her father fights against me now and is my enemy. Which makes that girl my enemy, too.'

Guilhem traced the soft line of Alinor's cheek,

a tantalising wisp of hair curling out from beneath her wimple, pure gold against her pale skin. He remembered those long tresses spread out around her naked body, snaking across the bedclothes as she had lain beneath his hot, blatant gaze, oblivious to his scrutiny. His mouth tightened. She was explaining something to Eleanor, her hands flung out in a graceful arc, demonstrative. Her voice rang out, lilting, melodious. He remembered how his name sounded on her lips, how his heart responded. How when she glanced at him, a runnel of sweet desire pierced his very core. 'Your enemy?' he responded gruffly. 'Have a care, Edward. She's hardly that.'

'She is by default,' Edward replied grumpily. He scratched at his elbow, considering. 'I know the women and children are all innocent in this stupid civil war, but even so…' He trailed off suddenly, his expression fixed. Before Guilhem could stop him, the Prince strode forward, chainmail glinting, and grabbed Alinor's arm, his grip cruel. 'Stand up!' he barked at her.

Guilhem sprang forward, pulling Edward away easily. 'No!' he growled. 'You do not treat her like that! Stay sat!' he roared at Alinor, who had half-risen in her chair, her eyes round and worried. She sank back down tentatively, glancing at Bianca, who responded with a confused shake of her head.

Scowling, Edward dusted down his arm with a studied, fastidious action on the spot where Guilhem had held him. 'A little over-protective, I think?' he said slowly. 'What is going on here?'

'Nothing,' replied Guilhem. 'I only ask that you treat the lady who rescued my sister with more respect.'

Edward raised his eyebrows in mock disbelief. 'Then forgive me for thinking there is more to this than meets the eye,' he said.

Guilhem folded his arms across his broad chest, creasing the pale-green wool of his clean tunic, mouth set in a stern line. 'There is nothing going on,' he bit out.

Edward laughed, shrugged his shoulders. 'Fine, if you say so. I only sought to ask for her help in a small matter.' He turned to Alinor. 'Forgive me, my lady, but do you know where your father is at this precise moment?'

Alinor rose to face the Prince, her palms clammy with sweat. Tension shimmered in the chamber; even the Queen's ladies had paused in their duties, watching Edward from the corners of the room. She pressed her hands down the front of her skirts, the silver embroidery of the fabric glinting in the firelight. Her breath seemed caught in her lungs, stalled, waiting. Guilhem stood a little behind Edward's lean, imposing figure and she caught the tiny, unmistakable shake of his head.

But what could she say to the Prince but the truth? Surely there was no harm in that?

'My father is in Wales,' she replied quietly. 'Fighting for the King. For you.'

'Wrong!' Edward smiled nastily. 'That is the wrong answer!'

A faint uneasiness trickled through her, weakening her knees. 'I... I beg your pardon, my lord?'

'Your dear father has changed sides, Alinor. Your stepbrother, too. Didn't you know?'

She staggered back, her eyes fluttering upwards in surprise, her hand scrabbling back to grasp at some sort of support. 'I...'

'Does it look like she knew, Edward? For God's sake, stop tormenting her.' Guilhem pushed past Edward, took hold of Alinor's arm before she fell. She leaned against him gratefully. Thank God.

The Queen swept forward in a rustle of silk skirts. 'What is going on, Edward? What are you talking about?'

'Her family fight for the rebels now, Mother,' Edward barked out. 'Claverstock is against us.'

'God in Heaven!' The Queen threw her hands in the air. 'When did this happen? Why was I not informed?'

'You couldn't have known, Mother. Nobody knew, not even Lady Alinor from the look of her. I have only just found out myself.'

The Queen shook her head, dismayed. A creeping tide of colour, bright red, flooded her cheeks. 'And I thought it would be a good marriage for Bianca.' She turned back to the girl sitting by the fire. 'I'm so sorry, my dear. It seems like you were almost married to a rebel family.'

Bianca rose from her seat. 'My lady, I...'

'Thanks to the quick thinking of Lady Alinor, that didn't happen,' Edward cut across anything Bianca was about to say. 'And, due to the situation we are in, I wonder if we might call on her to help us again?' She caught the musty sift of his breath as his face loomed close hers.

Instinctively, she shrank back into Guilhem's hold, the powerful curve of his arm. 'I'm not sure...' she hesitated.

'Let me rephrase that,' Edward said, fixing his peculiar washed-out eyes on Alinor. 'You *will* help us.' He clapped his hands together. 'Now, I intend to rid myself of this infernal chainmail and have a long, hot soak. I will speak to you tonight, at the evening's feasting. Make sure you sit next to me.' He grinned up at Guilhem, a triumphant expression playing on his lips, then walked out of the solar, his step light and jaunty.

'What does he want with me?' whispered Alinor, her fingers clutching at Guilhem's forearm.

Tight-lipped, he shook his head.

* * *

In a riot of pink-and-orange streaks, the sun dipped below the western horizon. Vast, elongated shadows stretched across the grassland at Knighton: dark contorted images of the huge oaks in the deer park. In the great hall, a fire had been stoked up in the hearth, the candles and torches lit, trestle tables laid with pewter plates and goblets. The hall was alive with colour: the expensive garments of the nobles, their glittering jewels, the gleaming surcoats of the knights embellished with family crests. Woollen tapestries, with scenes of hunting and feasting fashioned from hundreds and hundreds of tiny stitches in rich, vivid colours, adorned the white-plastered walls.

'Alinor, the Queen believes you. We all believe you. The look on your face when Edward told you! I thought you were going to faint. You shouldn't look so worried, especially as I'm so happy.' Looking down into the bustling hall from the raised dais where nobles and royalty sat, Bianca raised her goblet and took a delicate sip. 'The Queen has arranged everything for me: a full escort back to France and a maidservant in attendance! And did you hear, Alinor? She even said she would give me some of her clothes so I would be able to change into clean garments for the journey! Her own clothes!' She pressed her hand excitedly against Alinor's sleeve.

'It's good news, Bianca,' Alinor agreed dully. In front of her, on the white linen, her plate was laden with food: thick slices of roast pork, steamed root vegetables, bread. Candles, set into heavy ornate candlesticks, shed their flickering light across the table, reflecting benignly on the smiling faces of the chattering nobles. Her stomach churned with anxiety. She couldn't even remember placing the food on her plate. The chair next to her remained empty; Prince Edward had still not appeared and neither had Guilhem.

'By the way...' Bianca leaned conspiratorially into Alinor, nudging up against her arm. 'What was going on between you and my brother earlier?'

'Earlier?' Alinor flushed, scrabbling to comprehend Bianca's meaning.

'I came into your room before, when you were sleeping. Guilhem jumped up like a scalded cat! I swear I have never seen him blush, but he was blushing then; I think I must have startled him. He looked so guilt-stricken, and then he yelled at me, as if I were in the wrong!'

'I don't remember...' Alinor trailed off, trying to clear her befuddled mind. Guilhem had been standing over the bed and she had been wrapped in a towel, with a cloak thrown on top. The cloak had covered everything, surely? She had been so tired. A blankness flowed through her brain;

she couldn't seem to recall anything. Her fingers fiddled with the napkin in her lap, smoothing the linen flat, then crumpling it once more into a ball. Across the great hall, a group of musicians began to assemble, tuning up their various instruments with a discordant sound, off-key.

'Well, no matter,' Bianca said. 'It was obviously nothing if you can't even remember it.'

Alinor shuffled her hips uncomfortably against the dark wood of her polished seat. How long had Guilhem been standing there, whilst she slept?

The door leading directly on to the high dais from the royal apartments opened suddenly, dragging across the flagstones with a scraping sound, menacing. Guilhem strode in, heading for the seat beside Alinor, followed by Edward trailing behind at a more languid pace, raising his hand in greeting to the people in the hall, a sly smile playing across his lips. Stepping back, Guilhem allowed Edward to sit next to Alinor, then threw himself into the chair next to him, his jaw set in a stiff, inflexible line.

Alinor recoiled at the rawness in Guilhem's expression; her hands began to tremble and she placed them carefully on the tablecloth in front of her, fingers spread wide to stop the shaking.

'So, Lady Alinor, I have a proposition for you.' Edward's voice possessed a jubilant ring. He edged forward, resting his elbows on the table. 'I have been chasing my tail around this wretched countryside trying to track down the elusive Simon de Montfort and quite frankly, I'm tired. Bored. I need a rest. Someone else needs to do the work for a change. And that person, my lady, is you.'

Alinor's eyes sprang wide in horror. 'I... I beg your pardon, my lord?' she stuttered out. Perspiration clung to the base of her neck.

'You, Lady Alinor, are going to help me.'

Beside him, Guilhem scowled, one large fist curling on the tablecloth. 'You can't do this, Edward,' he growled out. 'You cannot take advantage like this.'

'Oh, but I can, Guilhem. I am the Prince, and, while my father is held captive, I am in charge. She'll be absolutely fine if you go with her.' The Prince addressed Guilhem, but he kept his pale-blue eyes pinned to Alinor's face.

You go with her. Shock coursed through Alinor's veins, hot and cold tremors that rattled down to the very core of her. What did the Prince mean? Through a fog of panic, she glanced at Guilhem, at his stark, forbidding profile, at the spike of dark eyelashes framing his sparkling eyes. He knew already. He knew what the Prince was going to ask her and he didn't like it one little bit. Had they argued? Tension clogged the air between the two men, suffocating.

'I want you to find out where Simon de Montfort is and infiltrate his inner circle. That should be quite easy for you, given that your father is with him,' Edward sneered down his long sharp nose at her. 'Prise him away from his knights, from any sort of protection, so that Guilhem and my other knights can take him prisoner. They will bring him to me. Along with my father as well, hopefully.'

'And then what will you do?' Alinor battled to keep the wobble from her voice.

'Why, I'll run him through with my sword for all the trouble that he's caused this country!' Reaching towards a silver platter, Edward lifted a piece of meat with his fingers; dangling the slice above his mouth, he took a huge bite. Grease dripped down from the side of his thin mouth.

Her vision blurred, her plate brimming with slowly congealing food swam before her eyes; she sagged back in the chair with the impact of Edward's words. What Edward was proposing was cold-blooded murder. But how could she defy the orders of a prince? 'I...'

'I can make life very difficult for you if you refuse to do this' Edward smirked. 'For example, I could arrange for you to marry Eustace of Claverstock, just as your stepmother wishes.'

His outrageous words soaked through the cloying numbness of her brain, driving out her gathering anxiety. A wild, scalding anger whipped through her veins, an unstoppable fire. How dare he? How dare he blackmail her like this, after everything she had striven for? He ordered her about like a common cur, a thrashed dog on a leash!

She stood up violently, banging her hip against the edge of the table. A pewter goblet full of wine tipped dangerously, threatening to spill. 'No, you can't do that!' Her tone was jagged, accusatory.

'Oh, yes, I can, Lady Alinor.' Eyes intent on the feast laid before him, Edward began to pile food on to his plate, his manner dismissive. She had been given her orders and he was confident she would carry them out. But he paused for a moment, eating knife poised in the air, his gaze absorbed by a rust-coloured stain on the tablecloth. 'And there's no point pleading to my mother, she agrees with me. De Montfort has held the King prisoner for nearly a year now. It's time he came home.'

Dimly, as if from behind a padded screen, she was aware of the Queen's voice, gently reassuring, murmuring something behind her: an apology, perhaps, for what they were asking her to do. Boiling anger shook her slim frame; she wanted to kill Edward, she wanted to wipe that smug, self-satisfied expression from his mean, pinched features, from that sloppy, wet mouth.

A hand wrapped around her upper arm. 'Come

with me, now,' Guilhem's voice ordered her, quietly. A command, not a request. Somehow he managed to extricate her from the table, pulling her between the high-backed chairs. Her gown snagged on a splinter; he twitched the material away with a calm, decisive movement, then clamped her to his side with one brawny arm. The split hem of his pale-green tunic splayed out as he moved forward, Alinor stumbling at his side. She dragged against his hold, angry at his intrusion, his interference, wanting to yell and scream and shout.

'Stop it.' Guilhem tilted his head down to hers. 'Do you want to be thrown in the dungeons?' He marched her firmly down the steps and into the lower area of the hall, where the trestle tables thronged with peasants, knights, serving maids—all manner of classes eating, gesticulating with raised knives, pointing fingers, their voices raised against the lilting jig played by the musicians.

Passing beneath a fluted stone arch, he bundled her down a narrow passageway; light streamed in from outside, radiating off the white-plastered walls, forcing her to screw up her eyes against the brightness. Wind scurried through the constricted space, racing over the uneven flagstones, cold and nippy, rippling and lifting Alinor's skirts. The chill breeze brushed her legs; she shivered. Guilhem held her hand now, tugging her relentlessly, out into the courtyard gardens, neat rectangular beds of earth filled with herbs and vegetables. The scent of lavender permeated the air. In sheltered spots, insects spun, zig-zagging crazily in the low sunlight. The sound of music chased after them from the great hall: the fiddle and the harp, muted, then a spurt of laughter. Beneath an arbour heavy with climbing roses, she managed to pull away from him, digging her heels in. 'How can he do this to me, Guilhem? How can he?'

Guilhem crossed massive forearms across his chest, observing her slowly. His eyes were the colour of a flat, calm sea, pewter-brilliant. 'Because he's the Prince, Alinor. His command is the law.' A single rose petal, dislodged from the chaotic jumble of rose branches above him, spiralled down and landed on his shoulder.

A furious sob ricocheted through her chest. Her voice was high, shrill. 'How can he be allowed to do such things? To blackmail me like this? Surely the Queen doesn't agree with his decision? I have to go back in and appeal to her!' She turned on her heel, her thin-soled slippers grinding into the flagstone path.

'Alinor, stop.' Guilhem's voice held a warning. The strengthening breeze caught his tawny hair, rippling the thick, glinting strands, and sent a scurry of petals downwards, a shower of pink-silk scraps. 'Without the King the Queen has no power over Edward; he can do what he likes. Don't go back in there.'

'But it's outrageous what he's asking me to do!'

'I agree. But Edward has a volatile temperament, I would not like to see you punished for this.'

'Oh, he wouldn't!' she flashed at him boldly, sticking her chin in the air. The shadows from the rose trellis criss-crossed her face, making her eyes more intensely green, bottomless pools of emerald. The pulse in her throat thrummed frantically against gossamer-white skin. Despite her outward show of bravado, she was frightened.

'He would,' Guilhem said sternly. 'He has sent women to their death before, for less than you have done today.'

Her lungs emptied with a sudden whoosh of air; her hands fluttered upwards, touching her face, the wrap of cloth at her neck. His arms came forward, hands curling about her upper shoulders, supporting her. 'My God,' she ground out bitterly, 'the man is a monster! Why in Heaven's name is he your friend? Why do you remain loyal to him?'

Guilhem paused. Beneath his fingers, the woollen stuff of her sleeves was buttery-soft, the warmth of her flesh diffusing through. He rubbed his big thumbs against the fabric. Above them, a buzzard circled and wheeled, vast wings vibrating in the chill wind. 'Because he helped me once. And I will always be grateful to him for that.'

'What? What did he do? I can't believe a man like that would do anything other than to help himself!' she blasted out, trembling in his hold. 'It would have to be something pretty impressive, I'm sure, for you to stick with him like this.' Her tone was scathing. 'He must have saved your life, at the very least, for you to remain so loyal to him!'

Guilhem's eyes swept over her, darkening to midnight blue. Riven with sadness. Despair surged through him, bleak and wretched.

She saw. Her breath caught. 'My God, what happened to you?' Her body slumped in his grip; she remembered. He had been in a prison, for months. Her heart plummeted; suddenly all the bluff and bluster, the anger against Edward, was knocked out of her by the stark look of pain on Guilhem's face. 'I am so sorry,' she whispered, clasping her arms about her chest, teeth beginning to chatter. 'He saved your life, didn't he?'

'Aye, he did,' Guilhem murmured.

'When you were locked up?'

His gaze roamed across her sweet face and wondered whether he should tell her. What he should tell her. Not everything. Not at this moment, when she needed his help. There would be time enough for her to hate him later. 'Yes, I was,' he said, finally. 'It was Edward who secured my

release. Took me home.' He closed his eyes at the
memory: his starved emaciated body, covered in
sores, barely able to stumble a few yards.

Alinor touched his cheek, palm silky against
blond stubble. 'I'm sorry,' she murmured. 'I had
no intention of stirring up bad memories.'

He knew he should remove her hand, place it
gently away, but instead he turned his cheek into
the velvet cup, inhaling her faint perfume. Inadvertently, his lips brushed her skin, tickling the
sensitive inner flesh of her palm. She sensed the
loss, the hurt that ravaged his strapping frame.
Instinct drove her, even as her mind clamoured
for self-restraint. Leaning forward, she wound her
arms about his waist, drawing him against her
slenderness, wanting to comfort him, needing to
drive out by her simple gesture the sheer desola-
tion, the pure despair in his eyes.

It was a mistake.

Chapter Fifteen

Desire, scrappy and volatile, stalked him like a wolf: trickles of igniting fire. A stern voice told him to step back, to step away, his own conscience warning him. He tried to heed it. Gritting his teeth, he stared bleakly out over the top of Alinor's head as her lithe figure crushed against his, delicious, pliable.

Tipping her head up, she smiled at him. Beneath Guilhem's tunic, his waist was hard muscle, firm, pressing into her forearms. Her fingers linked in the inward curve of his back, knuckles grazing the powerful flexed rope of his spine. Her intention had been to comfort him, but now, as he crushed against her, honed chest muscles brushing against her breasts, that intention had changed. Every nerve ending was charged, quivering with a latent, flickering excitement. She wanted this moment to go on for ever, but she knew she must release him. She ran her tongue across dry lips.

Release him now, she told herself sternly, *before you embarrass yourself.* Clamping her mouth in determined resolution, she unclasped her fingers and made to pull away.

'No,' he murmured. 'Stay.' His fingers tightened around her upper shoulders. He stepped closer, muscled legs buttressed against her own, tangling with her skirts.

She glanced up, surprised. Her heart thudded treacherously, blood hurtling against the surface of her skin. 'They will be wondering where we are.' Her voice was husky.

'Let them.' A curious light entered his eyes, the colour of a shimmering sky at dawn. He lowered his head, mouth brushing hers, light, sensual. A tentative softness. He could not help himself. Self-control fled, ragged as the icy breeze.

Her eyelids fluttered down; she tipped her chin upwards, her mouth meeting his. Sensation rocked her, driving shards of hot, burning ice into her very core. His lips roamed along hers, seeking, teasing, puncturing any last fleeting protests of resilience. Her chest shuddered. Blood pounded in her eardrums, her mind clearing of anything but the sweet insistence of his mouth. She clung to him like a slender willow sapling, graceful yet strong, bending into the curve of his body, clutching at his shoulders, drawing him down.

He groaned, opening the supple plushness of

her mouth with delicious force, bruising, demanding. She tasted like honey. Her heart sang, danced, skittering with delight. His arms cradled her waist, winding her tight against him; she was conscious of every tightly packed muscle, every corrugated ridge of his frame. Her chest heaved, then plummeted again with an odd, blistering awareness. So be it. She would deal with the consequences. All that mattered was his mouth against hers.

Then, through mounting layers of pleasure, she heard a sound. An iron latch clicking upwards. She stiffened against him.

Through sinewy arms, he sensed the sudden tension in her body. Reluctantly he dragged his mouth from hers. 'What is it?' His eyes glittered, midnight pools of smouldering desire.

'Someone's coming,' she murmured, lips tingling. Hot colour suffused her face as the cold reality of her illicit behaviour slammed her. Why, she had behaved like a wanton, draping herself all over him; he was like a drug, an addiction of which she could never have enough! Stupid, stupid girl! Staggering back, she collided with the trellis. Rose thorns poked through her dress, pinching cruelly at her shoulders. Fluttering with agitation, her fingers rose to her mouth, then touched her cheeks, her hair. Regret crashed over her, a bitter taste against her tongue.

Guilhem turned his head to look down the

path, raking one hand through his tawny hair, breath punching from his lungs. Desire dragged at his loins, heavy, unspent. What would have happened if they hadn't been interrupted? But he didn't even need to ask himself that question; he knew the answer already.

Bianca appeared at the entrance to the rose arbour, blue silk glimmering in the half-light. Petals blew across her path, sporadic snowflakes of pale pink. She snagged her veil with one hand to stop it flying in the breeze. In the time Guilhem and Alinor had been out in the gardens, the sun had dropped below the horizon and the wind had strengthened. Neither of them had noticed.

'Oh, there you are!' she called out, her face breaking into a wide smile.

Guilhem fixed his gaze on the flagstone path, traced the jagged lines of pale lime mortar between the stones. Alinor barely managed to hold herself upright, clinging desperately on to the trellis behind her, knees shaking.

'The Queen was anxious to know where you had gone.' Bianca bustled forward, threading her arm through Alinor's, drawing her away from the snagging rose. 'What's the matter with both of you?' Her eyes bounced from Guilhem to Alinor, a puzzled frown drawing her brows together. 'Why are you so quiet? Have you argued?'

Nodding jerkily in response to Bianca, Alinor

allowed herself to be walked back along the arbour. Shamefaced, Guilhem watched them go. How could he go on like this, trying to resist her beauty, but failing miserably at every turn? Maybe he should just bed her and be done with it. The thought disgusted him. No, he would never do that. He respected her too much. To use her, then discard her. She was worth ten of him, nay, a hundred of him; the thought was inconceivable! But how could he ride by her side to find the King, and protect her, without wanting to possess her, love her, at every moment of the day and night? He was not to be trusted, yet he trusted no other man with such a precious possession.

Returning to the great hall, Bianca hanging on her arm, Alinor was relieved to see that Prince Edward was dancing. The trestle tables and long benches had been pushed back against the walls. The cleared space thronged with people, sweaty-faced and smiling, linking hands to form a chain that skipped first one way, then the other, bouncing in time to the music. Edward's tall, whip-thin body dominated the crowd, pale-blond head bobbing above the rest. Everyone seemed drunk and happy, the air thick with the smell of cooling meat grease, smoke and honeyed mead.

'Alinor, you look so sad. Are you quite well?' Bianca murmured in her ear as they walked towards the high dais.

Her lips burned, a lingering reminder of Guilhem's mouth upon hers. 'I'm scared, Bianca, if
you must know.' Scared of how I feel about your
brother. Her heart closed up, bereft, hopeless. She
wanted to glance around, to see if he followed
them, but instead she pinned her gaze steadfastly on
the wooden steps to the dais, the rickety banister.

'But if you do this for the Prince, you will gain
his protection, not to mention his admiration.'

'It's not a case of "if". I have no choice, Bianca.
Look at the alternative—marriage to Eustace. I
should never have come here.' An enormous feeling of entrapment washed over her, a vulnerability
that she despised. She thought back longingly to
the freedom she had enjoyed when garbed in her
nun's habit, the ability to roam about the countryside unimpeded. If only the Queen hadn't arranged Bianca's marriage to Eustace, then none
of this would have happened. But then, she would
never have met Guilhem. Would that have been
preferable?

Bianca clutched at her arm with the air of a
conspirator. 'I could smuggle you away to France
with me—just like you helped me at Claverstock.'

'Don't even think about it.' Guilhem's voice
barked down on them both.

Alinor's heart jumped; he was right behind
them.

As they approached the top table, the Queen

rose and came towards Alinor, hands outstretched. Worry cleaved her face. 'I am so sorry about this.'

Alinor linked her fingers with the Queen's, allowing herself to be led back to the table. Bianca slid back into her own chair.

'Today's events have shaken me, I'm afraid.' The Queen turned to her. 'The news about your family...' She trailed off. 'And Edward's request to you.'

Alinor bit her lip. Shame flooded through her, shame at what her father had done. Her shoulders hunched, as if trying to protect her from the prying eyes of the great hall—did everyone know what she was now? That her family were traitors to the crown?

'But you will help us, my dear, by doing this. We need to put a stop to the rebel cause, bring stability to the country again. Guilhem will look after you; you have nothing to fear from him.'

Alinor glanced over to the steps where Guilhem had stopped to talk to another knight. *Yes, I do. I fear the loss of my heart.* She plucked at the hem of the tablecloth, hanging down across her lap.

'He is one of Edward's finest knights and would never break the code of chivalry. You are safe with him.'

No, I am not. Her heart beat frantically in her chest, so fast that she feared it would escape and leap out on to the table before her, so all could see her shame, her bewilderment, her love for the man just a few feet away from her. Nausea roiled in her belly. The chaotic music, the smoke rising thickly in the hall stifled her; a tightness dragged at her chest.

'I think, if your lady permits it, I would ask leave to retire please.'

The Queen inclined her head, granting permission. 'Of course. You will ride early on the morrow...is that the plan, Guilhem?' She raised her eyes as he approached the table. 'That you will leave early?'

He nodded. Moving behind Alinor's chair, he pulled it back as she rose unsteadily.

'Oh, don't go up just yet!' Bianca said. 'I wanted to dance.'

'Stay and dance.' Alinor smiled. Tiny lines of fatigue fanned out from the corners of her eyes. 'I think the day is catching up with me. I will come and see you before I leave tomorrow, to say goodbye.'

She walked stiffly towards the stairwell, aware of many eyes upon her, then looked askance at Guilhem, who fell into step beside her. 'What are you doing? Aren't you staying here?'

He held open the narrow door for her, one muscled arm laid flat along vertical oak planks; she caught his tangy scent as she sailed past him, chin in the air, spine straight and rigid. He must not see how he affected her.

'I thought I would make sure you reached your chamber unscathed,' he said, following her up the spiral staircase. Flickering torches slung into iron brackets lit the steps, casting a jittery nervous light across the damp, gleaming stone.

She turned abruptly, one step above him. Her eyes met his on the level and she recoiled slightly, devastated by the blue intensity of his gaze. 'You don't trust me!'

Guilhem grinned, holding his palms up towards her. 'Correct.' He tapped a finger against her forehead. 'I can see right in here, Alinor, and I know you're trying to think of a way out of Edward's plans for you.'

She whisked away from him, marching up the stairs, skirts bouncing briskly in her wake. 'Do you blame me?' she lobbed back, her speech bitter and scathing. 'Why does it always have to be like this, women bending to the will of men? Caught, trapped, in thrall to them. I should take the veil; at least then I would have some freedom.' She disappeared through the carved archway on to the first-floor landing, heading for her chamber.

He caught up with her, easily matching her impatient stride, almost squashing her into the wall as he took up the breadth of the corridor. 'Why would you choose such a life?' he murmured. 'Never to know a man, to bear his children, to have a family growing around you? It's seems a poor choice to me.' In the shadowed half-light of the corridor, his hair gleamed like a burnished flame.

She stopped, folding her arms across her breast, stifling the flare of desire in her belly. How had they managed to end up talking about this? 'Not if it means my head is my own and my decisions are my own to make!'

He laughed, his upper arm nudging hers. 'You're too headstrong, Alinor. Marriage is all about sharing, about discussion and joint decisions.'

She laughed, but the sound was hollow, brittle. 'It's never bcen like that. Marriage is a business, brides bartered for land and estates.' She lifted one shoulder, a gesture of futility. Her neckline gaped fractionally, revealing the delicate sweep of her collarbone.

'It doesn't have to be.' His thoughts raced forward, to a distant future, hazy, brimming with possibility. Alinor as his wife. The mother of his children. He played with the idea for a moment, until the black guilt came crashing down around him and he watched as hope disintegrated, breaking up into a thousand raw-edged splinters. An impossible dream.

'It's *always* like that,' she corrected him, her

mouth set in a stubborn line. 'I can't think of one marriage where the couple actually *like* each other, let alone love each other.'

If only it could have been different between them, he thought. If only he had met her before, before that awful time at Fremont, when he had been a different, better man. He would not wish his arid heart, his damaged soul, on anyone. 'Maybe you're right,' he said brusquely. 'I suspect it's a matter of luck if you manage to marry a good husband.'

'Oh, and that would be you, would it?' she blurted out without thinking.

Guilhem held her gaze for a long time. 'No, not me,' he said, finally. 'Never me.' The blue of his eyes darkened, dulled, as if a fire had been doused. A shift of pain crossed his face.

Why not? she wanted to scream at him. *Why can't it be you?* Biting her lip, she hurried up the final steps to her chamber, snuffing out the questions that jumped in her brain. She clicked up the iron latch, pushing into the chamber. *Because he felt nothing for her, that was why.* But if he felt nothing for her, then why did he keep kissing her?

'Goodnight, then,' she said, slipping around and starting to close the door.

'Goodnight, Alinor,' he replied. 'Believe me when I tell you there is no way out of this plan. Don't even think about trying to run away. Edward would send his men out to find you and they would hunt you down, and drag you back.' He reached forward, fingers grazing the soft sweep of her jaw. 'And those men might not be me and they might not be as lenient. I would not want that to happen to you,' he said. 'You are safer with me.' But even as he uttered the words, doubt scurried through his brain.

Surprisingly, Alinor slept well, waking in the early morning from a dreamless sleep. Birds clamoured outside her window, a high-pitched, excitable dawn chorus. Padding over to the oak coffer, she poured water into the earthenware bowl, scrubbed at her face. She shivered in her thin chemise. Drying her face briskly, she dragged on her undergarments and woollen stockings, sticking her feet into her slippers before she pulled on her gowns. The thin red leather was streaked and marred with dirt; these shoes were meant for gentle days inside, not charging about the countryside in all weathers. She wondered how long they would last until they fell apart. Tying her under-dress to her slim shape with leather lacings, she drew on her sleeveless gown that added another layer of warmth. She pushed her head through her wimple, the soft fabric covering her bare neck. Re-braiding her hair, she wound and pinned it into a low bun at the base of her neck,

pulling up the gathered folds of her wimple to secure it to the top of her head.

Positioning her circlet firmly over her veil, she
lifted her chin, catching sight of her reflection in
a rectangular piece of polished silver above the
coffer. Her face appeared pale and wan, despite
her uninterrupted sleep. She adjusted the wimple
self-consciously, tucking a stray strand of hair
behind her ear, then immediately chastised herself for her vanity. For whom was she making
herself look better? For him? Guilhem wouldn't
even notice. He held her at a distance, whilst she
sank ever deeper into a bewildering maelstrom of
emotion. How she had lowered herself by submit-
ting to him; why was she unable to simply push
him away? A wave of chagrin, of regret, pulsed
through her. Was she really that weak-willed? Or
was it simply that she yearned for the taste of his
mouth, the closeness of his body and would risk
everything, even her own reputation and his dis-
respect, in order to achieve such a thing? She was
like a starving bird, she thought bitterly, hopping
about the kitchen yard, waiting and hoping, until
someone scattered out a few stale crumbs for her
to feast on avidly.

She twitched away from the basin, gathering
up her cloak. She would do this thing for Edward,
without demeaning herself any further with Guilhem. She could resist him, she had to resist him,

otherwise she would go mad with longing and every kiss would make it worse, more unbearable. She hoped they would find Simon de Montfort quickly and then she could settle back into a quiet life at the Priory, away from any distractions.

As she descended the spiral staircase to the great hall, bars of strong sunlight poured through the arrow slits, lighting the confined space. Her hand brushed lightly along the curving metal banister, keeping her step sure and true. On the threshold of the hall, she hesitated, amazed by the amount of people crowding along the trestles; of course, it was still harvest time and the peasants had to be out early in the fields, gathering in the crops. In front of her on the high dais, Edward and Guilhem stood, heads bent over a square piece of parchment, a map, spread across the width of the table. The tablecloth from the previous evening had been removed and now the polished wood was revealed, chestnut-hued and glossy. Of the Queen and Bianca, there was no sign.

Catching her wavering movement in the archway, Edward looked up, a faint sneer curling his upper lip. Guilhem smiled at her. Her heart flipped stupidly.

'Er... I'll go and wake Bianca,' she said, backing away, unwilling to be closeted with the two men. Although she hated to admit it, Prince Edward scared her.

'No, come here, girl,' Edward barked. 'I'll tell you of our plan. I was about to tell Guilhem and I don't want to repeat it.'

Reluctantly, she edged forward to stand next to Guilhem, inhaling the piquant scent of horse-flesh. A stray length of straw clung to his braies—had he been to the stables already? Close to him, her heart jumped with treacherous awareness, but she forced herself to concentrate on the lines and squiggles of the map.

'Knighton Palace is here,' Edward was saying, jabbing the parchment with one long finger. His knuckles were oddly prominent: white and knobbly. 'And I have a feeling that de Montfort is somewhere around here, based on what my spies have told me.' He circled an area on the parchment.

'That's an area covering some ten square miles,' said Guilhem drily. 'And most of it forest. Have you nothing more definite?'

'If I had then I would have him by now!' Edward snapped. 'And my father would be back in his rightful place, back on the throne of England!'

A thread of fear pulsed through Alinor at the Prince's volatile reaction. Guilhem's arm skimmed against hers; it might have been in error, but she drew confidence from his mistaken touch, from that discreet strength coiled in his muscled forearm.

'Calm down, Edward,' Guilhem said. 'I will probably be able to narrow the search area, eliminate the places where he would not strike camp. Here, for example, a vast flood plain of marsh and inhospitable ground; he would not go there.'

'Good man.' Edward slapped Guilhem on the back. 'Keep going like that and you'll have him.' He switched his watery gaze to Alinor. 'And you, young lady, do exactly what Guilhem tells you to do. I am sending six knights with you as escort, but when you find the camp, you will go in with Guilhem alone with a message for your father that your stepmother is very ill and he must come home immediately. That way Guilhem can get close to de Montfort and bring him out with a knife in his neck. No one will dare to stop them.'

'But Guilhem will be captured the moment they see him wearing the King's colours,' Alinor gasped out. Her heart hollowed; she couldn't believe she had agreed to such an outrageous plan, but what choice did she have? 'He'll be taken prisoner.'

'Ah, no.' Edward wagged his finger at her. 'Guilhem will be dressed as a peasant and act as your manservant. They will not suspect a thing; a lady of quality travelling alone would naturally have some sort of bodyguard. He's big and burly enough to act the part.' He started to fold up the map, failed, then pushed the mess of crumpled parchment irritably into Guilhem's chest. 'Sort that out, will you? Where's my mother? Where's breakfast?' He threw his lanky frame into a nearby chair, fed up with the minutiae of the whole affair. 'I'm famished.'

Chapter Sixteen

In contrast to the previous day, the stiff wind had dissipated, the bright sunshine blotted away; the air was surprisingly muggy. A low band of cloud pressed down on the land. Hazy clusters of midges rose up from the muddy track as Guilhem and Alinor rode in a north-westerly direction, three soldiers in front and three soldiers behind. The further Alinor drew away from Knighton Palace, the greater her sense of relief; the Queen was expecting the arrival of her stepmother and Eustace and she had no wish to face them and become embroiled in the retelling of Wilhelma's crime.

Bianca had been tearful, clingy, when she had finally descended into the great hall that morning; after breaking their fast together, Guilhem had hugged his sister, reassuring her again that she had the best escort back to France. Bianca was due to leave that day and ride towards the port on the south coast. A ship would carry her back home on the high tide in the evening. But Bianca's fingers had gripped Alinor's tightly as she rose to leave. A wave of sadness passed over Alinor; in the past few days, Guilhem's sister had been a good friend to her. Would they ever see each other again?

She peeked at Guilhem, surprised at the difference in his appearance now he wore rough peasant clothes. He still wore his fawn woollen leggings and calf-leather boots, but the richly embroidered blue surcoat had been replaced by a square-cut tunic of mud-coloured wool, coarsely woven and ripped in some places, patched up in others. One sleeve was coming adrift at the shoulder, the stitches stretched and pulling. He wore a short cape and hood, pushed back to fall in stout gathers at the nape of his neck. All the trappings of his profession had disappeared: the chainmail, the helmet, even his sword and scabbard, replaced with a short knife stuck into the leather belt around his waist. But even wearing such clothes, there was no mistaking his size and power—the tunic stretched across his bulky shoulders and ended at mid-thigh, revealing the bunched strength in his long, lean legs.

'Where did you find those clothes?' Alinor asked, breaking the long silence between them. Guilhem seemed content to ride without conversation, but she felt jittery, unsure in his presence, not knowing how she stood with him, or even what he really thought about her.

He turned his head. The grey-lit day dulled his burnished hair to dark gold. 'One of the kitchen servants has a husband about the same size as me,' he explained. 'It wasn't difficult.'

'You look so different from your normal self...' She trailed off, unsure. As if by making a comment upon his outward appearance, her words became too intimate, too personal. Above her, a blackbird trilled, singing its melancholy tune on a swaying branch. What was she trying to say? That he seemed more approachable, without the fearsome accoutrements of war? She knotted her hands into the bridle, sticking her heels down firmly in the iron stirrups, lacking the confidence to finish her sentence.

He laughed, throwing his head back. 'I'm not sure what you consider my normal self to be, Alinor. All I know is that I reek to high heaven of soil and sweat. And not my own, which makes it all the more unpleasant.' His midnight eyes glittered with amusement.

She smiled at him, a soft tilt to the corner of her mouth. 'I can't smell anything.'

His heart lurched. God, how beautiful she was: that faint rose tint to her cheeks, her lush rosebud mouth. 'Then either there's something

wrong with your nose, or you're just being polite,' he shot back, raising his eyebrows in mock
surprise.

Her heart warmed beneath his teasing, a great
slug of air releasing suddenly from her chest.
This was fine; she could do this, she could be
with him and maintain this easy camaraderie
as long as they kept a reasonable distance from
each other.

'Oh, all right,' she admitted, pressing her hands
down on the horse's neck to raise her weight, adjusting her hips in the leather saddle. 'I was just
being polite.' She rode astride, the position providing better balance with her damaged arm; her
long skirts hung down on each side of the horse,
wings of gathered cloth. Flicking her skirts down,
her fingers brisk, decisive, she furrowed her brow.
'Smelly or not, do you think it will work? Do you
think we can get into de Montfort's camp?'

He read the anxiety in the pale, wan lines of her
face. Guilt swam over him for taking her into such
a potentially dangerous situation, one to which he
was accustomed and to which she was not. 'Look,
Alinor, I don't like this plan one little bit, but I
think it will work.'

'Will Edward really kill Simon de Montfort?'
she murmured, low enough for the others not to
hear.

'No,' Guilhem replied. 'His bark is far worse

than his bite. He will keep him prisoner until the King is released.' He grimaced. 'Unfortunately, he will also do the same with your father.'

'I suspected as much.' Her voice held a strange hollowness.

'Eustace and your stepmother will already be... with the Queen.'

'You mean locked up.' Alinor paused. 'It doesn't matter. I... I know you are shocked, that I should be more upset by the thought of them being punished...but all I can feel is a sense of relief.'

'I'm not shocked.' Guilhem's voice hardened. 'It's completely understandable after what they have done to you.'

'My father has done nothing.'

'He has failed to protect you.' *Or even care for you*, he thought.

She read the kindness in his face and her heart scythed with raw poignancy. 'Don't pity me, Guilhem. Please. After all of this, I will be all right, truly.'

Throwing him a bright smile, she tapped her heels into her horse's rump and trotted away from him, down a narrow path which prevented him from riding alongside her. He fell behind, staring at the slim, narrow curve of her spine, the gentle indent of her waist.

I don't pity you, Alinor, he thought. *I love you.*

* * *

They rode for hours, skirting possible areas where the de Montfort army might be, riding up steep hills to scan the vast expanse of countryside for any telling signs of a gathered army: trails of smoke, the white canvas of tents, the flash of chainmail, or sword. So far, nothing. Not a trace. Alinor's muscles were cramped and sore from having been in the saddle for most of the day; she wondered if she would even be able to dismount. At last, after what seemed like an interminable amount of time, Guilhem raised his arm and called a halt to the soldiers. They had stopped in a forest clearing, the sound of water nearby, a sparse covering of spindly grass, luminous green in a pool of light.

'We'll stop here for the night,' he announced, swinging down easily from his horse. Leading the animal to the edge of the clearing, he looped the reins over a low branch. Wilting with tiredness, Alinor listened to him rapping out orders to the soldiers: make a fire, prepare some food, tend to the horses. The business of setting up camp was second nature to him and his commands held the underlying ease of habit. Alinor rubbed at her eyes, gritty with dust from the road; the dirt seemed driven into the fine pores on her face. Mixed with a faint sheen of sweat, it made her skin feel claggy.

'What do you want me to do?' she asked, lifting her head slowly as Guilhem approached.

'Well, dismounting would be a good start.' She looked completely exhausted, he thought. Purpling lines of fatigue extended down from the corners of her eyes; her body curved forward in the saddle, drooping before his gaze. They had ridden too far and too fast for her, he realised, a pall of shame washing over him. He should have taken more care of her, looked out for her. 'Can you?'

'Of course!' she flashed back. Placing her hands on the horse's mane, she leaned forward, attempting to swing her right leg backwards over the horse's rump. Her muscles screamed out in agony; she gave a tiny hiss of pain. Why did this have to happen, now, in front of Guilhem? 'I need some time to do this,' she said, irritably. 'You go off and do whatever it is you have to do.'

'Place your hands on my shoulders—' he ignored her words '—and I will help you. You've been riding all day and you're not used to it. Sore muscles are nothing to be ashamed of.'

Annoyed, she glowered at the frothing mane of her palfrey, then shrugged her shoulders, admitting defeat. Twisting in the saddle, she positioned her hands on his wide shoulders. Circling her waist with his hands, he lifted her off gently, easily, setting her down on her feet in front of him.

'Ouch!' she cried out, clutching on to him as

her feet hit the ground. It was as if someone had hammered metal rods down the back of each leg. 'That hurts.'

He grimaced. 'Keep flexing your muscles,' he advised. 'They should become less sore over the course of the evening.' What she really needed was a hot bath. It wasn't right that he should be dragging her about the countryside in this heathen fashion; she was not a soldier, born and bred into this way of life, she was a lady. What on earth had Edward been thinking when he had set her on this course? What had *he* been thinking, ever to agree to it?

'Come and sit by the fire,' he said, 'and have something to eat. It might make you feel better.'

Well, she doubted it could make her feel worse. To her utter chagrin, she found she had to place a hand on Guilhem's arm to even be able to walk over to the spot where the soldiers had lit the fire. Smoke curled up through the gap in the tree canopy from the pile of damp wood like a messy skein of white-grey wool, spitting fretfully. She sank jerkily to the blanket that someone had spread on the ground, gritting her teeth against her screaming muscles, throwing an ashen smile to the soldier tending the fire.

'Thank you,' she murmured up to Guilhem. He had lowered her down as if his arm was a rope and she still clung to it. She dropped her hand, kneading her fingers into her lap. 'I've never known riding to be quite so painful before!' She laughed half-heartedly, trying to cover her embarrassment.

'We covered a lot of ground today, Alinor. You did well.'

'What you mean is; I did well for a woman.'

'No,' he said frowning. 'You did well. Full stop. Look at the men around you—they're all tired out.'

For the first time, she glanced round the camp. Guilhem was correct. His soldiers all lay around the camp in various stages of relaxation—some lying completely flat on their backs with their eyes closed, some seated, talking quietly with their companions.

She tipped her head up at him, tilting it slightly: the faintest sign of agreement.

'You see?' He smiled down at her. 'You don't need any excuse for how you feel. It's normal to feel tired after a day like this, it's not a weakness.' God, most women would have started to complain after the first hour or two of riding this morning. Alinor had been in the saddle for the whole day.

She shrugged her shoulders, staring doubtfully into the fitful flames. 'If you say so.' Why was he being so nice to her? It made him harder to deal with; her heart flared beneath the gentle admiration in his voice.

'I do say so, Alinor.' He laughed at her uncertain expression. 'Stop being so hard on yourself. You have done well today; you should take pride in that.'

She shivered, wrapping her cloak more firmly about her, trying to damp down the surge of happiness that rose within her at his praise. 'You'd better stop now,' she said, 'otherwise all this flattery might go to my head.'

He hunkered down beside her, surprisingly graceful for such a big man, balancing easily on the balls of his feet. 'You deserve it, Alinor. Now, have something to eat and then you can sleep.'

A large, jagged stone poked uncomfortably into Alinor's right shoulder. Maybe that was what had woken her? Keeping her eyes tightly closed, she rolled over on to her left side, hoping to find a more accommodating spot on the lumpy ground. Her hands gripped the edges of her cloak, wrapping it more securely across her body, and she held her arms in a cross-wise fashion across her chest, hoping it might be warmer that way. Her toes were freezing, the chill night air sneaking through the thin leather of her slippers, her fine silk stockings. In the process of rolling over, the edge of her cloak had become caught beneath her hip; she sighed in frustration, reluctantly tugging it back into place. She had to go to sleep! She must! But even as she closed her eyes, her mind worked frantically, scooting along runnels of worrying thoughts, haphazard, annoying.

An owl hooted suddenly, breaking the sifting silence of the woodland.

Irritated, disheartened by her inability to sleep, Alinor sat up abruptly, drawing her knees to her chest and wrapping her arms around her shins. A small kernel of flame still burned in the centre of the fire, a trail of smoke rising listlessly. Her eyes swept the camp, struggled to focus on the sleeping shapes around her; the earlier cloud had cleared away and the moon, a slim curved wedge, hung low in the star-studded sky. All around her the soldiers slept, rolled on the ground in their cloaks, breaking the silence with stuttering snores, occasional mutterings in their sleep. She envied them their dreams, their blissful unconsciousness.

'Can't you sleep?'

She lurched forward in shock, jumping at the familiar voice behind her. Hunching around, she saw Guilhem a few feet away, his back propped against the trunk of a giant oak, one knee raised.

'No,' Alinor whispered. 'And I don't know why not!'

He chuckled at her childish exasperation. 'Are you cold?'

'Well, I am,' she admitted. 'But that normally doesn't stop me sleeping. I don't suppose you have a blanket anywhere?'

'I don't,' he replied slowly. 'Unfortunately soldiers tend to travel light. I do have a suggestion, though.'

'What is it?'

'If you come over here, you can lean against me. It will make you warmer.'

She frowned at him, absorbing the full import of his words. A thread of excitement fluttered along her veins. 'Guilhem, are you mad? I can't! It's out of the question, after—' She stopped, abruptly, her face flushing with embarrassment. What had she been about to say? That every time she came too close to him, they seemed to end up kissing? She couldn't say such things to him! Besides, if she did, it sounded as though she expected him to do such a thing. As if she wanted him to kiss her! Her heart quailed in self-doubt at her last outrageous thought: who was she trying to hoodwink? She wanted him to kiss her again.

He held his hands up in mock innocence. 'Alinor, this is no time for maidenly modesty. I can see you're shivering. Come over here and take advantage of an honourable offer. I promise I will keep my hands to myself; we have an audience, after all.' He quirked one eyebrow at the sleeping soldiers. A sudden, unbearable longing gripped his belly as she began to move; he knew he was taking a chance.

'Here, sit against me, lean back,' he ordered

gruffly, as she crept over to him. He would maintain a stern, distant attitude towards her. 'The ground is drier beneath the tree.' Alinor slid down beside him, her hips nudging his, slim legs against his own. Even through her veil, he could smell the sweet lavender fragrance of her hair, her skin. His heart quivered with delicious anticipation; he bit his lip, steeling his resolve.

'How many layers are you wearing?' he asked sternly, trying to ignore the sweet press of her body.

A luscious warmth spiralled through her, a warmth spiced with masculine scent: heady, invigorating. An exquisite feral heat curled across her shoulders and down the icy length of her spine, making her shiver, making her warm.

'One chemise, one under-gown of silk, one over-gown of wool, my cloak,' she chanted out, stretching out her legs along the grass in front of her, wriggling her toes to try and warm them. 'Stockings, inadequate shoes. Surely that's enough?' Her veil rustled against the coarse wool of his tunic as she moved her head fractionally.

His cheeks warmed as she named her garments and he visualised each one of them. The vision of Alinor clad only in her diaphanous chemise at Claverstock, when he had hurriedly left her chamber, charged across his mind. 'Aye, it should be,' he managed to croak out. 'Try to go to sleep now.'

She made a small sound, a sigh of contentment and nestled her head into the crook of his arm. Something poked sharply into his skin through his borrowed tunic.

'What is this?' he said, exasperated. Putting his hand on her head, he encountered her silver circlet, complete with knobbly filigree-silver decoration. 'I'm going to take this off,' he declared. 'It's jabbing into my shoulder.'

'No, don't, my veil...'

But he had already removed the circlet from her head and her veil, unsecured, slid down across her shining hair and fell to the ground in the puddle of light silk.

'...will fall off,' she finished lamely, self-consciously lifting her hand to the hastily pinned wimple.

'Do you normally sleep with that on?' He gestured to the length of cloth gathered around her neck and the sides of her face. Her skin gleamed, lustrous alabaster in the moonlight.

'Of course not.' Alinor laughed. 'But I must keep it on in company.' She glanced over to the soldiers.

'They won't even notice, they're all asleep. It's probably all that stuff on top of your head that's keeping you awake,' Guilhem said.

'I meant you,' she replied, significantly. 'You count as "company" as well.'

'Oh, me?' he answered, a little too breezily. 'It doesn't affect me one way or the other. I just think you'll be more comfortable, that's all.'

Her heart closed up a little at his statement. It made sense that he would be completely unaffected by whatever she did, or whatever she wore, or didn't wear. He was completely immune to her. And the sooner she came to terms with that, the better.

'So be it,' she muttered. Her fingers pulled at the few pins holding the wimple in place. In a matter of moments, the long cloth wrap was folded and set on a neat pile consisting of her veil and circlet. She scattered the hairpins on top of the wimple. 'There,' she declared. 'Now maybe you'll be able to sleep.'

Guilhem tipped his chin up in the air, resting the back of his head against the trunk, feeling the woman settle against him. Alinor's body was warm and supple, her golden hair glistening like ropes of spangled stars a few inches beneath his chin, her light fragrance permeating the air beneath his nose. This was a test, a test of his own devising: the ability to withstand such temptation at close quarters. Sleep was something that evaded him for a long, long time.

Chapter Seventeen

〜〜〜

Alinor woke early; it was dark. She shivered, though her body was warm, cradled securely against Guilhem. His thick arm was braced around her shoulders, curving below her armpit, forearm nudging deliciously against the sensitive skin of her breast. His hand rested on her hip. Keeping her eyes pressed shut, Alinor expelled the air from her lungs, luxuriating in the feeling of contentment, wanting to hold on to, to savour the sensation. If only it could always be like this; if only she could wake up like this every morning, with the man she loved.

With the man she loved. The words scoured her heart, ripping at the tender flesh. How foolish she was to even imagine such a scenario; Guilhem had made it perfectly clear what he thought about her, so why did she keep on torturing herself with impossible dreams? Her eyes popped open, stung by the horrible reality of her situation. This was no idyllic trip into the countryside, despite the hopeful, misguided route of her thoughts. This was Prince Edward giving an order to Guilhem which he would carry out, despite his own misgivings. She was stupid if she even thought otherwise.

Her breath puffed out, a pall of white in the chill air. The moon threw down a soft glow, enough light for her to discern the sleeping bodies of the soldiers, bundled like large rocks around the smouldering wood of the fire. Above her head, the branches of the trees criss-crossed like lace against the velvet sky, stars sparkling high. And from somewhere over to the right of the clearing, Alinor could hear water, the trickle of a stream gurgling over stones.

She licked her lips. Her throat was sore and parched. Suddenly it seemed imperative that she should drink, then wash her face and neck before everyone woke up. Despite the cold night, the journey yesterday had been hot and gruelling; dirt clogged the pores on her face with a slick coating of dust and sweat. Surely the stream was not that far away; the sound of the water was loud, close.

Slowly, with infinite care, she lifted Guilhem's arm from her lap, placed it gently on the ground. Not wanting to wake him, she shuffled forward on her hips, skirts bunching up around her knees, and managed to extricate herself from the muscled loop of his other arm. The damp grass scuffed the underside of her heels. Turning, she rolled herself on to all fours, wincing. Her stiff muscles protested, screamed out with the movement, aching from the day before. Lifting her head, she peered up at Guilhem, expecting him to be asleep.

His eyes were wide open, his dark-blue gaze sparkling down at her, amused.

'I thought you were asleep!' she whispered, the edge of accusation in her voice. He must have witnessed all her careful movements in trying to extricate herself. 'I was trying not to wake you!'

He quirked one eyebrow upwards. 'Going somewhere?' In the moonlit shadows, the planes of his face seemed carved, more sharply delineated.

'Not really,' she said hastily. 'I was going to the stream, to wash and have a drink.'

'I'll take you there,' he offered, pushing one hand through his tousled hair.

'Really, there's no need; it's only over there.' She pointed vaguely to a spot through the trees.

Guilhem laughed softly. 'No, it isn't.' He jerked his head in the opposite direction. 'It's over there, much further than you think. I wouldn't want you to lose your way.' He rolled away from the tree, an easy movement, and on to his feet.

Alinor sat back on her heels, brushing off a dried leaf from her skirts. 'You mean you don't want me to run off,' she murmured quietly. Her hair gleamed, a wrap of pale-gold silk around her head: rippling, vibrant.

'That, too, although I don't think you'd be that stupid.'

'Don't worry, Guilhem, I realise I have no choice in this matter.'

He stared at her bowed head, shoulders hunched, defeated, and hated himself for what he was forcing her to do. She was one of the bravest, most intelligent, most beautiful people he had ever met.

Alinor cocked her head on one side, regarding him with her huge, clear eyes, pools of limpid green. 'Although,' she said slowly, smiling, 'you could just say you lost me. I promise you, I would completely disappear and Edward would never find me.'

Guilhem laughed. 'He would never believe me.'

She folded her arms across her chest. Jammed beneath her hips, her toes were beginning to prickle and she wriggled them, trying to increase the blood flow to her feet. 'Couldn't you say you slipped up? Took your eyes off me for a moment?'

'It would never happen.' He shook his head.

'Why not? Because you're such a perfect knight, because you never make a mistake? Everyone is fallible, Guilhem, even you.'

His heart coiled with grief, sadness. How right she was.

'Enough,' he growled at her, eyes darkening.

'You can goad me all you like, but it isn't going to happen. You and I are going to find de Montfort together.' He extended his hand. 'Come now, if you want to wash before the others wake up.'

She chewed miserably at her bottom lip, but accepted his help, allowing him to pull her up from the ground. 'I hate this,' she whispered as she stood beside him. 'I hate what Edward has asked us to do.'

'I know,' Guilhem said. 'But it won't be as bad as you think it is. And I will be with you, all the time.'

Alinor reached down to scoop up her wimple.

'Leave it,' Guilhem advised. 'It will be easier to wash without. ' His gaze lingered on her uncovered hair, the pure-gold strands silvery in the moonlight, twisted into the plaited coil at the nape of her neck, the wispy curls tickling her ears. With the encumbrances of fashion removed—the wimple, the veil, the circlet—her glowing innocence was evident for all to see.

Alinor followed his confident stride through towering thickets, the low-growing shrubs and arching ferns that grew in the damp, spongy soil beneath the trees. Her skirts rustled and snagged against fierce, wayward brambles and she wrenched at the material time and time again to free herself and keep up with Guilhem's fast-receding back. At last, they reached the stream, a wide, shallow river, with trees poking out at odd angles from the bank, roots undercut and exposed by the vigorous force of the water in times of flood. But now, the water level was low, expanses of small stones shining white and dry in the middle of the river.

'Here,' Guilhem said, stepping down a series of uneven, lumpy ridges, stopping halfway to help Alinor down. Lifting her skirts, she clung gratefully to his fingers, placing her small feet where he had placed his, until they stood at the water's edge on a level, gravelled area, crunchy underfoot with flinty stones. Releasing Alinor's hand, Guilhem pulled his leather flagon from his belt and crouched down, filling it before offering it up to her, water sluicing over his hand. Alinor took it and drank.

The water was ice-cold, delicious, flooding her mouth and throat with sweet-tasting liquid. She gulped greedily, wiping the stray droplets away from her lips, and grinned at him. 'I cannot tell you how good that tastes.' He smiled, taking the flagon from her, replacing the stopper.

Dropping to her knees at the water's edge, skirts splaying out from her hips, Alinor plunged her hands into the flowing water. Cupping the liquid into her hands, she splashed her face, rubbing away the dust and dirt and grime from the day before.

'This might help,' said Guilhem, handing her a square linen handkerchief. 'It's clean.'

She dipped the white fabric into the water, watching the fabric swirl in the shallows, before wringing it out and wiping the back of her neck, her throat. Conscious that Guilhem was watching her, she rinsed the handkerchief and wrung it out, intending to give it back to him.

'Thank you,' she said, hitching around.

Guilhem was pulling his tunic over his head.

Blood pulsed in her chest, a great tidal wave of desire; she jerked her head back, stunned. 'What are you doing?' she squeaked. Her fingers dug into the wet handkerchief like a lifeline. She scrabbled to her feet, stumbling on the loose stones, hem soaked with river water.

Guilhem threw the borrowed garment on to the gravel beach, a look of disgust crossing his face. 'I need to wash, too,' he said, 'especially after wearing that stinking thing.' He laughed, stepping forward towards the water, braies snug across his slim hips, his roped thighs.

'Keep your braies on!' she blurted out, her voice bossy with panic.

He chuckled. 'Of course, Alinor, I have no intention of offending you.'

Her heart fluttered; she felt loose, untethered, as if someone had cut her adrift from her moorings and pushed her out into a wild, unsteady sea. Her stomach wobbled, a sweet anticipation, unfulfilled. She couldn't look at him, yet, somehow, she seemed unable to drag her eyes away. He bewitched her. The moon, with its rich, luminous light, bathed his torso in a sheet of limpid silver, highlighting the iron-clad expanse of honed, ridged muscle, the flat stomach. His skin glimmered, like polished marble, a god of old, an Adonis.

Her knees sagged treacherously; desire hummed along her veins, growing, threatening to burst. Her fingers itched to touch, to trail across that silky stretch of skin, to test the warm muscle, to feel… 'I will go back,' Alinor muttered. Wrenching her gaze from him, she stared hazily at Guilhem's tunic, lying in a crumpled heap. Her hands were shaking.

Guilhem had knelt by the river, ducked his head under. He turned towards her, droplets flying from the wet ends of his hair. 'No.' he said, 'I've finished.' Water sluiced down his powerful arms, the ripple of muscle, as he stood, and she watched helplessly as the trickles of water streamed across the shadowed cleft of his navel, disappearing beneath the waist of his braies. Her stomach churned; she felt as if her heart would burst. How much longer could she endure this? How much longer could she stay in his company without revealing that she cared for him? Before she made an idiot of herself?

Picking up the hated tunic, Guilhem dried his skin roughly. 'See,' he said cheerfully. 'I told you I wouldn't be long.' The water smelled fresh on his skin, a clean invigorating scent.

'Let's go then,' she said, her voice jagged with emotion.

He caught her arm, loose fingers encircling her sleeve. 'Wait, what's the matter? Have I done something to offend you?'

Shaking her head, she smiled faintly. 'No, it's nothing. Thank you for bringing me here, I feel much better.'

Hearing the false note in her speech, too formal, he tipped his head to one side, the now-damp tunic crumpled in one fist. 'That's not it. It's something else, isn't it?'

Yes, she wanted to scream at him, it is something else! I desire you! I love you! The words bubbled up in her chest, building and building until she thought she would explode.

Her lungs compressed, releasing one long slow breath as she tried to rein in her rapid, insane thoughts. 'Your wound,' Alinor said, reaching out for something, anything to say: a distraction, a diversion from her true feelings. 'I noticed it was looking a bit red—is it healing properly?' She glared purposefully at the faint line on his bare shoulder; there was nothing wrong with it, the skin had knitted together perfectly. 'And you've taken the bandage off!'

'What?' Guilhem said, surprised. 'Is that all you're worried about?' The low moonlight slanted across his face, highlighting the shadowed hollows of his cheekbones.

She tried to adopt a tone of brisk, practised efficiency. 'Does the wound feel hot?'

He shrugged his shoulders. 'No.' His eyelashes, wet from the river, stuck out like black feathers around his eyes.

Steeling herself to stop her shaking fingers, Alinor placed her palm flat on the wound; the skin was cool, dry. Flicking her hand away, she tucked it down beside her skirts. 'It's fine.'

'Well, that's good then,' he said, his tone suspicious. 'If you're sure that's all you're worried about?'

She nodded, the movement jerky, unrestrained.

Clutching his tunic, Guilhem turned, bent down to pick up his leather flagon from the grass.

Alinor gasped, clapped her hand across her mouth in shock. Across Guilhem's back, cruelly accentuated by the stark, unforgiving moonlight, was a huge white scar, the skin raised and puckered, running in a diagonal line from shoulder to waist.

Her heart opened, flew to him. 'Sweet Jesu, Guilhem, what is that—that scar on your back?'

He spun around, all levity dissipated, his face a dark mask, eyes hollow. Pulling the tunic roughly over his head, he yanked it down across his hips, his thighs. 'It's an old wound,' he muttered.

'My God, what happened to you?'

He shook his head, a slight movement. His mouth twisted, an expression of distaste, disgust. 'Something that I'm not proud of.' His words held finality.

'It looks like a burn,' Alinor said, almost to herself. Peering up into the midnight depths of his eyes, she scanned his face, searching for some clue, some hint as to what happened to him.

'It is,' he confirmed.

'Why did no one treat it properly?' Her voice rose a notch, outrage colouring her speech. 'Did no one put salve on it?

'It was difficult,' he replied slowly, his voice struggling to find the words, the explanation that had remained silent for so long. 'There was no one around to treat it. My commander threw me in prison for what I had done.'

'What did you do?' she whispered.

'I defied orders.'

'How?'

He sighed.

As if by their own volition, her fingers reached

up, touched the shadowed curve of his jaw, a gesture of comfort. 'Tell me,' she whispered. She wanted to know what had happened to him, what made his eyes burn cold with that blank, hostile fire; what cruel, determined shadows haunted the inner depths of his mind.

Guilhem's voice, when it came, was hollow, clipped. 'My commander ordered me to set fire to a castle on the borders of Gascony. I asked him if anybody was in it; I had no intention of burning anyone alive, even if they were our enemy. He assured me the castle was empty.' His voice shook slightly. 'But it wasn't empty, Alinor, it was full of women and children. As the smoke rose, billowing out of the windows, I heard their screams. I ordered my own men to go in and pull everyone out.' He cupped her hand that curved around his face, kneading her knuckles with the broad pads of his fingers. 'And we did pull everyone out. Everyone, apart from one little boy,' he said, bitterly.

Wrenching away from her, he picked up his belt from the glimmering grass, buckling it roughly, angrily, around his waist. 'The child died in the fire, Alinor, and for that, I cannot forgive myself. I couldn't save him, the fire was too strong, the heat too intense. A burning roof beam fell across my back and I couldn't go on. And all the time the boy's mother was outside, screaming and screaming…'

'Stop now,' she whispered. 'Stop torturing yourself, Guilhem, you did everything you could.'

'Did I? Every day I question myself. Could I have done more, could I have saved him?'

'Guilhem, you nearly lost your life in that fire; you were lucky that the burn didn't fester and end up poisoning your blood, killing you in the process.'

He shook his head. 'Maybe that would have been for the best.'

His dull words hit her, a stunning side-blow; shock bubbled up in panic, liquid, searing. 'No!' Alinor blurted out at him, her voice shrill, un-even; her eyes sparked green fire. 'No! I forbid you to say such an awful thing!' She thumped him, hard, the flat of her palms smacking against his chest. 'How dare you?' she spluttered out, her throat muscles closing up in choking disbelief. She pushed at him, again, shoving against his chest.

His chin jerked up at her frantic admonish-ment, the trembling emotion in her voice. 'Alinor, stop, calm down, what's the matter with you?'

Her fist snared a handful of his tunic, gripping the fabric, as she dragged herself close to him. 'I never want to hear you say such a dreadful thing again,' she said, her heart looping danger-ously. A lead weight dropped right to the bottom of her belly and now it pulled her down, a boul-der wrapped in fear.

'What's wrong with you?' he asked. Her beautiful face, skin lustrous, pearl-like, tipped up to him like a flower, like the fresh white petals of a rose. The worst was over. He had told her and yet, curiously, she hadn't run away or turned her face from him in disgust; instead she clung to him as if her life depended on it. 'Alinor, why are you acting like this? What I did was...unforgivable.'

'No!' Her fist pushed into his chest once more. 'What you did, Guilhem, was amazing, honourable and courageous. Your commander wanted all those people to die and yet you rescued them. How many lives did you save?' Alinor was yelling at him now, one slender hand slashing at the air to emphasise her speech. 'I bet you didn't count those. And yet you judge yourself on the loss of one life, beating yourself up for that, chastising yourself. Anyone who knows you, Guilhem, would have known that you would have done your utmost to get that child out. No man should have to live with such guilt and certainly not you.'

Guilhem was silent, an odd expression on his face. Moonlight dappled the taut skin across his cheekbones.

Breathing heavily, air tearing at her lungs, Alinor stopped abruptly, chest tight with emotion, wavering on the spot. The aftermath of her high-pitched yelling rang in her ears, obscuring the soft burble of the river. She focused on her hand, clutched tightly in the coarse weave of Guilhem's tunic, and reddened, snatching her fingers away. He was so quiet, his mouth set in a stern, forbidding line; she couldn't decipher his thoughts. What had she said? She couldn't even remember even half of her words; they had poured out of her so quickly, a torrent of emotion. She patted her hair, then folded her arms tightly over her belly, fingers knotting into the soft fabric of her gown, unsure of herself. She stepped back, away. 'I'm sorry,' she mumbled.

A strange lightness danced about his heart. The faintest shimmer of hope. He watched the rapid pulse at her throat, saw the wild flush of colour in her cheeks. She was like a fierce little tigress defending her cubs, except that she was defending him, fighting for him with every word that she spoke. She was on his side. The dark crust around his heart shifted slightly, fracturing; the taut muscles in his belly softened with release. He had never heard anything like it, never heard a woman speak thus, with such force, such vehemence.

'My God,' he said softly, reaching out to touch her hair.

She jerked her head back, away. 'I've said too much,' she whispered, ducking her head with embarrassment, and turned on her heel to walk hastily back to the camp, to the relative safety of the other soldiers.

* * *

Why on earth had she allowed herself to become so carried away, her words tripping and scampering over each other like some madwoman screeching in the corner of a market square? What must Guilhem think of her? She had allowed her emotions to overpower her, to affect her self-control; thank God she had stopped herself when she did. Her heart shrivelled with shame. What if she had blurted out her true feelings for him? This way, at least, she could slink away after they found de Montfort with some element of her dignity intact. And Guilhem would be none the wiser. She kicked her horse to follow the lead soldiers up the escarpment, trailing after the glossy horses' rumps on a diagonal line, the bristly gorse reaching up to brush at her skirts. When she and Guilhem had returned from the river this morning, all the soldiers had been awake, the fire stoked up and water boiling over the flames in a blackened pot. With admirable speed, the men had packed and cleared the camp before the sun had barely moved an inch upwards in the sky, bundling their bedrolls and stamping out the fire. After her fiery outburst earlier, Alinor had remained silent on the journey, barely exchanging one word with Guilhem, who rode behind her.

One of the soldiers at the top of the hill raised

his arm to halt the line, then rode back down past Alinor, to Guilhem.

'We've reached Skelton,' the soldier announced, pushing back the shining visor of his helmet. His face was streaked with sweat and dust. 'The town is down there, in the valley.'

'A known de Montfort stronghold,' said Guilhem, moving his horse alongside Alinor's. His knee brushed against hers; she twitched at the reins to steer her horse away, but was prevented by the steep slope on her right-hand side. 'You soldiers can't go into the town, it's full of de Montfort's spies and sympathisers; you'll be murdered in your beds. Stay the night up here and wait until we return with information. Alinor and I will go into the town, alone. De Montfort's camp must be near here; we'll ask around.'

His eyes, shifting to Alinor, held an odd piercing light, as if he could see into her very soul. 'Are you happy with that?'

She inclined her head in agreement, her heart sinking with trepidation.

Chapter Eighteen

'Are you ready to play your part?' Guilhem said, as they plodded down the lee escarpment of the ridge towards the town: a makeshift huddle of houses strung out along the valley bottom, clustered around a market square, a church. The lowering sun caught the smoke rising from the chimneys: thin trails rising haphazardly up into the softening twilight.

'Part?' echoed Alinor, leaning back in the saddle to counter the horse's downward gait. Her gaze had been trained on Guilhem's back, tracing the strong muscled rope of his spine beneath the makeshift tunic. The scar beneath. The depths of horror that Guilhem must have endured. She shivered, severing her mind, and her heart, from such thoughts. The saddle-back, rigid leather, dug into her hips and she lurched sideways as her palfrey slipped on a loose stone.

'Yes.' Guilhem laughed, twisting around in

the saddle to look at her. 'You are the noble lady, remember, accustomed to giving orders, to getting what you want, and I am your humble servant.' Sitting on his horse with the natural grace of one accustomed to riding almost every day of his life, his broad frame bristling with honed muscle, Guilhem was the picture of vibrant health and vitality: a knight, a noble. He couldn't look less like a servant if he tried.

'Try to look a bit more humble then,' Alinor muttered, flicking the reins at the flies clustering around her palfrey's mane. Despite the clear skies, the air was warm and moist, clouding with small black midges.

'Aye, mistress, that I will.' Guilhem touched his forelock, a mocking gesture of subservience.

'Your horse is a dead giveaway,' she said, some of her anxiety leaching away. All morning her mind had danced about, waiting for him to refer to the manner in which she had spoken to him earlier. How could she have said such things to him? Behaved in such an outrageous way, smacking him in the middle of his chest? But he had said nothing; she hoped fervently that he had forgotten about it. 'And your expensive leather boots. You should be walking barefoot.'

'You're enjoying this.' He grinned at her, the curve of his generous mouth lighting up his features. Alinor had been outspoken this morning, rattled and out of control, her reaction to his guilt-ridden confession completely unexpected. And yet since then, her manner had been quiet and withdrawn, her eyes continually darting away from him as if she couldn't bear to look at him, for to look at him would remind her of the terrible thing that he had done. His heart trembled, folding in on itself with sadness. She had had time to think about what he had told her and take in the full impact of his words. He had dared to hope, but now that hope fizzled, blown away like spent ash on the breeze.

The town was busy, crowded with people who had decided to stay for the night after market day, before taking the long journeys back to far-flung villages, estates. Dismounting on the outskirts of town, Guilhem proposed to lead both horses in. True to his word, he had muddied his boots, pulling a stained, floppy leather hat over his head. With Alinor in the saddle, he held both sets of reins in one hand, marching at the horses' heads, leading them across the loose-planked bridge and along the main cobbled street of the town. Rubbish lay everywhere, littering the streets and gutters: old caskets, spent straw, piles of dung from a cattle sale. Dogs prowled, searching for scraps of food, heads hunched down below thin, bony shoulders. Fat women, thick beefy arms crossed over massive bosoms, gossiped to each other out of the sides of their mouths, rheumy eyes tracking the progress of Alinor and Guilhem as they passed along the street.

At last, an inn came into sight, a wooden sign swinging across an open courtyard. Guilhem led the horses in, hooves clattering noisily in the enclosed space, the sound bouncing off the grimy white walls. A stable lad darted out from a covered passageway, hair lank with grease, sleeves flapping high on his forearms, too short. The landlord appeared at the door, his manner initially boisterous, belligerent. Then his eyes alighted on Alinor and his smug, slouching demeanour disappeared. His bloodshot eyes rolled over her, noting the fine quality of her garments, the rippling silk, the ornate silver circlet.

'A room, my lady?' He bowed his head. 'I have a private chamber which I'm sure will suit you.'

'Two rooms, please,' she said. 'One for me and one for my servant here.'

The innkeeper's face clouded. 'I am completely full, my lady. Apart from one private chamber. Your servant can sleep in the stable, along with the rest of them.' He laughed hoarsely, his cackle descending into a phlegmy fit of coughing. A lock of dirty grey hair fell across his ridged forehead and he smoothed it back with a slow carefulness.

'Is there anywhere else?' she asked. She had no wish for Guilhem to sleep in a filthy stable.

The landlord glanced at her curiously. What had she said? 'No, my lady, I'm afraid not. This is the only inn in town.'

'I'm sure that will be fine,' Alinor replied carefully. She hoped it would be. Guilhem stood at the head of her horse, head bowed, handsome features obscured by the large hat, saying nothing, mute.

The landlord rubbed his hands appreciably. It had been some time since a lady of quality had deigned to stay at his inn. He racked his brains, trying to remember the last time the sheets had been changed in the private chamber. 'If you would come this way, my lady?'

Guilhem released the reins, came around the side of her horse. 'This place is not good,' he murmured. 'I think we should ride on, find somewhere else.'

'You heard him,' Alinor hissed down to him. 'There is nowhere else.' She bit her lip, her words hesitant, unsure. 'Or we could sleep in the open again?'

He heard the doubt drag at her voice, noted the bluish tinge of exhaustion beneath her eyes. He shook his head. He didn't want her spending another night outside again, but he wished he could have found her somewhere with fresh linens on the bed, decent food. 'No, no, it's fine, but we need to be careful in a place like this.' His hands circled her waist to lift her down from the horse and the stable lad led the animals away.

'This way, this way.' The landlord waved his hand in front of him dramatically, the upper half of his body almost bent double from his waist in an effort to please. Alinor stepped up into the hall of the inn, wrinkling her nose in disgust. The smell permeating the air was vile: the stench of cheap tallow candles mingling with stale beer, sweat. Men, and it was all men, she realised in horror as her gaze swept the high-raftered hall, swivelled their eyes towards her, tankards stilled on slack mouths, glistening wet.

'Is there no other way to the chamber?' she asked, stalled in the doorway. 'Must I be paraded in front of all and sundry?'

'Of course, of course!' The innkeeper shooed her backwards again, his pasty fingers flapping towards her. 'Forgive me, madam, I wasn't thinking! Go back down the steps; we'll go the other way!'

Spinning around, she came face to face with Guilhem on the step below her. Alinor flushed. 'It's a madhouse in there!' she attempted to explain her fast retreat. 'The landlord says there's another way to the chamber.'

The landlord puffed his way up a rickety stair-case bolted to the side of the inn, pressing one thick arm against a narrow door to open it, indicating with a rough sideways jerk of his head that Alinor should enter. She squeezed past the sweating, obnoxious bulk of his body, which no doubt was his intention, and into the chamber: a confined, dismal space occupied by one small bed, a coffer set with the cracked earthenware jug and bowl.

'You need to pay me, now,' the landlord said, holding out his palm, fleshy lines filled with black grease. 'I can't bring you any food if you don't have the money.'

'Here,' said Guilhem, slapping a pile of loose silver into the innkeeper's open palm. The innkeeper counted the coins fastidiously, then moved out of the way so Guilhem could enter.

'Stables are down there if you want to sleep,' the innkeeper said, narrowing his gaze at Guilhem. 'I can fetch you a blanket if you like.'

Guilhem shut the door in the innkeeper's face. The door rocked against its rotting frame as he slammed it, a shower of woodworm dust clouding downwards from the sagging lintel.

'This place is intolerable,' he grumbled. The chamber stank of pork fat, of foul-smelling grease and rotting vegetables; the kitchens must be nearby. He glared at Alinor. Stripes of sunlight crept through the makeshift shutters across the one window in the room, crossing her slender frame.

'It's not bad,' said Alinor. 'I'll be all right in here.'

'Not bad!' He strode over to the bed. 'Have you seen this?' Exasperated, he tore off the covers, one by one. A threadbare blanket, two linen sheets, damp and stained, a limp feather-filled pillow—all landed on the dusty floorboards in a heap. The mattress, or what was left of it, was revealed: a thin layer of very old straw stuffed on top of the bed frame. No doubt it was full of lice, or some other hideous blood-sucking insect.

'No,' he said, almost to himself. God, she deserved better than this! He wanted crisp linens for her, a tub of scented water so she could wash herself, not this smelly, filthy room, more akin to a pigsty than a bedchamber. He thought longingly of his home in the mountains of France, the huge windows open to the clear, pine-scented air, the airy bright-lit chambers, the sound of cow bells tinkling down from the meadows. If only she could have that, if only they were there and not here in this rank, dingy chamber. It made him angry, irritated, that she was unable to have such things, to see her bright angelic face glow in such dismal surroundings. After what he had been through he could endure almost anything. But Alinor? No, not her. She had endured enough.

'Stay here,' he told her. 'And bolt the door behind you. I won't be long.'

She flew to the door as he left, struggling to fit the unwieldy bolt into its hasp. His heavy boots thudded down the stairs and then she heard the sound of his voice, raised in anger with the landlord. She frowned. What on earth did he think he was doing? Surely the last thing they needed was to call attention to themselves?

Moments later, Guilhem returned, carrying a large bucket of hot, steaming water, a linen towel trapped beneath his elbow, the fabric patched, but clean.

She stared wistfully at the water. 'How did you get that?'

He smiled, tipping the bucket up. Water swilled and splashed into the earthenware bowl. 'Money has its uses, Alinor.' He pushed the towel into her hands.

'Oh, Guilhem, you needn't be running around fetching things for me!' she laughed, protesting. 'You must remember, I am used to the frugal ways of the nuns. When I stay with them, we have much less than this.'

'But I bet whatever you had was clean.' He ducked his head beneath the lintel, his big body half-obscured by the door. 'I'm off to fetch some more things; I might be a bit longer this time.'

Ensuring the iron bolt was in place, she moved towards the basin, dappling her fingers experimentally across the water's surface. It wouldn't hurt to wash, would it? Guilhem said he would be a little while. Lifting her arms, she removed her circlet and veil, unpinning her travel-stained wimple, now more mud-coloured than white. Her scalp was sticky, hot; damp fronds of hair clung to her forehead. She pulled out the pins securing her plaits, letting them drop, then untied the leather laces from each curling end. Once released, the gold tresses fell nearly to her hips; she raked her fingers through her loose, knotted hair, trying to separate the strands, to shake out the dust and dirt from the road. In the embroidered pouch that hang from her girdle, she drew out a small comb fashioned from deer horn, the shaft inlaid with pearls, and began to drag it through her hair.

Someone knocked at the door. Shock bolted through her. Guilhem! Already? Hurriedly, she placed the towel over her head, a makeshift veil to cover her hair, grasping the material closed with one fist at her neck. The tines of the comb dug into the sensitive skin of her palm on her other hand.

'You said you were going to be…!' She unbolted the door, the protest dying on her lips. The innkeeper stood in the doorway, smiling lasciviously.

'I saw your man go out,' he said, staring greedily at the bare patch of flesh at her neck that the towel failed to cover. His eyes bulged outwards, mouth saggy, lewd. Fear prickled through her veins.

'And he'll be back soon,' Alinor replied bossily, attempting to shut the door. One bulky foot shoved into the narrowing gap as she tried to close it.

'I came to see that you had everything you need,' he said. 'We don't often have ladies staying at this place.' He emphasised the word 'ladies' with a sneer.

'I'm not surprised,' she replied, her voice shrill with false bravado. 'The place is a dung heap.'

'Beggars can't be choosers,' he replied, a sharpness erasing his earlier drawling tone. 'I can tell you have no choice. There's something not right about you two. Are you on the run from somebody?'

'Go away,' said Alinor rudely.

The innkeeper took a step into the chamber, shoving up against her, expression brimming with lecherous intent. His sour breath wafted over her as he wrenched the towel from her head with thick pudgy fingers and flung it to the floor, feasting his eyes on her loosened hair. 'My, my, what a beauty you are, hidden beneath all that cloth. You and I are going to have a fine time together.'

'Go away, get away from me before I shout and scream for help.' Openly terrified now, Alinor felt her knees sag alarmingly.

'And who's to hear you, little lady?' the inn-keeper taunted.

'Me.'

Guilhem. Thank God.

Caught in a spiralling web of panic, Alinor had the briefest impression of the landlord spinning backwards, his pudgy bulk disappearing down the steps in a series of thuds and curses. She heard Guilhem shout down at him, a volley of threats and curses. Staggering backwards, her whole body trembling, she plopped down on the mattress, pressing her face into her hands. Tears burned the inside of her eyelids, threatening to spill.

'Why, why does this keep happening to me?' she wailed miserably, her voice muffled. 'Why am I so stupid, so unable to protect myself? I thought it was you at the door, Guilhem, that's why I opened it. I'm sorry.'

She heard him bolt the door, come over to her. Kneeling down, Guilhem placed the pile of new bed linen that he had just purchased on the dusty floor. He reached for her hands, tugging them gently away from her tearstained face. 'Alinor, stop this. Stop blaming yourself. It's I who should be sorry. I should never have left you alone in such an awful place.'

Hands ensnared by his, Alinor hunched her shoulders by way of protest. Her long hair spun out from her delicate features like threads of gold filament, silky and light as cobweb, spilling across the white skin of her throat and neck, over her slim shoulders. 'I'm annoyed,' she said, voice hitching a little. 'I used to be able to fend for myself, fight my own corner...but now... I don't understand why it keeps happening, first Eustace, now...him!' She jabbed her finger angrily at the doorway. 'Why will they not just leave me alone?' Her voice trailed away, hollow, bewildered.

Guilhem cleared his throat, brushing his knuckles against her cheek. 'Do you really have no idea?'

'About what?' Her expression was blank.

'You're a beautiful woman. You draw the admiring glances of men wherever you go—'

'Stop teasing me,' she cut off his sentence, standing abruptly. 'You're talking rubbish. Wilhelma constantly told me I was too outspoken for my own good, too scrawny, and that no man would ever want me!' Even as the words tumbled from her lips, her eyes widened in horror and she clapped her hands across her mouth. 'And there you have the proof.' She wrenched her hands from his. 'I just cannot keep my mouth shut.' She stalked over to the earthenware bowl on the coffer, dunking the linen flannel furiously into the rapidly cooling water. Her shoulders sagged. Why in hell's name had she said such an outrageous thing? To him, of all people? The man whom she loved. The man whom she could never have, because he thought nothing of her.

'And you believe Wilhelma?' Guilhem rose to his feet. Breath snapped in his chest. Alinor stood with her back to him, the glorious curling tendrils of her hair brushing her hips. His loins gathered heat, a dangerous foreboding.

'It's the truth, isn't it?' Eyes glittering with unshed tears, Alinor whirled around vehemently, the soaking washcloth clenched between her fingers, spinning water droplets, sparkles of light across the dingy chamber. 'Why do you torment me like this?' The blue of his eyes was intense, flicking out from the gloom like the vivid flash of a kingfisher's wing; she pivoted back again, grimacing down at the bowl, not wanting to see the pity, the compassion in his gaze. God forbid that he should ever feel sorry for her!

He acknowledged the fierce set of her head, her shoulders, hunched and fragile, almost obscured by the magnificent sweep of her hair. How could she not realise how enchanting, how desirable she was? The need to comfort her, to tell her she was wrong, so mistaken, propelled him towards her, two swift strides across the narrow chamber. His hands settled lightly on her shoulders. Alinor jumped, startled at the sudden contact. With her mind raging, she had failed to hear his quiet step. Warmth radiated from his body, engulfing her. Every vertebra in her spine, every ligament, whipped taut, quivering with awareness. Her stomach muscles shuddered, then softened.

'Don't,' Alinor managed to croak out, almost sobbing beneath the sweetness of his touch. 'Please don't. I don't want your pity.' She battled to hold her body rigid, unmoving, as if by keeping herself so tightly bound, she would not crumble beneath the scorching power of his touch.

'I don't pity you,' he said, his voice rough, guttural. *I desire you. I love you.* The unbidden thoughts stabbed through him, firing his blood, sending any thoughts of comforting her straight to oblivion. *He wanted her.*

The air in the chamber became suddenly denser, thickening.

His breath, hot, seductive, brushed her ear, nudged the flesh: a whisper of promise, of delight. The race of her blood picked up speed. Anger dropped away. Her mind slackened, cast adrift, conscious thought bobbing helplessly. She didn't want to think any more. Flesh thrummed, her body teetered, wavering, about to fall.

With one hand, he swept her hair to one side, exposing the delicate curve of her neck. His big body pressed against her spine, her hips, the back of her thighs. Her body ricocheted, arching, thrilling beneath the jolt of his unexpected touch. His lips touched the sensitive skin beneath her ear; the breath punched from her lungs, hunted, ragged. Hunger ripped through her, incandescent, glorious.

Self-control wobbled, then plummeted, dropped away to nothing. The faintest trill of doubt clamoured feebly from her conscious, logical mind; she smashed it away, smithereens of glass against stone. She had no wish to question his motives, or to ask aloud why he was doing this, for this might be the one time, the only time they could be together. There would be time for regret, for recriminations, later.

Twisting in his loose hold, she raised her hands to clasp the carved shadows of his face. Water dripped from her fingers, glittering like diamonds in the strips of sunlight pouring through the broken slats across the window. Raising herself on tiptoe, she scuffed her mouth against his, a tentative touch, hesitant. His lips were cool, firm, the tangy scent of his breath mingling with hers. Her behaviour was brazen, foolhardy, but she cared not. She had nothing to lose. Excitement laced through her, pooling dangerously, surging darts of newborn feeling stabbing through her belly. Her breath bubbled up in short, panicky gasps, yet she was exhilarated, flesh humming with anticipation, nerves strung taut, dancing on the fringes of…she knew not what.

At the silken touch of her lips, Guilhem groaned,

crushing hard against her, pressing her back against the oak coffer. His mouth slewed across hers, unsparing, wild. She gasped out loud at the ragged invasion and his lips sank closer, demanding, incisive. Desire catapulted through her, a catalyst bursting in a shower of stars, shaking her, driving her body to clamour for more, more of him. Her hips knocked violently against the earthenware bowl; it lurched dangerously, then fell, crashing to the floor and breaking, water flooding the wooden boards, spreading darkly. He told himself there was still time, time to stop what he was about to do, time to cease this insanity. His sensible, ordered mind cried out for self-restraint, even as his desire dashed the plca away, torching the thought to ashes.

Muscled thighs braced against the soft flare of her hips, Guilhem's mouth traced hers, trailed lines of white-hot, splintering fire. Her hands wound around his neck, winching closer, nearer, fingers tangling in the short, curling ends of his hair; his thick arms snaked around her waist and he lifted her against him. Dragging his mouth away, he pressed his forehead against hers.

She clung to his shoulders, pleading silently, *Please don't let this be over. Not now.*

'Sweet Jesu!' His lips moved against her cheek. 'I cannot trust myself around you! Stop me now,

Alinor, for I cannot stop myself!' Blunt desire scuffed his voice.

'No.' Her breath puffed out against his skin. 'I don't want to.'

'Alinor, you know what will happen.' Guilhem drew back; midnight eyes, liquid-soft with passion, grazed hers. A ruddy colour dusted the top of his cheekbones.

She nodded.

His big arms rounded her shoulders to haul her close, lips tracking a line of fire across her mouth. Self-control flew from him, flapping off into the distance like a crazy bird, vanishing. He did not watch it go, gathering her against him. They moved as one, falling to the pile of linens spread across the floor, Guilhem plucking at the strings that held her gown together like a man possessed. She laughed as he pulled the undergown over her head, reaching out to help him tear off his tunic. Kicking his braies into the corner of the room, he threw himself down on her, shockingly naked, virile. His powerful limbs gleamed in the half-light, roped muscle like carved, burnished wood.

Her chemise was the only barrier between them, the material flimsy, insubstantial; her pink skin glowed like a pearl through the white, gauzy fabric. Guilhem's hand moved up from her waist, rounding the outward curve of her breast, and she gasped at the delicious sensation, her slight frame shuddering to a point of being unable to cope, reduced to a quivering mass of need, unable to think, to see. Reality dimmed, reduced to a visceral, beating passion. His thumb smoothed across one blossoming nipple; she arched upwards, crying out with sheer delight, clawing at his shoulders. Caught in an eternal moment of fierce, unbridled lust, time fractured, lost its edge.

He wrapped her tight in his arms, the hot crush of her slender frame against his own, mouth plundering her, a savage invader, ruthless, feral. She thought she would ignite beneath his touch, a massing whirlpool of need swirling dangerously within her. She could not think, she could not speak: she was lost.

And then suddenly he was in her, hot and solid, moving steadily, quietly, giving her time to adjust. He eased slowly through the fragile membrane of her innocence, taking care. There was no pain, only a mild discomfort. His breathing was rapid, hoarse against her ear, his hands knotting savagely in her pure gold locks as he fought to slow himself, to check the hectic race of his desire. Her arms flung out wide, flailing, thrashing, seeking support. Breath scampered in her chest, chasing air. Her eyes snapped open, clung to his, her fingers clutching the sides of his face, aghast and overwhelmed at the vast tide of passion surging through her, the vortex of need that spiralled dangerously through her heart, her blood, her belly.

Muscles straining, he moved within her, starting to increase his pace, every movement suffusing her body with the growing promise of shuddering ecstasy. The burgeoning fullness built slowly, intensified; she pitched beneath him, mewling softly, dancing to his sweet rhythm, matching each powerful thrust with an astonished eagerness of her own. Clenching desire spun tighter and tighter, narrowing to a tiny point where it could go no further; darkness flittered along the periphery of her consciousness. Her mind frayed, loosened, breath rasping out in short, truncated gasps as he drove her on and on, pushing at her until her body, the very core of her, erupted in a jagged mass of terrible violence. A million shooting stars exploded, pulsating through her, pulverising her; white-hot splinters of light arcing across her stunned brain.

She cried out then, as did he, shouts of utter joy and pleasure; Guilhem threw his head back, throat and chest slick with sweat as he roared out his release, shuddering within her. 'Sweet Jesu! Alinor!' he yelled out, sprawling over her, his body sated, replete.

Chapter Nineteen

Alinor's eyes popped open. For a scant moment, bewilderment clagged her sleep-sodden mind: *where was she*? Memory flooded in, a sudden rush, the vivid images sending a wave of colour across her cheeks. Sprawled across her, Guilhem, fast asleep, his slow, even breathing tickling her ear, stirring her hair. One arm was thrown across her breasts, solid, possessive. Thick, muscular legs tangled with hers. The sweet-smelling linen, now strewn and mussed across the dusty floor, pillowed her spine. Every inch of her flesh hummed, vibrated; her limbs were heavy, satiated. Every muscle felt as if it had been pulled and stretched, as if on tenterhooks, until the strings had been cut, bringing instant, joyous release. Her body held the imprint of him: a new fluidity. How could she have known it would be like this? She had no prior information; her mother had never spoken of it and the nuns had no idea about such things.

Moonlight sneaked through the shutters, casting a faint, eerie light across the chamber. No noise emanated from the rabble in the inn below; it was late and all was quiet. What would it be like, she thought, to wake up every day with a man such as this? To share his thoughts, to laugh and cry, to bear his babies? Her heart leaped with joy, with hope. Children bundling into a big, wide bed, squalling and chattering, rolling around like puppies. In the darkness, beneath the dense warmth of his limbs, her mouth turned up in a faint smile; she shivered a little with excitement, with hope—was it a possibility?

Her eyes tipped downwards, following the polished line of his naked flank to his hip, a narrow curve, and then to the roped outline of his hefty thighs. His skin shone, smooth like marble. The twining of their bodies was shocking, intimate; excitement burst deep within her belly, firing her blood once more. She wanted to stay like this for ever: Guilhem crushed against her, packed tight, flesh pressed against flesh, her chemise rucked up around her hips. The cool night air touched her bare legs, her feet. She shivered, not with the cold, but with the sheer delight of being with Guilhem.

Above her, he shifted suddenly, lifting his head, propping himself up on one elbow, fearsome eyes glittering down at her. Her glorious hair fanned out across the stark white linen, a rippling flag of gold. His face was wretched.

'Are you cold?'

She shook her head, watching him carefully: the stern set of his mouth, the hollowed-out look of his eyes. Her heart crimped in on itself. Don't say it, she wanted to cry out, don't say anything to spoil what has just happened.

'Alinor, I'm so sorry. What have I done?'

His muttered question tore into her, ripping her hazy-edged dream of a future together to limp, dangling shreds. *No, please, no!*

Curling away from her, he stood up abruptly, dragging on his braies.

Shifting her hips, she yanked her chemise down to cover her exposed thighs, an awkward, jerky movement. Heart wobbling, she sat up, tears shimmering. Hope smashed, an earthenware pot bursting into a thousand shards. He did not want her. He did not love her. Why, he couldn't have phrased his feelings more plainly. The grim apology; the bitter-edged question. She grimaced at her toes, feeling like a piece of flotsam, discarded, unable to look at him, fighting back the hot, prickling tears that threatened to spill. What had she expected? A marriage proposal? No, of course not—she had lain with him in the knowledge that she would receive nothing in return. She had expected nothing. She had fully believed that she would have the strength to withstand the grisly aftermath, the backlash, any rejection; but now, with a failing heart, she realised she had not. She was weak. What a fool she had been.

Lifting the edges of the linen sheet around her shoulders, she eyed him squarely, schooling her features into a pale, rigid mask, gathering the scant remnants of dignity about her. 'Nothing, Guilhem. You've done nothing.' Her voice, when it emerged, was clipped and brittle, masking her sadness.

He glared at her, eyes like piercing daggers. 'I've ruined you, Alinor. I've taken your innocence.'

She hunched her shoulders forward, drawing up her knees to clasp them. 'Which I gave freely. I have no regrets.' She would squirrel the memory away: the tangled limbs, the staggering pulse of release, the tumbling intimacy. She would keep it safe for ever, remember it for eternity.

'No regrets? Alinor, are you entirely aware of what has just happened?

'Of course.' She straightened, drawing herself up to her full, diminutive height. 'We lay together.'

'Is that all you can say?' His mouth set in a furious line.

Eyeing him firmly, she strove to maintain levity in her tone. 'That's what happened, isn't it?'

'No one will marry you now!'

I want only you.

'I have no wish to marry. I've told you that already,' she countered more firmly, her voice gathering strength.

He raked her expression for some sign, any sign of regret at what they had done, shaking his head in disbelief. Why, he had behaved no better than her stepbrother, a boor and an oaf, plundering her sweet, innocent body like one possessed. The Devil incarnate. He had devoured her, gorged on her, like a man in the desert on the fringes of starvation. She should be ranting and raving, beating his chest with her small fists for what he had done to her and yet, there she sat, chin stuck boldly into the air, arms folded tightly across her chest, absolving him of his sins.

'Are you quite well?' he asked, his voice softening as he hunkered down beside her. His bare chest gleamed, taunting her with its beauty, pectoral muscles defined like honed chunks of armour plating. 'Did I hurt you?'

'I'm fine.' Her speech juddered, wavered, a flickering candle.

'Alinor, talk to me, what I have done to you...' His fingers drifted to her hair; she stiffened. 'You should have stopped me.' His hand fell away.

'I didn't want to stop you, Guilhem, don't you understand?' A lone tear tracked down her cheek, a silver thread.

'No,' he said, sitting back on his haunches, 'no, Alinor, I don't understand.'

Air gripped in her lungs. Her fingers knotted into her linen chemise, pleating the fabric incessantly. 'I wanted you, Guilhem, I wanted to be with you, I wanted to lie with you! To know what it was like, between a man and a woman…'

Astounded, he stared at her, incredulous at her blunt, outspoken speech. He had never heard a woman speak thus, with such simple honesty, such frankness. 'Alinor, you're not making any sense…to give your innocence away like that… to someone like me…'

'It's not like I will ever have another opportunity.' Her smile was lop-sided, self-deprecating. 'I wanted it to be you.'

Her declaration drove him to his feet. Shoving one hand through his hair, he drew his thick brows together in a savage frown. 'Why, Alinor? You don't even know who I am! I have nothing to give you!'

You can give me your heart.

To her surprise he dropped to his knees beside her, seizing her chin between thumb and forefinger. 'Stop trying to absolve me of my sins, Alinor, or make me feel any better about what has happened. You know what sort of man I am; you know what I have done. I am not worth it.'

You are! You are! she wanted to scream at him.

But staring into the hollowed-out ravages of his eyes, the grim lines carving down the sides of his mouth, she knew that she had lost him. Her chest heaved, a huge dry sob clenching at her lungs, twisting cruelly in her gut like a knife. By taking the first tentative step towards the promise of an uncertain future, she had risked her heart, laying it open on a slab only for him to then tear it apart, bit by bit, leaving the remnants scattered across the ground, torn and destroyed. He had batted her words back to her, unwilling to hear, still caught in the guilt-ridden snare of his past. She had wanted him to believe her, to trust her words, to love her. But she had failed. She had risked everything, body and soul, and had lost it all.

Curled into a tight, miserable ball, Alinor lay on the sagging, makeshift bed, her spine turned stiffly towards Guilhem. She shivered in her thin layers, her chemise, the sheet wrapped about her shoulders. Her heart ached. What was worse? To have remained chaste and to have never known what it was like to be with a man? To be with *him*? Or to toss prudence away and plunge into a visceral world, unknown, full of hot shivering delight, joyous abandon. To lie with a man who did not want her.

The coarse plaster covering the wall swam before her vision. Strands of bristly horsehair poked

out at angles from the thick layer of mud and animal dung, hard-packed, dry. What would happen
now? She would have to go through with helping Guilhem extricate the King from de Montfort's grip, if only to gain freedom from Prince
Edward's threat to marry her to her stepbrother.
But after that? Then she could run, run away to
some wind-whipped, isolated place and lick her
wounds in private. She would survive.

Sitting upright, propped up against the wall,
Guilhem glared at the taut line of Alinor's back.
Shame, like thick burning tar, slopped through
him, trailing fire. He tipped his head back, closing his eyes again. He sighed. Sleep continued to
evade him, and, judging from Alinor's constant
shuffling and hitching about on the straw mattress, he suspected she was awake as well. The
image of her face, intense and fierce, her green
eyes blazing, refused to leave his mind, spinning
round and round, taunting him. The sound of her
voice. *I wanted it to be you.* His heart plummeted
crazily with the knowledge, those astonishing
words dropping from her lips. Was it the truth?
Her speech drove through the blackness of his
mind, flaring down to his heart, igniting the vast
frozen lump of his heart. Wrapped around her soft
pliable limbs, he had become whole again, bit-
terness and despair obliterated by her utter trust.
And how had he repaid that trust? By gripping it

round the throat and wringing every last drop of pleasure from it.

In the darkness, he scowled. How could he have done such a thing? He cursed himself, over and over again, for allowing his guard to drop, for possessing what was not his to possess. She should hate him for what he had done, and yet all she seemed capable of was forgiveness. That morning, when he had told her the story behind his awful scars, Alinor had been on his side. He hadn't dared to acknowledge it then, but in her fiery defence of his actions, a flash of hope, new-born and wavering, had flickered through his heart. The flimsiest possibility of something more between them. He should have coddled that possibility, nurtured it as tenderly as a baby, but instead, what had he done? He had stamped cruelly on it, snuffed it out, like a spoiled reckless child.

A sharp tap on the door, decisive, disturbed the troubled progress of his thoughts. Springing to his feet, he lifted the iron latch. One of his escort soldiers stood outside.

'We've found de Montfort's camp!' the man said excitedly. In the grey pre-dawn light, the gold embroidery shone out from his scarlet tunic. Three golden lions: the crest of Prince Edward.

Seizing his arm, Guilhem hauled him into the chamber, shutting the door quickly. 'How?'

The soldier's eyes glittered in the shadows.

'From where we set up camp on the hill, we were able to see down into the whole valley. John noticed the smoke from their campfires, not far from the outskirts of town. We sent him down to investigate, and it's definitely de Montfort. The banners are flying and everything.'

'You took a risk, coming down into the town,' Guilhem said sharply, frowning at the soldier's tunic, the identifying emblem shining out from the red cloth. 'How did you find us?'

The soldier grinned. 'There's only one inn, my lord. I stuck my head in downstairs and figured you and the lady would not be sleeping there.' He wrinkled his nose. 'I made a lucky guess.'

'How soon till sunrise?'

'Not far off. If we ride now, we'll reach the camp as the light arrives. The soldier peered past Guilhem to the silent figure lying on the bed, the flimsy sheet revealing the delicate jut of Alinor's hip. 'Maybe, when you're ready, you could meet us and we can escort you there?'

Guilhem folded his arms across his chest, movements precise, decisive. 'Go back to the other men and send one of them back with a message for Prince Edward, tell him you've found the camp. Lady Alinor and I will join you as soon as we can.'

The soldier left, and Guilhem turned towards Alinor. 'Are you awake? Did you hear what he said?'

'Yes,' she said, twisting around to sit up. His voice had been gruff, businesslike. Devoid of emotion, it cut into her, lacerating her flesh like a knife. She swung her bare toes down to the floor. 'I will dress.' Her expression, evasive, wary, tore at his heart. Her eyes touched his own, briefly, then slid away.

'Alinor, I am sorry—'

'No!' She bit off his words, her voice shrill, strained. 'Don't speak of it. I don't want to hear another word. What's done is done, Guilhem. And I, for one, am glad of it. Please don't wallow in self-pity on my account.'

Stunned, his head knocked back at her blunt, autocratic speech. She was putting him firmly in his place. Curiously, he wanted to laugh; here she was, bossing him about how he should speak, how he should feel towards her, and yet she was the one who should be full of self-pity. She was the victim here, yet she staunchly refused to step into that role. Admiration swept through him at her fervent courage, her whole-hearted bravery. She had given herself to him, freely, and wanted nothing in return. With her words, she was releasing him from any obligation. He should have been relieved, but strangely he was not.

'This isn't finished between us, Alinor,' he said quietly, strapping on his leather belt around his slim hips, securing the short knife in its scab-

bard. 'But we have a job to do. I'll wait outside.'
He ducked his head beneath the lintel and disappeared.

Why did he insist on prolonging this agony?
She wanted an end to it, otherwise her heart would
shrivel away with sadness. Pitching forward
from the bed, Alinor fumbled for her clothes,
spread chaotically across the floor. Their disarray mocked her; her utter abandonment to Guilhem had been so overwhelming that she scarce
remembered the moment they had fallen to the
floor. That time seemed so far away now, another
lifetime. Her vision blurred, cloudy with tears.

Simon de Montfort's camp lay some ten miles
east down the river from the town of Skelton;
a collection of white canvas tents, patched and
stained from years of campaigning, of being bundled up and tied to the rumps of warhorses. Now
they were pitched on the flat ground of a vast
flood plain stretching out to a point where the
valley sides became steep, banners flapping in
the brisk wind. Trickles of smoke rose, hazing
the clear air, wriggling up into the first fingers of
light pushing across the valley. Although easily
found, de Montfort's men were also able to see
any threat coming from a long distance; the camp
was heavily guarded, with soldiers set at intervals
on the outskirts, battle-ready.

Hidden within a copse of ageing oaks, Guilhem surveyed the layout of the camp, narrowing his eyes. From this point he and Alinor would go in alone, whilst their escort soldiers remained behind in the trees. He shifted forward, his saddle creaking. 'I don't like this,' he said. His breath puffed out white in the chill morning air. 'I don't like this at all. De Montfort's men are too quick to fire off their arrows.'

'They wouldn't shoot at a woman, Guilhem.' Alinor rubbed at the leather rein between her fingers. 'Look at me; I'm hardly a threat.'

His jaw tightened. He didn't need to look at her, that slender, proud figure sitting bolt upright on her horse. Every enchanting line of her body, every soft delectable curve, was imprinted on his brain, etched, gouging into his conscience. Whilst he had waited outside the chamber at the inn, she had dressed with remarkable speed, somehow managing to lace herself into her garments without help, pinning up her hair into a tight, plaited bun. Her veil, circlet and wimple were all in place, fixed and secure, stabbed with numerous hairpins. Her manner was brisk, efficient, almost to the point of brittleness, her speech minimal, as if by holding herself in so securely, no outward emotion would reveal itself.

He had done this to her. He had turned the brave, smiling Alinor into this tense, constrained shadow. And if he stayed around her much longer, he would surely make it worse.

'Guilhem?' Her voice nudged at him, brought him back to the present.

At the edge of the woodland, a group of magpies swooped down, chattering excitedly, an aggressive, guttural sound, their wings blue-black, glossy.

'It's too dangerous,' he replied darkly, scowling across the sunlit fields, dew coating the grass like a cloth of diamonds, to a point where a soldier, dressed in Montfort colours, stood guard. About half a mile behind him the canvas tents flapped and bowed. This whole situation was so wrong. Every instinct told him to bundle Alinor away and carry her to a place of safety, where no one could ever harm her. Where he could look after her, care for her. But after what had happened between them, would she have him?

Alinor shifted her position in the saddle as her horse sidled gently beneath her. She leaned forward, patting the palfrey's neck. Her fingers were slender, nails like pink shells against the grey frothing mane of the animal. 'Guilhem, I'm not frightened, if that's what you're worried about. And it's my only option; I have to do this, or Prince Edward will force me to marry Eustace.' Her voice was clipped, toneless. 'What's my alternative?'

Marry me. The insane thought popped into his head, unbidden. He blinked in surprise, then shook his head. What utter madness.

'My own father is in that camp, remember? I can ride up alone and approach the guard first. Nothing is going to happen to me.'

He gritted his teeth. Her reasoning made sense, although it went against every code of chivalry to allow a woman to enter into a military camp unarmed, alone. 'All right,' he agreed reluctantly, 'but the moment that soldier grants you access, beckon me forward.'

Alinor kicked her heels into the palfrey's rounded flanks, as if she couldn't wait to be away from him.

Trotting forward through the sparkling grass, bridle clicking in time to the horse's pace, Alinor let out a long slow breath of release. Her chest throbbed with sadness, a dull, widening ache. She was almost there, almost at the point where she could break away from Guilhem and hide. She couldn't go home, or return to the Priory and the welcoming arms of the nuns she knew and loved, much as she wanted to. No, she would head north and find another nunnery willing to take her in. It couldn't come soon enough.

Following a stunted hawthorn hedge, she made her way towards the soldier, making sure that she was visible at all times. She knew the man had spotted her, by the immediate way he stood to attention, one hand moving to his sword helm. Planting a wide, fixed smile on her face, she slowed the horse to a walking pace, hooves whispering through the thick verdant grass. Through the slits of his shining helmet, the soldier watched her approach calmly.

Alinor reined in the horse, a few feet away from the soldier. The hem of her lavender-coloured gown rippled in a low curving arc along the horse's flank. 'Are you with de Montfort?' she asked, her voice high and imperious.

The soldier bowed, then tipped his head up to her. 'Who wants to know?'

'I am Lady Alinor of Claverstock, and I believe that my father, Peter, the Earl of Claverstock, is in your camp.' She gestured towards the cluster of tents. 'It is imperative that I see him, for I have urgent news to convey.' Let the soldier think the worst, for at the moment, her brain was too scrambled to think what her 'urgent news' might be.

The soldier shifted his feet slightly. 'Are you alone?' he asked.

'I have my manservant with me,' she explained. 'But he stayed by the trees for fear that you might shoot him. Can I beckon him to come forward?'

'Is he armed?'

'A short knife on his belt. For my protection,

that is all. You don't think I would travel completely undefended?' She raised her eyebrows, expression faintly condemning.

Behind his helmet, the soldier blushed, nodding his assent. He watched as she raised her arm into a graceful half-circle, and a man pulled away from the shadows of the trees, a tall man with huge shoulders, dressed in a ripped, threadbare tunic.

'Take me to my father,' Alinor instructed the soldier, as Guilhem moved up to her horse's head and grabbed the bridle. 'My manservant will lead me in.'

The soldier marched off down the trackthat ran alongside the river. Checking that he was far enough ahead of them not to overhear, Alinor leaned forward and touched Guilhem's shoulder. A surge of longing whipped through her, leaving her shaken. It was the first time she had touched him since they had lain together.

Snatching her fingers away, she tried to dampen her bubbling emotions. 'How are you planning to get de Montfort out of there?' She eyed the tents doubtfully. There must have been above a hundred, each sleeping about twenty soldiers.

Slowing his pace so that he could walk alongside her, Guilhem shrugged his shoulders. 'I'm not sure at the moment,' he replied casually. 'I'll work it out once I'm in there, facing him.'

Alinor peered at him, incredulous. 'Is that what you normally do?' He seemed so calm about the whole thing, so casual. Surely all battles and campaigns had to be planned in advance, with weeks of preparation.

'Yes.' He smiled grimly. 'I think better on my feet.'

'And what do I do, Guilhem, while you "think on your feet"?'

'Stay back behind me.' He scowled, as if suddenly remembering that she would be there, too. 'Stay back and stay alive, Alinor. That's all I ask of you.'

Chapter Twenty

Most of the tent flaps were laced securely, braided rope threaded into eyelets and fastened in a criss-cross fashion; the hour was early, and only a few soldiers were awake, peering at Alinor covertly with curious, sideways glances as she and Guilhem moved through the camp. Her heart thudded with trepidation; she was not afraid for herself, but for the man leading her horse, his tall broad-shouldered figure striding confidently into an enemy camp. What would these soldiers do to him if they realised his loyalty to Prince Edward? They would surely slaughter him where he stood! Pressing her toes down in the stirrups to give her extra leverage, she hauled on the reins, halting the forward progress of her horse.

'Guilhem, this isn't safe!' she whispered urgently, leaning forward in the saddle. Her white veil floated around her head, diaphanous, caught in a sift of air.

He turned to her, placing one hand on the palfrey's neck. His lean fingers, tanned and sinewy, ruffled the animal's mane. The rough peasant hood, pushed back, emphasised the corded ruggedness of his neck, the muscle-bound hollow of his throat. 'Alinor, I'll take care of you, I promise,' he said. His eyes were the intense colour of a twilight sky, violet-blue.

Worry blossomed across her heart. 'I meant for you!' she hissed at him, conscious that they were drawing attention to themselves by stopping. 'These people will cut your throat if they find out who you are!'

A fleeting smile crossed his face at her concern; his fingers touched her hand, a gesture of reassurance. 'You mustn't worry about me, Alinor. No one knows me here.'

His words did little to comfort her, but she allowed the reins to run through her fingers so he could lead her once more. At last the soldier they were following stopped outside one of the tents at the far end of the camp.

'Your father, the Earl of Claverstock, is in here. Shall I wake him for you?'

Alinor gulped, a heady panic frothing through her veins. This was it. Her father was going to be very surprised to see her and no doubt angry; he had no idea that she knew about him swapping allegiance. And yet, via a peculiar, tricky route, she had been brought to this point by her father's stubbornness: his insistence that she inherit the estate and that she should marry Eustace. She knew he cared little for her; it was doubtful that he would ever forgive her for what she was about to do.

She fixed the soldier with a hard stare. 'Yes, thank you,' she replied. Perspiration pooled in her armpits.

Guilhem swung her down easily from the horse; pleasure rushed over her as his hands grasped her waist. God, if she carried on like this she would be a snivelling wreck in his presence! Guilhem's hands dropped away as soon as she was steady and she toed the ground nervously, waiting for the tent flap to push back and her father to appear.

A sharp exchange of words, then curses, emerged from the inner confines of the tent and she smiled tersely. Her father didn't like to be woken early at the best of times. His face appeared through the tent flap, eyes bloodshot, face pudgy and mottled with sleep, thinning hair stuck out in all directions.

'Alinor? What in God's name are you doing here?' he yelled at her, stepping out into the wet grass. A blanket was wrapped around his spare rangy figure, the creased white hem of his long shirt poking out above bare pallid shins. His gaze raked the slim, diminutive figure of his daughter. 'How did you even know where I was?'

'You changed sides, Father. How could you?'

His head rocked back at her accusatory tone. 'Not that it's any of your business! Is that what you came here to tell me?'

She tightened her mouth at his customary flare of anger. 'No, I came to talk to you about Wilhelma.'

His eyes flew to Guilhem, standing silently at her side, huge arms crossed over his chest. 'And who is this?' he continued in a dismissive tone as he took in Guilhem's dishevelled garments. 'Is he from Claverstock? I don't recognise him.'

'I needed an escort, Father. I wasn't going to travel alone.'

'You'd better come inside. Can't stand out here providing entertainment.' He held back the thick canvas, indicating that Alinor should enter, then followed her in, rudely dropping the flap in front of Guilhem's nose so he was forced to make his own way inside.

The air inside the tent was heavy, stale, reeking of sour male odours. Three knights, bundled into their cloaks, appeared to be sleeping, stretched out on the rush matting which provided some protection from the damp, lumpy ground.

'You'd better keep your voices down,' her father said. 'Like me, the others don't like to be woken too early.'

'De Montfort?' Alinor whispered, desperate

to get the worst part of this whole business over with. Was one of those sleeping figures the main enemy of the King and Prince Edward? She hovered by the tent opening, conscious that Guilhem stood very, very close to her, his hip nudging hers. She welcomed the contact, drew strength from the big, powerful man at her side.

Her father frowned. It was a curious question for her to ask.

'No, he sleeps alone. He's in one of the other tents. Why do you want to know anyway? I thought you came to see me.'

Her mind emptied. Caught in her tense web of anxiety, she couldn't remember the lie she was about to tell. A boiling weakness sapped the strength in her knees, and she would have fallen forward if Guilhem hadn't discreetly cupped her elbow, holding her upright. 'Wh-what?'

'Are you completely deaf, maid? Why are you here?'

Beyond her father's shoulder, a flicker of movement snagged Alinor's gaze. The smallest rustle of fabric. Through the gloom, she peered intently at the sleeping soldiers. One of the men had opened his eyes. To her complete shock, he was staring at Guilhem, hooded eyes sparkling, intense. A knowing look of recognition crossed his stern, battle-hardened face. Panic laced through her, hopping crazily about her tense body. She shuffled closer to Guilhem, positioning herself slightly in front of him, as if to protect him from potential threat, she knew not what.

'You must excuse me for a moment, Father,' she blurted out hurriedly. 'I need a quick word with my manservant outside.' Ignoring her father's look of irritation, she spun on her heel, placing the palm against the flat hard muscle of Guilhem's stomach, pushing him back, out of the tent, out into the fresh, chill air. He resisted slightly, not understanding her actions, and she shoved harder, desperately, not caring what it must look like.

'What are you doing?' he demanded as they bundled through the opening together.

Her horse stood idly outside the tent, cropping the short grass with a rough, tearing sound. She grabbed the reins and clutched Guilhem's hand, starting to march towards the exit of the camp with a decisive, fast-paced stride. 'Walk,' she gasped at him softly. 'Don't protest, don't look back, just walk with me.'

'What is it?' Side by side, the palfrey following behind, they zig-zagged through the tents, Alinor's skirts swishing briskly through the long grass, the hem soaked dark with dew. 'We can't leave now, Alinor,' he protested, 'not when we're so close.'

'Someone in my father's tent recognised you,' she rattled out, her voice wobbling slightly. Her green eyes were huge, concerned. In the distance lay the oak forest where they had left Prince Edward's knights. If only they could reach that point, reach the safe cover of the trees before anyone came after them.

'Are you sure?'

'I'm certain of it.'

Behind them, there was a shout. Then another. Then, as if from nowhere, an arrow flew past Alinor's ear, a sickening whine.

'My God!' Guilhem bellowed, immediately realising the severity of the situation. 'We need to run!' He tightened his grip on Alinor's hand, his long legs pounding across the tussock-strewn grass, heading for the point at which they had entered the camp: the straggling group of hawthorn. Hampered by the voluminous skirts of her gown, Alinor struggled to match his long stride, air tearing in her lungs. She was fit, but not as fit as Guilhem.

Another arrow whizzed past them. Then another.

'Give me the horse!' Guilhem shouted as they ran side by side. 'We can make this! Once we are in the trees they will never find us!'

She threw the reins at him and he caught them deftly. Fear gave her energy, firing the muscles in her legs. With one hand available to lift her skirts high, her slippered feet sprung over the sparkling grass, the spongy ground, matching Guilhem's loping pace. A horrible whirring noise buzzed behind her, too close, then something hard glanced against the back of her head, just above her left ear. She stumbled forward slightly, her eyes watering at the fiery spreading pain, but Guilhem yanked her along again and she knew, for his sake, that she had to go on. Gritting her teeth, she forced herself to ignore the pain fanning across her skull.

Panting hard, they reached the shelter of the trees. She had no time to protest as Guilhem released the reins and sent her horse galloping off through the corrugated trunks with a sharp slap to her rump, murmuring tersely that they would 'fetch her later' before they tore off into the welcoming shadows. The forest was quiet, motes of sunlight tunnelling down through the branches, pooling patches of light on to the soft, uneven ground. The sounds of shouting, of arrows flying through the air, died away, drifting off into the distance. Pulling Alinor with him, Guilhem wound a torturous route upwards through the snagging undergrowth: a mess of brambles, exposed tree roots sticking out like pale, broken limbs. He climbed steadily up to an outcrop of rock, moving around the outside of the huge stone. Alinor stumbled after him, clambering up the slope, feet sliding on the dry leaves, the loose soil, silk slippers filling with earth and small, sharp stones until at last they reached the top, lungs bursting, clamouring for breath. Releasing Alinor's hand, Guilhem threw himself down on to the flat top of the rock, crawling low on his hands and knees to the very edge. Despite his size, his body moved with quick, efficient movements, graceful, snaking forward like a cat after its prey. From this point, through the high canopy of the trees, he had an excellent view of the whole valley. De Montfort's soldiers were nowhere to be seen.

'It looks like they may have given up on us.' Rolling over and sitting up, he grinned over at Alinor. Sweat glistened on the carved contours of his face. 'Let's hope so.'

Shadowed by the huge oaks, Alinor stood at the point where the solid rock butted up against the forest floor, thick with spent leaves. The lavender colour of her gown shone out incongruously against the drab colours of the woodland, the dull browns and greens. A greying vagueness shimmered around the edges of her eyes; her head felt light, insubstantial.

'That was some run.' Guilhem sprung to his feet and came towards her. 'Thank God you spotted that man when you did. It was probably someone I have fought before...' he murmured, almost to himself. 'I'm not unknown, being a friend to the Prince. Even so, I didn't think any-one would recognise me, dressed like this.' He cupped her shoulders, his blue eyes soft. 'You saved my life, Alinor, when you realised what was happening, by pulling me out of there when you did.'

'Guilhem... I...'

'Oh, God,' he said suddenly, his chin jerking upwards, staring at a point beyond her shoulder. 'That's all we need.' He squeezed her arm, a gesture of reassurance. 'Wait here.'

As he moved passed her, Alinor turned around. Her head swam, but she had no inclination to raise her fingers, to assess the damage at the back of her head. She doubted the wound was serious, otherwise she would have passed out by now. Squinting through the trees, her gaze following Guilhem's broad back, she gasped, fear bolting through her. No, no, not him! A group of knights walked their horses slowly along a faint track, bridles jingling, chainmail flexing like rippling snakeskin. Heading up the twenty-or-so men was Edward, his red surcoat shining out, immaculate. The three golden lions embroidered across his chest gleamed out in the shadowed gloom. Bringing up the rear were the same knights who had escorted them from Claverstock, leading Alinor's grey palfrey.

Alinor's heart tightened, compressed with anxiety. Edward would make her go back in there, back into the camp again, back to face her father. Folding her arms across her chest, she strove for balance, fought to keep her breathing steady. Don't panic, she told herself. Keep control of yourself. The urge to run, to sink back under the cover of the trees, loomed large, but something held her back. Something kept her feet pinned to the spot. She couldn't leave without saying goodbye to Guilhem.

'Edward.' Guilhem strode towards the Prince. Edward reached down, clasping Guilhem's fingers with his chainmail-covered hand.

'Good God, look at the state of you,' said Edward, taking in Guilhem's dishevelled appearance, the grimy peasant clothes, the streaks of dirt across his square-cut chin. The Prince pulled off his helmet, handing it to the soldier next to him, and pushed back his chainmail hood. His wispy hair stuck to his scalp with perspiration.

Guilhem sighed. 'What are you doing here, Edward? I thought you were going to stay at Claverstock?'

'I got bored,' Edward drawled, slapping away a fly buzzing idly around his neck. 'Sitting around with the ladies all day, throwing meat bones to the dogs, it's not for me. When you sent that message back that you had found the camp, well, I had to come.' He scanned the forest, arrogant gaze touching the pale, silent figure of Alinor, before whipping back to Guilhem. 'Where is he, then, de Montfort? You have got him, haven't you?'

'No.'

'Why not?' A streak of angry colour mottled Edward's gaunt features. 'Did she give you any trouble? Did the chit give you away?' He jerked his head towards Alinor.

'No, nothing like that. Someone recognised me, Edward, and it was Alinor who made me leave, before we even found de Montfort. He is there, though.'

Edward swung himself down from his horse, booted feet sinking down into the soft vegetation, the litter of decaying leaves and moss. 'Then she can go into the camp again, with someone else. Someone who won't be recognised.'

Alinor's knees sagged at his words, muscles like wet rope. Her hand flew out, seeking support, something to clutch at, to hold her upright, but there was nothing, only air. She tottered back a few steps, but managed to keep her balance.

'No.'

Edward frowned, his pale, red-rimmed eyes searching Guilhem's hard features. 'What do you mean, "no"?

'What I mean, Edward, is that she's done enough. You can't blackmail her like this. Now you know where the camp is you have enough resources to go in there and find de Montfort for yourself.'

'Are you refusing my orders?'

'Yes.' Guilhem laced big arms across his chest. 'Edward, you are my friend and a loyal one at that. What you did for me in France was above and beyond that call of friendship and I shall always, always, remember what you did for me. But this? I cannot go along with it. Alinor has done too much already, she needs some rest...'

Edward glared at him, hard. Irritation flickered across his face. Then suddenly, his expression cleared and he threw back his head, roaring with laughter. 'Oh, my God, man, I never thought I would see this!' Shaking his head with amusement, with disbelief, he clapped one hand on Guilhem's shoulder, raising his eyes towards Alinor's slender figure standing quietly beneath the trees, the sun dappling her blue skirts. Her features were pinched, all colour drained from her skin, so that her face shone out, like a pale moon, from the shadows. 'What's the matter with her, anyway?' Edward said sharply.

Guilhem's head whipped around. Took in the deathly white of Alinor's face. He sprung over to her, clasping her shoulders. 'What is it?'

'It's nothing, really.' She touched the point on her head where the pain was. Her fingers came away, covered with a sticky wetness.

Guilhem stared at her hand covered with blood, dripping from her fingers. 'Sweet Jesu!' He spun her around. Blood soaked her veil, weighing down the light, silken fabric. 'How did this happen?'

'I'm not certain,' she replied. Her voice was distant, muffled, as if someone else were saying the words, not her. 'I think an arrow might have caught the back of my head.'

'Is she all right?' Edward strode up. His keen gaze took in the blood-soaked veil, her deathly pallor.

'No, of course she's not all right!' Guilhem roared. Panic ricocheted through him, a cold sliding knife, digging into his heart, brutal, savage. For the first time in his life, he knew fear, pure, undiluted fear, at the thought that this woman, this reckless, courageous woman whom he had come to care for so much, whom he loved, could be hurt so easily. And all because she had taken a risk for him. She could have easily begged her father for help in that tent and exposed his true identity, yet she had not. She had protected him, Guilhem, and in the process, become hurt herself. 'I must get her to a physician!' Seizing her fingers, he started pulling her towards the horses.

'Guilhem, stop, calm down.' Alinor hung on to his upper arms, fighting to remain conscious through the sifting layers of mist suffusing her brain. She tilted her aching head, drawing strength from the taut planes of his face, those twinkling pools of blue. 'It's not that bad.'

'Not that bad!' he yelled down at her. 'Alinor, you're bleeding everywhere!'

'Listen to the maid, Guilhem, she knows what's best for her. You can help her.' Edward's voice was calm, purposeful. 'I will take my soldiers and make camp at the bottom of this hill. If you need us, you know where we are.' Returning to the horses, he mounted up and, with his helmet in place, gave the order to move out.

Clutching on to Guilhem, Alinor watched them go, the glossy rumps receding through the trees. What words had been said between Edward and Guilhem to make the Prince leave so quickly? She had been so convinced that he would force her to go back into that camp again.

A wave of nausea rolled over her. 'I must sit down,' she gasped suddenly. Guilhem held her as she sank slowly into a puddle of skirts. Her head lolled forward, but she made a supreme effort to lift it again, to speak. A strange rigidity gripped the muscles in her neck. 'Take off my veil, and have a look at the wound.' Her voice, although quiet and trembling, held authority.

Crouching beside her, Guilhem removed her circlet, lifting the veil away gently from her head. Blood matted the pure gold strands of her hair.

'Is it still bleeding?'

Carefully, he parted the strands on her head. The cut sliced across the pale skin of her scalp, red blood oozing slowly in a thin line. 'No,' he replied, relief clouding his voice. His hands were trembling. He was used to dealing with wounds on the battlefield far greater than this, yet here he was, fingers shaking over her neat head, quivering. He knew why. The thought flooded over him, a great surge of emotion, engulfing, devastating. This woman meant more to him than anything, anyone, in the whole wide world; he couldn't bear it if anything happened to her.

'You see,' she said, her voice soft, lilting. 'I told you it wasn't bad. The arrow only grazed my skin.' Alinor twisted around and smiled; the sweetness of her expression astounded him, knifing him through the heart. He had hauled her around the countryside against her will, kissed her, bedded her. And still she smiled at him.

'Now, have you any alcohol?'

'What…? Yes, in my flagon.'

'Pour it over the cut to clean it.'

As the brandy touched the open wound, she sucked her breath in sharply, hunching forward to clasp her knees when Guilhem replaced the stopper. 'That will do for now,' she managed to say. 'If it's stopped bleeding, then it won't need any stitches.' Her head swam; exhausted and weak from the whole ordeal, she wanted to sleep.

Guilhem knelt in front of her. Beside him, her ruined veil lay cast on to the layers of decaying leaves, the gauzy whiteness like a swirl of mist across the ground. 'You stood there, saying nothing, whilst I spoke to Edward, yet all the time, you were injured. Why didn't you tell me the moment this happened, Alinor?'

She frowned. 'Because you would have stopped, Guilhem; it happened as we left the camp, before we were even halfway to the trees.'

'You kept on running,' he murmured, incredulous.

Her eyes sparked emerald fire. 'Yes.' She laughed. A light blush hazed her cheeks. 'They would have killed you, Guilhem. I couldn't let them catch you!'

'Why not?' His face was wretched. 'Surely that would have been preferable for you? I've caused you nothing but trouble, and yet, unbelievably, you stick by me. I don't understand—why do you do it?'

'Don't you know?' She breathed softly. A shaft of sunlight flickered down through the last fluttering leaves, bathing her skin. She closed her eyes briefly, velvety eyelashes sweeping down across the recovering bloom of her cheeks. She had nothing to lose by telling him how she really felt. Was she brave enough? The worst that could happen was that he would laugh in her face, but she was willing to take that risk.

He picked up her hands, lying limply in the folds of her skirts, smoothing the skin on her wrists. Beneath the pale, fragile flesh, he could see the trace of her veins, a net of blue. Her pulse bumped steadily against his thumbs. 'Maybe I do,' he said slowly, tentatively, as if in a dream. He couldn't quite believe what she might be about to say. 'But tell me anyway.'

She paused, chewing fretfully on her bottom lip. 'I love you, Guilhem. I have loved you from possibly the very first moment I met you.'

His heart squeezed tight, a wrenching twist of acknowledgement. He touched her cheek, the wispy golden curls of hair drifting over her forehead, incredulous, astounded by her simple admission. Those heartfelt words. My God, *she loved him*. Sheer, undiluted pleasure leaped through his veins, punching him straight in the gut. *She loved him*.

She shrugged her shoulders, slumping forward. 'There, now you know. I know it doesn't make much difference to you, but maybe it explains my behaviour. Guilhem, I would do anything for you. I would follow you to the ends of the earth if you asked me.' She frowned, clamping her lips together. Her fingers curled into the pile of loose leaves beneath her, worrying at the crisp foliage till it disintegrated into tiny pieces, waiting for him to laugh at her, to mock her. She braced her body, prepared for the onslaught.

High above them, two buzzards wheeled above the trees, great wings feathered out against the blue sky, their haunting cries piercing through the still air.

'My God...' he breathed.

'Go on, then...' Alinor tilted her head, her mouth pursed in a grim line '...tell me what a fool I am. Why would anyone like you love anyone like me?'

'Why would they not?'

Her head jerked up.

'Alinor, you are the most beautiful, wonderful, adorable thing that has ever happened to me. I mean that.' The rough melody of his voice soaked through her, percolating through her body like a warm balm. 'When I first met you, on the bridge that day, wielding a sword that was far too big for you, defending your sacks of grain, my heart already knew, even if my head did not.'

'What did your heart know?' A fluttering, newborn joy seized her. Lowering her gaze, she fixed her eyes on the hem of her dew-soaked gown. If she looked at him now, if she peeped into those magnificent, midnight-blue eyes, she might break this spell, this dream that she was in. She patted her gown into place across her raised knees, an awkward, self-conscious gesture.

'That I love you, Alinor. I was hurt, guilt-ridden, from what had happened in Gascony. I carried it round with me like an iron cloak across my shoulders. I was not worthy. But your kindness towards me, your generosity of spirit—my God, Alinor, everything about you made me realise that I can love someone. And that someone is you. You have given me back my heart and now that heart belongs to you.'

She swayed beneath the quiet determination of his words, delight singing through her veins, shoving away the last remnants of sadness, the misery that had stalked her since his awful rejection after they had lain together. Hope danced in her heart, a real possibility, a chance of a future together after all.

Concern crossed his face, a shadow of doubt. A muscle twitched in the sculptured outline of his jaw. 'Will you have me, Alinor? After everything I have done?' The hesitation, the lack of certainty in his voice plucked at her heart.

'Oh, Lord, Guilhem, how can you even ask such a question?' Alinor laughed out loud, the sound tinkling through the trees. Throwing her arms about his neck, she pulled his head down to meet hers, her small frame overflowing with happiness. 'I never thought this could be... Oh, God, how I wished for it, yearned for it, but I never thought...'

With a low rumble of pleasure, Guilhem laughed, lowering his head. His mouth claimed hers, raw and possessive, in a kiss that would hold them together, for ever.

* * * * *

*If you enjoyed this story,
you won't want to miss these
other great reads from Meriel Fuller:*

*INNOCENT'S CHAMPION
THE KNIGHT'S FUGITIVE LADY
CAPTURED BY THE WARRIOR
THE WARRIOR'S PRINCESS BRIDE*

MILLS & BOON®

HISTORICAL

AWAKEN THE ROMANCE OF THE PAST

0716/04

MILLS & BOON®

Mills & Boon have been at the heart of romance since 1908... and while the fashions may have changed, one thing remains the same: from pulse-pounding passion to the gentlest caress, we're always known how to bring romance alive.

Now, we're delighted to present you with these irresistible illustrations, inspired by the vintage glamour of our covers. So indulge your wildest dreams and unleash your imagination as we present the most iconic Mills & Boon moments of the last century.

Visit **www.millsandboon.co.uk/ArtofRomance** to order yours!